INSPECTOR HADLEY

THE DIAMOND MURDERS

by

PETER CHILD

Benbow Publications

Copyright 2009 by Peter Child

Peter Child has asserted his rights under the Copyright, Designs and Patents Act, 1988 to be identified as the author of this work.

All rights reserved. No part of this publication may be reproduced, stored in a retrieval system, or transmitted in any form or by any means, electronic, mechanical photocopying, recording or otherwise without the prior permission of the copyright owner.

Published in 2009 by Benbow Publications.

British Library
Cataloguing in Publication Data.

ISBN : 978-0-9558063-2-2

Printed by Lightning Source UK Ltd
Chapter House
Pitfield
Kiln Farm
Milton Keynes. MK11 3LW

First Edition

OTHER TITLES BY THE AUTHOR

ERIC THE ROMANTIC

THE MICHEL RONAY SERIES:

MARSEILLE TAXI

AUGUST IN GRAMBOIS

CHRISTMAS IN MARSEILLE

CATASTROPHE IN LE TOUQUET

RETURN TO MARSEILLE

THE INSPECTOR HADLEY SERIES:

THE TAVISTOCK SQUARE MURDERS

THE GOLD BULLION MURDERS

THE TOWER OF LONDON MURDERS

THE AMERICAN MURDERS

NON FICTION

VEHICLE PAINTER'S NOTES

VEHICLE FINE FINISHING

VEHICLE FABRICATIONS IN GRP

NOTES FOR GOOD DRIVERS

NOTES FOR COMPANY DRIVERS

NOTES FOR GOOD DRIVERS

NOTES FOR COMPANY DRIVERS

ACKNOWLEDGEMENTS

Once again, I wish to gratefully acknowledge all the help and assistance given to me by Sue Gresham, who edited and formatted the book and Wendy Tobitt for the splendid cover presentation. Without these talented and patient ladies this book would not have been possible.

Peter Child

INTRODUCTION

In the autumn of 1881, Klaus Detrekker, owner of the Transvaal Diamond Mining Company, arrived in London from South Africa with two assistants and a sealed box containing four large uncut diamonds of incalculable value. Within twenty four hours of his arrival, Detrekker's mutilated body was discovered floating in the Serpentine Lake in Hyde Park and his two assistants, along with the diamonds, had disappeared from the Piccadilly Hotel. As Inspector Hadley and Sergeant Cooper began the investigation into the murder, a Prussian aristocrat, Count Erik von Rausberg, arrived at Scotland Yard to see the Commissioner and inform him that the German Government had secretly purchased the diamonds from Detrekker and if they were not recovered quickly, it would cause a serious diplomatic incident between Germany and England…

Characters and events portrayed in this book are fictional.

CHAPTER 1

Inspector James Hadley left his home in Camden in a light-hearted frame of mind and hailed a Hansom cab to take him to Scotland Yard. Although the London traffic was busier than usual for a Wednesday morning in August, the cab made good time to the Embankment and when Hadley stepped down from the Hansom, he stood for a few moments gazing at the fast flowing Thames with its myriad of boats plying along the glittering waterway. He felt proud to be an Englishman, living and doing his duty in London, the very centre of Queen Victoria's Empire. He breathed deeply, sighed and entered the Yard just as Big Ben struck nine o'clock.

Sergeant Cooper was already at his desk and smiled when Hadley stepped into the office.
"Good morning, sir."
"Morning, Sergeant, and what a good one it is" replied Hadley as he sat behind his desk.
"It looks like another hot day, sir."
"It does indeed, so I think as we haven't much on at the moment, we can afford the luxury of an extended and refreshing lunch, Sergeant."
"At the Kings Head, sir?"
"Where else?" queried Hadley with a smile as George, his affable clerk appeared and asked if he was ready for a pot of tea.
"Need you ask, George?"
"I was only being polite, sir" replied George with a smile as he winked at Cooper. Hadley nodded and looked idly through several folders on his desk, but nothing of interest caught his attention and when the tea arrived he sat back in his chair.
"I think, as we've got time on our hands, that we ought to review our filing system, Sergeant."
"Why, sir?"
"Well it seems to me that we could speed up our paper chases if we could get George to bring in a quick cross reference system for ongoing investigations."
"It would mean more work for him, sir, I think at the moment

he does very well."

"Yes, he does but what if…" Hadley was interrupted by Mr Jenkins, Chief Inspector Bell's clerk, entering the office.

"Good morning, sir, the Chief Inspector would like to see you and the Sergeant immediately" said Jenkins.

"Right, lead on" replied Hadley and as they followed the clerk out, Hadley said to Cooper "I wonder what this is all about?"

"We'll soon find out, sir."

Chief Inspector Howard Bell looked more harassed than usual as, without greeting them, he waved them to sit and said "early this morning a man's body was found in the Serpentine by a gentleman walking his dog, a constable was summoned and he managed to recover the body from the water…"

"Good man" interrupted Hadley.

"Quite so, the deceased was obviously a gentleman, well dressed in expensive clothes, but he had nothing on his person except a gold fob watch and a letter addressed to him at the Piccadilly Hotel."

"So we know his name, sir."

"Yes, Hadley, the dead person is Mr Klaus Detrekker, and here is the letter that was recovered from his coat pocket" replied Bell as he handed the envelope to Hadley

"If he had been the victim of a robbery, the watch would have been taken" said Hadley.

"That's very true."

"So was it an unfortunate drowning accident, sir?"

"No, Hadley, the man was murdered and his body mutilated, I don't know anything more than that."

"Anything important in the letter, sir?"

"Yes Hadley and that's why you're investigating the crime" replied Bell as Hadley opened the envelope, took out the note, which was from Sir Robert Salisbury of Cavendish Square, and read it out aloud.

"Dear Klaus, I am pleased to know that you have arrived safely in London and I look forward to dining with you here on Thursday evening, when we can discuss matters of mutual interest. Yours, Robert."

Hadley looked up at Bell and said "I don't understand what's so important about that, sir"

"The note is from Sir Robert Salisbury" said Bell.

"So I see."

"He's the under secretary of state at the Home Office, Hadley."

"And you think he might be implicated in something illegal, sir?"

"Anything is possible, Hadley. I'm going up to brief the Commissioner on what I know so far whilst you begin the investigation and whatever you do, try and keep the Press from wild speculation because the news of the murder has already leaked out and they've been here this morning asking damn fool questions."

"Right, I'll do my best, where is the body now, sir?"

"It's been taken to the Marylebone and I imagine that Doctor Evans has it in the mortuary."

"We'll get over there right away, sir."

"Report back to me as soon as you can, Hadley."

"Yes, sir" he nodded as he arose from his chair and headed for the door.

Doctor Evans looked up from his paper strewn desk and smiled at the detectives as they entered his office.

"Morning, Jim... Sergeant."

"Morning Doctor" replied Hadley as Cooper nodded.

"I'm sure that you've come to view our foreign gentleman who decided to take a dip, fully clothed, in the Serpentine this morning" said Doctor Evans with a smile.

"Well, it is the weather for it" replied Hadley.

"Indeed it is, but it's a shame he'd been murdered first though" said the Doctor as he stood up and made for the door. They followed him out into the mortuary where the naked body of Detrekker was laid out on a marble table.

"How did he die?" asked Hadley.

"A single stab to the heart, but then, as you can see the killer slashed at his face and neck after he was dead" replied Evans.

"A maniac then" said Hadley as he peered down at the multiple knife slashes across the face.

"Possibly or the killer didn't want him recognised" said Evans.

"His face is sun tanned, but his skin is white everywhere else" said Hadley as he glanced at the body.

"Yes, so he was obviously living somewhere hot, like India."

"All we know at the moment is his name, it's Klaus Detrekker" said Hadley.

"Perhaps he's a Dutchman from the Dutch East Indies?" ventured Evans.

"We'll find out from the Piccadilly Hotel, where he was staying" said Hadley.

"Well let me know, I'm curious, Jim."

"So am I, Doctor" replied Hadley with a smile.

The cab ride in the morning sunshine to the Piccadilly Hotel was pleasant but Hadley seemed unaware of his surroundings as his mind was racing with questions about Detrekker and his murder. He did not speak to Cooper all the way and only asked him to pay the cabbie as he stepped down from the Hansom outside the hotel. The detectives entered the imposing marble floored lobby and approached the reception, where two young men were positioned behind the desk. The receptionist confirmed that Detrekker was staying there but the two other gentlemen who arrived with him had checked out of the hotel that morning.

"What are their names?" asked Hadley.

The receptionist consulted the register and replied "Mr Hans Boeker and Mr Dik Vervorde."

"Where are they from?"

"All the gentlemen are from South Africa, sir" replied

"And their forwarding address is?"

"They didn't give one, sir."

"Right, will you please call the manager" said Hadley firmly.

"Who shall I say is calling, sir?"

"Inspector Hadley and Sergeant Cooper of Scotland Yard."

"Right, sir, I'll just be a moment" he replied and hurried away from his desk leaving the other receptionist looking bewildered. Within minutes he arrived back with Mr Sloane, the manager, who after introductions, showed the detectives to his office.

"Mr Sloane, you had three guests staying at the hotel last night, two apparently have checked out this morning and the third one has been found murdered in the Serpentine" said Hadley.

"Good God!" exclaimed Sloane his face growing pale.

"So, first of all, I would like to have all the details regarding these guests."

"Yes, of course, Inspector."

"And I would like to search their rooms right away."

"I will arrange that immediately."

"Thank you Mr Sloane."

The rooms occupied by Boeker and Vervorde were completely empty but Detrekker's room still contained all his personal belongings. The detectives searched through the items carefully and then packed them up into Detrekker's suitcases and had them taken down to the lobby. Mr Sloane was able to give only the barest details about the guests and other than the fact that they had arrived from South Africa, were booked in for two weeks and Mr Detrekker would be responsible for paying the hotel bill for all three, there was nothing else. Hadley thanked Mr Sloane and the detectives left the hotel with the suitcases and hurried back to the Yard.

Whilst George was left to itemise and record everything contained in the cases, Hadley and Cooper set off to number 22, Cavendish Square to interview Sir Robert Salisbury. An elderly butler opened the door of the imposing residence and looked Hadley up and down before he asked "can I help you?"

"Yes, is Sir Robert Salisbury at home?"

"He is, but he doesn't deal with tradesmen, so you'll have to go round the back and see Mrs Figgis, the housekeeper" replied the butler.

"I'm Inspector Hadley and this is Sergeant Cooper of Scotland Yard, please tell Sir Robert that we're here and we'll wait in the hall if you don't mind" replied Hadley as he pushed his way past the wide eyed butler.

"I'm sorry for my mistake, sir, I'll let Sir Robert know that you're here" said the concerned servant as he closed the door behind them and hurried off.

"Why do butlers always think we're tradesmen, Sergeant?"

"I keep telling you, sir, it's your hat, it's seen better days and so has your coat" replied Cooper with a smile.

"Alright, alright, Sergeant, you need not be so forthcoming…"

"You asked me, sir" replied Cooper.

"Try to be more diplomatic in future."

"I will, sir."

"I'll put matters right before the winter sets in and sport myself to a new top hat" said Hadley.

"What about your coat, sir?"

"I'll have to give it some careful thought before I rush into that extravagance, Sergeant" replied Hadley as the butler re-appeared and said "Sir Robert will see you now, sir."

"Thank you."

They were led through double doors into an elegant drawing room where a tall, distinguished looking man of about forty stood by the fireplace and a young couple sat close by on a quilted sofa.

"The police, sir" announced the butler.

"Thank you, Meadows, come in gentlemen and please be seated" said Sir Robert.

Hadley thanked him and introduced himself and Cooper before sitting down. The couple were introduced to the detectives as Gwendolyn, Sir Robert's daughter and her fiancé, Mr Rupert Brandon-Hall.

"Now what's this all about, Inspector?" asked Sir Robert.

"I understand that you have invited Mr Klaus Detrekker to dine with you tomorrow night, sir" said Hadley as Sir Robert went pale.

"How the devil do you know about that?" he demanded in a shocked tone.

"Because we found the note you wrote to him, sir."

"Has anything happened to him?"

"I regret to inform you, sir that Mr Detrekker has been found murdered…"

"Oh God, no!"

"His body was discovered in the Serpentine this morning and removed to the Marylebone Hospital where it has been confirmed that the gentleman was killed by a stab wound to the heart, sir."

"Oh my God, oh dear God, no" said Sir Robert as he slumped down in a chair pale faced and began to shake.

"Oh, Papa, are you alright?" said Gwendolyn anxiously.

"I think I need a brandy" murmured Sir Robert as she went to her father's side and held his hand before turning to her fiancé.

"Get some brandy quickly, Rupert."

"Right away, my dear" replied Rupert and he went over to a

drinks trolley and poured a large measure from a cut glass decanter into a goblet. Hadley was concerned at the appearance of Sir Robert and asked "do you need a Doctor, sir?"

"No, I'll be alright in a moment" he replied as Rupert handed him the brandy. After drinking the reviver, Sir Robert regained his composure.

"This has come as a great shock, Inspector."

"I'm sure it has, sir."

"What do his colleagues have to say about this terrible tragedy?"

"I don't know, sir."

"Why is that?"

"Because they booked out of the Hotel this morning and have disappeared" replied Hadley.

"Oh, no" whispered Sir Robert as he grew pale once again.

"Have you any idea where they might have gone, sir?"

"No, no, Inspector" Sir Robert stammered.

"By the tone of your note, you obviously knew Mr Detrekker very well, sir."

"Yes, quite well, Inspector."

"And may I ask what you planned to discuss with him over dinner?"

"I'm afraid that's confidential, Inspector."

"Sir, I'm investigating the murder of a gentleman whom you know and had invited to this house for dinner and with regard to your position in the government, I advise you strongly to co-operate with me and tell me everything that may be relevant" said Hadley firmly.

"There is nothing to tell, Inspector, I assure you, my invitation to Klaus was for social reasons only" replied Sir Robert with a forced smile. Hadley remained silent and watched as Sir Robert began to sweat.

"Get me another brandy please, Rupert"

Whilst Rupert was pouring the drink, Gwendolyn said "Inspector, your news has been a great shock to my father and I think it would be sensible for you to leave now and return tomorrow if you have any more questions."

Hadley nodded and replied "very well, Miss, and I'm sorry to be the bearer of such bad news."

"That's understandable, you're only doing your duty, Inspector" she smiled.

"Thank you, Miss, I wish you all a good day" said Hadley as Sir Robert gulped another brandy and gave him a sickly smile.

As the detectives walked along the Square towards Regent Street, Hadley asked "what did you make of that, Sergeant?"

"I think Sir Robert is obviously hiding the true reason for his meeting with Detrekker and his murder could reveal something that Sir Robert would wish to keep a secret, sir."

"Exactly, Sergeant, now hail a cab and let's get back to the Yard."

When they arrived back in the office, an anxious George greeted them and said "thank heavens you're back, the Chief Inspector wants to see you both straight away, he says it's very urgent."

"Thank you, George" said Hadley

Bell looked up as they entered his office and said with a grim expression "the Commissioner wants to see us immediately."

"May I ask, what is it about, sir?"

"He has a Prussian Count called von Rausberg with him, that's all his clerk could tell me, so let's get up there straight away and find out, Hadley" replied Bell.

CHAPTER 2

The detectives followed Bell into the Commissioner's office where he sat stony faced behind his large desk, his side whiskers bristling. Seated opposite him were two men, one looked distinguished and well dressed, wearing a monocle, his close cut, iron grey hair and full beard gave him a mature and superior look. Beside him sat a younger man, well built with black hair and a moustache which half hid a duelling scar on his cheek. The Commissioner made the introductions with a wave of his hand.

"Gentlemen, this is Count Erik von Rausberg and his assistant, Mr Schoender." Bell and the detectives shook hands as the Commissioner introduced them to the Count and his assistant.

"Now, everything that I will tell you must remain strictly confidential and under no circumstances must any other person be told about this investigation, is that clear?" said the Commissioner.

"Yes, sir" they all nodded and replied in chorus.

"The Count has informed me that he represents the German Government in a delicate and secret matter, he is not attached to the German Embassy, in fact they don't know that he is in London" said the Commissioner.

"And they must never know" said the Count firmly in a thick accent.

"Quite so, now the Count came here to collect a sealed box, which is the final part of an international transaction, and take its contents to a specialist in the field before going on to Amsterdam to conduct further business" said the Commissioner.

"May we know exactly what the box contains, sir?" asked Hadley as Bell glared at him and the Commissioner frowned before he looked at the Count.

"In the box are four uncut diamonds" said the Count and there followed a few moments of silence as Hadley pondered the implications.

"In the circumstances, sir, perhaps you would like to tell my officers everything that you consider would be helpful in the investigation" said the Commissioner.

"Very well" replied the Count with a slight nod.

"Please pay great attention to what the Count has to say" said the Commissioner and they all waited patiently for him to begin.

"I have come to London to collect the diamonds from Klaus Detrekker, owner of the Transvaal Mining Company in South Africa, and take them to Solomon Isaacs in Hatton Garden for valuation and advice on how they should be cut, before going on to Amsterdam to see Van De Haas, an acknowledge expert on the cutting of precious stones" said the Count. Hearing that, Hadley knew that this investigation was probably going to be more difficult than he anticipated.

"Do you have the diamonds now, sir?" asked Hadley.

"No, and that is why I am here, Inspector" replied the Count in a firm tone.

"Please continue, sir" said the Commissioner as he glared at Hadley for his untimely interruption.

"I went to the Piccadilly Hotel this morning to meet Mr Detrekker and collect the stones but when I arrived the manager informed me that he had been found murdered and as there was no sign of the diamonds I have come here to report the loss and demand that you find the box containing the Imperial German Government's property" replied the Count firmly.

"We shall do everything possible to recover the diamonds, sir" said the Commissioner.

"I fear that you may not understand the gravity of this situation, Commissioner" said the Count angrily.

"I assure you that I do, sir and…"

"The diamonds are the purest white, the largest of which is approximately 80 carats, the others are 65 carats, 62 carats and 46 carats respectively, which makes their combined value when cut, incalculable!" interrupted the Count.

"Good heavens" said the Commissioner.

"And when I tell you that only one larger diamond, of 112 carats, has ever been discovered and that was in India in the seventeenth century, it gives you some idea of the importance of this find" said the Count.

"Indeed it does, sir."

"The Imperial Government has purchased these stones for an undisclosed amount and half the money has been paid as a deposit into the Swiss Bank Account of the Transvaal Mining Company. It is my duty to recover the diamonds, or the money, and as Swiss

Banks are bound by protocols of secrecy and Herr Detrekker is dead, I have no option but to find the diamonds or should I say, you do, Commissioner" said the Count.

"Yes of course, sir."

"I am sure that if you do not, then my Government will claim that you have failed in your duty and that will lead to a serious diplomatic situation between our two countries. I hope I make myself clear, Commissioner" said the Count firmly.

"You do indeed, Count von Rausberg" replied the Commissioner nervously.

"I am due to meet Van de Haas in Amsterdam next Wednesday and I am booked on the ferry from Dover at midday on the Tuesday, so you have until then to recover my Government's property" said the Count.

"That should give us plenty of time, sir" said the Commissioner in a confident tone as Hadley groaned silently.

"I am staying at the Savoy Hotel in the Strand until then, so you may reach me there, Commissioner."

"We will, sir, in due course."

"Good. Then I wish you all a good day" said the Count as he stood up and gave a little nod of his head before he and Schoender left the office.

"Well, gentlemen, we have until next Tuesday to recover the diamonds or Her Majesty's Government will face a humiliating and damaging diplomatic situation" said the Commissioner.

"We'll recover them, sir, you can rely on us" said Bell with confidence.

"What do we know so far about the murder of Detrekker?" asked the Commissioner.

"He was discovered in the Serpentine, stabbed through the heart, sir" replied Bell.

"And you traced him to the Piccadilly Hotel, did you find anything there of interest?" asked the Commissioner.

"No, sir, but I have suspicions about his two colleagues who left the Hotel this morning before we got there" said Hadley.

"Then it's obvious that they have taken the diamonds" said the Commissioner.

"Probably, sir" replied Hadley.

"Have you any idea where they have gone?"

"No sir, not at the moment" replied Hadley.

"Well you'd better get a move on and find them if you're to recover the diamonds by next Tuesday" said the Commissioner.

"Yes, sir, but I'd like to ask, do you know why the Count insists on keeping the theft secret from the German Embassy?" asked Hadley.

"Diplomatic reasons I suppose, but that should not hamper our efforts to find Detrekker's colleagues and the diamonds" replied the Commissioner.

"Quite so, and there is another fact that you should be aware of, sir" said Hadley.

"And what is that?"

"Detrekker had a note in his pocket from Sir Robert Salisbury inviting him to dinner tomorrow night, sir" said Hadley.

"What?" asked the Commissioner as he raised his eyebrows in surprise.

"That is so, sir, and that's how we traced Detrekker to the Hotel" said Bell.

"Do you mean our Sir Robert at the Home Office?" asked the concerned Commissioner.

"The very same, sir" said Bell.

"My God, this has very serious implications" said the Commissioner looking down at his desk as he searched his mind for an explanation.

"We will proceed with great care, sir" said Bell helpfully.

"By God, you need to, Chief Inspector, because if we get this wrong then we'll all have to take early retirement and reduced pensions" said the Commissioner.

"Indeed we will, sir" said Bell.

"Well you'd better get on with it and make sure you keep me well informed as once the Home Secretary hears of it I'm bound to be asked what's going on" said the Commissioner.

"Right, sir."

"And Bell…"

"Yes, sir?"

"I'll get a Press statement released later which will say that Detrekker was the victim of a murderous robbery in Hyde Park. We're looking for a vagrant seen lurking nearby and we expect an early arrest" said the Commissioner.

"Very good, sir."

"And make sure you all stick to that if any of the Press start asking questions."

"We will, sir."

As Hadley and Cooper descended the stairs, Bell had urged them to work day and night if necessary to recover the diamonds and Hadley assured him that they would.

When they were back in their office Cooper asked "what shall we do first, sir?"

"Telegraph all London stations with the details of our South African friends, Boeker and Vervorde and request their arrest on suspicion of theft" replied Hadley.

"And then, sir?"

"Give this situation some careful thought and make plans, Sergeant."

"Will you tell George, sir?"

"Yes of course, he needs to know" replied Hadley. The affable clerk was summoned and sworn to secrecy then Hadley told him everything before requesting a pot of tea.

It was nearly lunchtime when the detectives hailed a cab and set off for Whitechapel.

"An early lunch at the Kings Head, sir?" asked Cooper as the Hansom made its way along the Embankment.

"After we've called on Charlie Benton, Sergeant" replied Hadley and Cooper smiled. When they reached Whitechapel, Hadley asked the cabbie to take them to Lipton Street. Eventually they arrived outside the old corner shop with the sign in faded gold lettering that read 'Chas. Benton and Sons' and underneath 'Suppliers and buyers of fine jewellery'. Hadley knocked at the door with the 'closed' sign, whilst Cooper paid the cabbie and as he joined him, he heard the sound of bolts being drawn back. The door opened slightly and Charlie's face appeared.

"Morning, Charlie" said Hadley.

"Oh, blimey, it's you Jim, with the boy" replied Charlie as he swung the door open for them to enter his gloomy shop. After he closed the door and bolted it, they followed him to the back of the shop and through the red velvet curtains to the untidy gas lit room beyond.

"Take a seat" said Charlie as he sat in the creaking leather chair behind his desk which was covered with paperwork. When they were seated, the old man looked over his spectacles and asked "and to what do I owe the honour of this visit, Jim?"

"Charlie, we've a very delicate investigation in hand…"

"Is that in contrast to your usual clumsy ones then?" interrupted the old man with a grin.

"Charlie, this is serious" said Hadley firmly.

"Nah, nothing is serious, Jim, only death is and as I'm nearer than you to the Pearly Gates, I can tell you that you've nothing to worry about yet!"

"Charlie, I promise you…"

"Oh, stop promising me, Jim, you're beginning to sound like my old woman!" he interrupted as Hadley glanced at Cooper who smiled.

"Have you been up the Kings Head this morning?"

"Not yet, but I'll go with you now if you're buying!" said Charlie as Hadley shook his head and sighed before he said firmly "listen to me, Charlie!"

"Yes, Jim."

"What do you know about Solomon Isaacs in Hatton Garden?" The old man pursed his lips, waited a few moments, and replied "if you're asking about him, this must be a delicate and serious case, Jim."

"I told you so."

"Well, I know he's the top man in the Garden for uncut stones and over the years there have been little rumours about him…"

"What sort of rumours, Charlie?"

"He's a very wealthy man and some people wonder where he gets so many large stones from and so much money, Jim."

"Does he cut diamonds?"

"I'm told that he does cut some but the large ones he sends to Amsterdam, he deals with one man over there called House or something" said Charlie.

"Van de Haas?"

"That's him, Jim."

"That's very interesting."

"Let me warn you about Isaacs, he's got a lot of powerful

friends in high places and he guards himself with a couple of smartly dressed thugs who'll knock seven bells out of anybody at the drop of his hat" said Charlie.

"Thanks for the warning" said Hadley with a nod.

"So I guess that some large uncut stones have been lifted and are floating about London somewhere" said Charlie.

"Your guess is right as usual" said Hadley.

"In that case I'll keep my old ear to the ground and let you know anything I hear, Jim."

"Thanks Charlie, now tell me where I can find Isaacs."

"His place is at the top of the Garden, just a few doors down from the Clerkenwell Road, Jim."

The detectives left the corner shop and walked at a leisurely pace in the sunshine to the Kings Head pub. Vera and Oswald, the publicans, were behind the bar struggling to keep up with the midday drinkers from the docks. The detectives had to wait until Vera noticed them and left Oswald to cope with the others. They ordered stout and cheese with pickle lunches before Hadley wandered off with his pint towards the open door and glanced along the busy Whitechapel Road, leaving Cooper to settle the bill.

As the Sergeant joined him, Agnes Cartwright, a voluptuous lady of uncertain years who gave personal relief to discerning gentlemen for five shillings a time, (two and sixpence on Mondays to encourage trade), arrived at the pub accompanied by Florrie Dean, her young friend. Florrie was an attractive blonde girl who offered very special services to the more mature gentlemen, who were both relieved and grateful for the service.

"Hello, Jim… Sergeant, how are you today?" asked Agnes.

"As well as can be expected, Agnes" replied Hadley as he leaned against the doorway and smiled.

"Six penny gins for you both?" asked Cooper and the women nodded.

"You're a treasure, Sergeant, now whilst you get the drinks I'll find somewhere for us to sit" said Agnes as she made her way into the noisy pub and glanced around for a table. She found one that had just been vacated by a man and two women so she called for Hadley to join them. As he sat down Agnes said "you look a bit lost today, Jim, what's wrong?"

"I'm thinking, Agnes."

"What about?"

"That would be telling, but you could help me…"

"Don't I always, Jim?" she interrupted.

"You do indeed."

"So, what's it all about?"

"I'm looking for two foreigners…"

"Blimey, Jim, you're spoilt for choice round here!" she interrupted.

"I'm sure, but these two are probably well dressed, look like toffs and come from South Africa" said Hadley.

"Are they black?"

"No, Agnes."

"What makes you think they'd come down here?" asked Agnes.

"I don't know, but as you and the girls down the Lane know everything that happens, this side of the City…"

"That we do" said Agnes as Cooper arrived with the gins and sat down.

"It's a long shot but someone may see them about" said Hadley.

"We'll all keep our eyes open for you, Jim" said Agnes as she raised her glass to the detectives. As the women began to chat and gossip, which was always valuable to Hadley as background information, Vera arrived with their lunches. The detectives shared their meal with the girls, then left the pub and hailed a Hansom to take them to Hatton Garden.

Stopping the cab in the Clerkenwell Road they walked down the Garden looking for Isaacs' emporium, it was as Charlie had described, four shops along. The detectives stopped to admire the glittering array of diamond rings and necklaces displayed on blue velvet cushions in the small window. Entering the smart interior of the shop they were met by a serious looking young man who asked if he could help.

"We'd like to have a word with Mr Isaacs, please" said Hadley.

"Who shall I say is calling, sir?"

"Inspector Hadley and Sergeant Cooper of Scotland Yard."

"I'll inform him at once, sir" said the young man and he

disappeared through a door at the back of the shop. Hadley looked around at the display cases and was impressed by the contents and amazed at the prices.

"This is not somewhere that you could bring your wife, Sergeant."

"No, sir, it certainly isn't. At these prices the visit would be bound to end in tears of disappointment" replied Cooper and Hadley smiled.

"Only the Commissioner could afford to shop here" said Hadley.

"That's for sure, sir."

The young man re-appeared accompanied by a smartly dressed, thick set, hard faced man and Hadley guessed that he was one of Solomon Isaacs 'assistants'.

"Mr Isaacs will see you now. Please come with me, gentlemen" said the well dressed man firmly. The detectives nodded and followed him through the door and into a dark, narrow corridor, up a flight of stairs to a large landing and through a door at the end.

As they entered the spacious room, Solomon Isaacs arose from his desk and looked quizzically at the detectives. Isaacs was about fifty years old with a pale face, sleek black hair, cut short. His hard black eyes narrowed with curiosity as he said "please have a seat, gentlemen and tell me how I can help you."

Hadley thanked him and as he and Cooper sat on the two plush chairs in front of the desk, the Sergeant produced his notebook whilst the assistant stood with his back to the door.

"I understand that you are expecting a visit from Count von Rausberg…"

"He's already been here, Inspector" interrupted Isaacs.

"He was intending to bring uncut diamonds for you to assess."

"Indeed he was, Inspector."

"They were purchased from a Mr Klaus Detrekker of South Africa."

"So I understand, Inspector."

"And did he inform you that Mr Klaus Detrekker was found murdered this morning in Hyde Park?" asked Hadley.

"He said he was now dead but he did not go into any great detail, Inspector."

"You don't seem surprised, sir" said Hadley.

"Well I didn't know the man so his death means nothing to me" replied Isaacs.

"I find it hard to believe that you didn't know Klaus Detrekker, sir."

"Are you calling me a liar, Inspector?" asked Isaacs angrily.

"I'm merely pointing out that as Detrekker was the owner of the Transvaal Diamond Mining Company, and as you are closely associated with the purchase and sale of expensive diamonds, it is very surprising to hear you claim not to know him, sir." Isaacs face blushed slightly and he waited a few moments before he replied "I've heard of him, of course, but I didn't know him, Inspector."

"I see, sir. I understand that the Count arranged to bring you the diamonds purchased from Detrekker for your opinion on value and cutting, can you confirm that, sir?"

"Yes, that is so, Inspector."

"Were you aware of the size of these stones, sir?"

"I did not know their exact carat but the Count said that they were considerable" replied Isaacs.

"Indeed they are, sir, in fact they are the largest ever found in Africa" said Hadley.

"In that case, I should be pleased to see them in due course."

"Do you think you will, sir?"

"Inevitably, Inspector."

"Why are you so certain?"

"Because if they are ever to be cut, then I, or another person of my equal standing…"

"Such as Van de Haas?" interrupted Hadley and Isaacs black eyes narrowed before he continued "will have to examine them before advising how to make the cut, otherwise, as I'm sure you know, if an amateur attempts to do it, they may shatter and be lost."

"Quite so, do you know a Mr Boeker or Mr Vervorde?"

"No, Inspector, who are they?"

"Both gentlemen were assistants to Mr Detrekker and arrived with him from South Africa, sir."

"Well, I don't know them."

"If they should call upon you, would you kindly inform me at Scotland Yard?"

"Certainly, Inspector, but why should they come to see me?"

"Because it is possible that they may have the diamonds, sir."

Isaacs gave a curious smile and said "is that so, Inspector, well we'll have to wait and see. Now I'm a busy man, so if you will excuse me. My assistant, Mr Grenville will now show you out."

"Good day, sir" said Hadley as he stood up and followed Grenville down to the shop. When the detectives were outside in Hatton Garden, Cooper asked "back to the Yard, sir?"

"Yes, Sergeant, I think the games afoot and we must make arrangements to keep this place under constant surveillance!"

CHAPTER 3

As soon as the detectives arrived in their office, Hadley summoned the Duty Sergeant and made arrangements for two plain clothes officers to keep watch at Isaacs shop for the South Africans. If the wanted men are observed entering the premises then one of the officers should telegraph Hadley from the nearest police station. The problem was that Hadley did not know what they looked like and all he could assume was that they were well dressed, had tanned faces and carried a small box. That was precious little description for the young officers but they were keen so, after Hadley had briefed them, they set off full of confidence. George organised a pot of tea, which relaxed Hadley before he went up to brief Chief Inspector Bell.

The Chief looked up from his desk as Hadley entered his office and asked "have you found the South Africans yet?"
"No, sir, but I'm sure that we'll pick them up soon."
"I'm not as confident as you, I'm afraid."
"It is probable that they have the diamonds and either murdered Detrekker for them or disappeared for their own safety as soon as they knew he had been killed, sir."
"Well, why didn't they come to us for protection?"
"I don't know, sir, perhaps they are afraid of the police."
"Nonsense, Hadley, no one is afraid of us" replied Bell with a snort.
"As you say, sir. I've been to see Isaacs in Hatton Garden…"
"And what did he have to say for himself?" interrupted Bell.
"The Count had been there this morning and told him that Detrekker was dead and the diamonds were missing" replied Hadley.
"And what was his reaction to that news?"
"He seemed remarkably calm about the whole thing, sir."
"Then he knows something and is hiding it" said Bell.
"I agree, sir, so I've arranged for two plain clothes officers to keep the premises under constant surveillance in case the South Africans turn up."
"Well done, Hadley, now what about Sir Robert, what's

happening there?"

"He was very distressed when I informed him of Detrekker's murder and so I'm going to speak to him tomorrow morning when I hope he has recovered from the sad news, sir."

"Well for God's sake, mind how you go with him."

"Of course, sir."

"The Commissioner is very worried, Hadley, so as soon as you've spoken to Sir Robert let me have a report to show him so he can discuss it with the Home Secretary."

"I will, sir."

"This is all very delicate" said Bell as gazed at his clasped hands before him.

"I appreciate that, sir."

"Good, so is that all, Hadley?"

"It is for the moment, sir."

"Well, you can get on with the investigation and leave me to worry about the diplomatic incident if we don't recover the diamonds by next Tuesday."

"Yes, sir, I will" replied Hadley with a half concealed smile.

Hadley spent the rest of the afternoon writing reports with Cooper and making plans for the next day. The detectives left the Yard at seven o'clock and Hadley was tired when he arrived at his home in Camden. Alice had prepared a light dinner of ham with a salad as it was still a warm evening and his son, Arthur, poured him a refreshing stout. Hadley relaxed with his family and tried to put the investigation to the back of his mind but he found it difficult because of the serious implications caused by the missing diamonds and the murder of Detrekker.

When Hadley arrived in the office the next morning, Cooper was already there and anxious to get started.

"Any news from our boys outside Isaacs shop?" asked Hadley as he sat behind his desk.

"No, sir, they reported back after they were relieved by the night watch, and their notes are on your desk" replied Cooper. Hadley glanced down and read the brief report which told him that nothing suspicious had occurred before the shop closed and was shuttered up at six o'clock and the staff left the premises.

"And have they taken over from the night watch, Sergeant?"

"Yes, sir, at eight o'clock this morning" replied Cooper.

"Good, now we'll have some tea and then pay a visit to Sir Robert."

"At his office, sir?"

"Yes, Sergeant."

The detectives left the Yard and walked round to the Home Office in Whitehall at a fast pace. When they entered the august building Hadley asked the receptionist to let Sir Robert's senior clerk know that he wished to see him. A messenger was dispatched upstairs and soon afterwards the clerk arrived looking concerned. When Hadley informed him that he wished to see Sir Robert the clerk replied "he has not arrived this morning, Inspector."

"Is he usually here by now?" asked Hadley as he glanced at his pocket watch.

"Yes, he's always at his desk by nine o'clock, Inspector, and all I can assume is that he is unwell today" replied the clerk.

"Thank you for your help" said Hadley and the clerk gave a nod before the detectives left the building.

"Where to now, sir?"

"Up to Cavendish Square, Sergeant… hail a cab if you will."

The Hansom made fast progress through the busy traffic and arrived outside number 22, Cavendish Square in good time. Cooper knocked at the door which was eventually opened by Meadows. When Hadley asked to see Sir Robert, the butler replied "I'm afraid you can't, sir, because the Master is not here."

"Where has he gone?"

"To his country house, sir."

"When did he leave?"

"Late yesterday afternoon, sir."

"Was he alone?"

"No, sir, Miss Gwendolyn and Mr Rupert went with him along with the other two gentlemen" replied Meadows.

"Tell me about the two gentlemen if you would."

"Nothing to tell, sir."

"What are their names?" asked Hadley, his blue eyes hardening.

"I don't know, sir."

"Well how did you announce them?"

"I didn't have to, Sir Robert brought the gentlemen back to the house and they went straight into the study, sir" replied Meadows.

"Do you know if these men are foreign?"

"I did overhear them thank Sir Robert when they first arrived and they had an accent which sounded like a German or Dutch one, but I'm not sure, sir."

"Did their faces look tanned by the sun?"

"Possibly, sir."

"Did either of them carry a small case of any kind?"

"I didn't notice, sir."

"Right, now where is Sir Robert's country estate?"

"At Chieveley in Berkshire, sir."

"Is it close to a town?"

"Yes, sir, Chieveley Manor is some six miles north of Newbury" replied Meadows.

"Thank you very much" said Hadley before he and Cooper turned away and descended the steps to the pavement.

"Back to the Yard, Sergeant…"

"And then on to Chieveley, sir?"

"As fast as possible, Sergeant" replied Hadley as Cooper waved at a passing cab.

On their return to their office, Hadley asked George to find out the time of the next train from Paddington to Newbury and told Cooper to draw two revolvers and twelve rounds of ammunition from the armoury whilst he briefed the Chief Inspector on the latest development.

"Are you sure about this, Hadley?" asked Bell with a worried frown.

"I am, sir."

"Well supposing these two fellas who've gone with Sir Robert down to his estate are friends of his, I mean it all could be very embarrassing" said Bell with a shake of his head.

"It's a chance I'll have to take, sir."

"Well make sure you're diplomatic, Hadley."

"I will be, sir."

"The Commissioner doesn't want Sir Robert upset."

"I'm sure of that, sir."

"And what happens if these South Africans turn up at Isaacs place while you're away chasing around Berkshire?"

"I'll give instructions to detain them to help us with our inquiries, sir."

"Well make sure that you do, Hadley, we can't afford for these suspects to slip through our hands."

"Leave it to me, sir."

"I've no other option, Hadley, so just make sure that you recover these diamonds before next Tuesday, then we can all sleep soundly again" said Bell.

"I'll do my best, sir" replied Hadley with a grin.

The detectives caught the eleven o'clock train from Paddington that was due to stop at Reading, Newbury, Bath and Bristol. The express thundered through the countryside and as Hadley watched the steam from the locomotive drift lazily across the green fields, he remained deep in thought. Cooper knew that it was best not to interrupt his Inspector's deliberations and he remained quiet, until Hadley spoke to him suddenly, in a serious tone.

"Sergeant, I fear that as the stakes are high and the rewards so great in this case, we may face very desperate men who will kill anybody who gets in their way."

"Including us, sir?"

"Without a shadow of a doubt, Sergeant, so always be ready with your revolver. I don't want to have to attend your funeral and I certainly don't want you attending mine!"

"Do you think the South Africans murdered Detrekker, sir?"

"I don't know what to believe at the moment, Sergeant" replied Hadley as he gazed out of the window once again.

"It certainly looks likely that they are the killers, sir."

"Possibly, but we have to take the Count into consideration as well as Isaacs and Sir Robert, any of them may also have had a hand in the crime and the list of suspects grows longer each time I think about the investigation" replied Hadley as the train began to slow as it approached Newbury station.

The detectives hired a trap to take them from the railway station up the Oxford road to Chieveley. They passed through the picturesque village and then about a mile further on, the trap swung off the road through open ornate wrought iron gates into the drive leading up to Chieveley Manor. The Georgian residence nestled sedately amongst mature trees and was surrounded by immaculate lawns that led away from the house down to a small lake with weeping willows that shimmered in the gentle summer breeze. The trap pulled up outside the imposing façade and whilst Cooper made arrangements for the driver to return later, Hadley surveyed the Manor house. The detectives ascended the steps, passed through the columns to the large front door where Cooper rang the bell. The door was opened by an elderly butler who looked them up and down before he asked "can I help you, gentlemen?"

"Yes, we would like to see Sir Robert" replied Hadley.

"And who shall I say is calling, sir?"

"Inspector Hadley and Sergeant Cooper."

"Please come in gentlemen and I'll inform Sir Robert that you are here" said the butler as he stood back and allowed them to enter the spacious hallway. When he disappeared through double doors into the drawing room, Hadley and Cooper looked about the opulent hall. The Italian marble floor gleamed and gave reflected light to the gilded ornate mirrors above the half moon wall tables and the splendid staircase swept up to the landing above where paintings of Sir Robert's ancestors were positioned at regular intervals. A huge chandelier was suspended from the ceiling and it shimmered in the sunlight that streamed through the upstairs windows. The butler soon re-appeared and said "Sir Robert will see you now, gentlemen." They followed him through into the large drawing room where he announced them.

"Thank you, Wilson" said Sir Robert as he stood to greet the detectives.

"Good day, Sir Robert, thank you for seeing us so promptly" said Hadley.

"Not at all, Inspector, please come and sit down" replied Sir Robert.

"Thank you, sir" said Hadley as he and Cooper sat on a plush cream sofa.

"Wilson, would you bring us some tea" said Sir Robert as he sat opposite the detectives in a large armchair. The butler nodded and withdrew as Sir Robert gave the detectives a quizzical look.

"I expect you're wondering why we have come to see you so soon, sir" said Hadley.

"It did cross my mind, Inspector" replied Sir Robert with a wry smile.

"As you know I am following up lines of inquiry concerning the cruel murder of Mr Detrekker…"

"Yes, and how can I help, Inspector?"

"You know that Mr Detrekker had two colleagues with him when he arrived in London, sir."

"Yes, I was aware of that, Inspector" said the knight hurriedly.

"They were staying at the Piccadilly Hotel with him but left the morning that Mr Detrekker was found in Hyde Park, sir."

"Have they gone back to South Africa?"

"I don't know, sir, but I was hoping that you may be able to shed some light on their whereabouts."

"Me, Inspector, how should I know where they are?"

"According to Mr Meadows, you left your London house with two foreign gentlemen late yesterday afternoon, sir" said Hadley and he watched how pale Sir Robert became.

"That is true, Inspector" he said anxiously.

"Do you mind telling me who they were, sir?"

"Not at all, Inspector, they were Herr Konigsberg and Herr Stumpfel from the German Embassy."

"And where are they now, sir?"

"They returned to London this morning, Inspector, so I'm afraid you've just missed them." Hadley felt totally deflated by Sir Robert's explanation and he was not sure whether to believe him or not so he remained silent for a few moments to gather his thoughts.

"Would you mind telling me why the gentlemen came down here to stay just for one night, sir?"

"Herr Konigsberg is an under-secretary at the Embassy and is a keen breeder of thoroughbred horses, he has very fine stables at his schloss in Austria, and he came with his assistant, Herr Stumpfel, to see my stallion, Hercules, to discuss the possibility of breeding from him."

"Why did he have to leave so quickly, sir?"

"Because he was recalled to Berlin to report on a diplomatic situation that had just occurred, that's why he left in a hurry" replied Sir Roberts as Wilson arrived with the tea on a large silver tray. After tea had been served, Hadley asked "is your daughter here, sir?"

"Yes, she is, why do you ask, Inspector?"

"I'm just interested to know if she journeyed down with you, sir."

"Yes, she did and her fiancé, Mr Brandon-Hall is with her, they are out riding at the moment" replied Sir Robert.

"How very pleasant on such a lovely day" said Hadley with a smile.

"Indeed it is."

Hadley waited for a few moments before he asked "did your German guests leave anything with you for safe keeping, sir?" and this sudden change in questioning seemed to unsettle the knight.

"Er, no, no, nothing, Inspector" he replied anxiously.

"Were you aware that Mr Detrekker had brought priceless uncut diamonds to London which he had sold in secret to the German Government, sir?" asked Hadley and saw Sir Robert begin to perspire.

"I knew he had brought diamonds with him, he usually does, Inspector, but I did not know for whom they were intended" replied Sir Robert.

"I must inform you in the strictest confidence, sir, that the diamonds are now missing and their loss has been reported to the Commissioner by an interested party on behalf of the German Government" said Hadley.

"Well for the life of me, I know nothing of this and don't know how I can help you, Inspector" said Sir Robert in an anxious tone.

"Indeed, Sir Robert" said Hadley and he thought that it would be unwise to press any harder, remembering that he had to be both careful and diplomatic.

"It seems you've had a wasted journey, Inspector."

"Not at all, sir, you've been most helpful" replied Hadley with a smile.

"Is there anything else, Inspector?"

"No sir, but may I ask, do you intend to return to London soon?"

"Yes, possibly tomorrow, Inspector, why do you ask?"

"When I visited your office this morning your clerk told me that you were absent because he believed that you may be unwell, sir" replied Hadley and Sir Robert paled once again but before he could say anything, Hadley continued "but as we can see, you're fit and in the best of health, sir."

"Yes I am thank you" replied the knight in an anxious tone as he blushed.

"Well we'll take our leave now and thank you for your help, Sir Robert, good day" said Hadley.

"Good day, gentlemen."

Hadley saved his comments until they were alone in a compartment on the train back to Paddington.

"I think that our Sir Robert is up to his neck in this mystery, Sergeant."

"I agree, sir."

"I'm not at all sure if the foreigners were not our South African friends and possibly they have left the diamonds with him for safe keeping."

"Why would they do that, sir?"

"They know that we're searching for them in London, Sergeant."

"What do you expect next, sir?"

"I think that if it is the case that they murdered Detrekker for the stones, they will want to get them to De Haas in Amsterdam as soon as possible."

"And Sir Robert is the man to help them, sir."

"Precisely so, Sergeant, with his contacts he could get the diamonds taken in a diplomatic bag to Amsterdam without any difficulty."

"What about Isaacs, sir, why wouldn't Sir Robert have them taken to him?"

"Too risky, Sergeant, the man is too well known and too close to our inquiries for safety."

"Right, sir."

"When we get back to the office we'll find out if Herr Konigsberg and his assistant have left for Germany, and if not, we'll question them carefully about their visit to Chieveley."

"Is that wise, sir, seeing that we have to be very diplomatic?"

"We're investigating murder and the theft of priceless diamonds, Sergeant, and everything else must take second place to that!"

As soon as they arrived at the office, George told them that the Chief Inspector wanted to see them immediately.

"I thought he would have gone home by now" said Hadley as he glanced at his fob watch, it was almost seven o'clock.

"No, sir, he told me to wait for you and tell you that it was urgent."

"Right, thank you, George, you can go home now."

"Thank you, sir."

Chief Inspector Bell looked up, his face grim and anxious as they entered his office.

"One of the South Africans has been found…"

"Where, sir?"

"Behind the elephant house in Regents Park zoo with his throat cut" replied Bell.

"Good God, when was he found, sir?"

"Late this afternoon by a Mr Arthur Spraggs, the elephant keeper."

"Do you know which one he is, sir?"

"Yes, he had various papers on him as well as business cards that identified him as Dik Vervorde" replied Bell.

"So it must be Boeker who's got the diamonds" said Hadley.

"Possibly, and may I remind you that while you were gallivanting around Berkshire on another wild goose chase, Vervorde was murdered. The Commissioner became even more worried by the whole affair and I expect the Press have been busy composing the most lurid and toe curling comments for tomorrow's papers, Hadley!"

"Situation normal then, sir."

"Don't be so flippant and cavalier with me, Inspector!" thundered Bell.

"I'm sorry, sir."

"If we don't get some positive results soon there will be a serious diplomatic situation for the Government to deal with and you'll be on horse traffic duties until you retire!"

CHAPTER 4

Hadley returned to his office where he drafted a telegraph message to all London police stations advising them of the murder of Vervorde and requesting the search and arrest of Hans Boeker. Cooper took it to the telegraph office and when he returned he found Hadley sitting at his desk deep in thought.
"Are you alright, sir?"
"Yes, thank you, Sergeant, just a bit tired."
"I'm not surprised, sir, it's been a very busy day."
"With not much accomplished, I fear."
"Perhaps we'll get a break in the investigation tomorrow, sir."
"I hope so, Sergeant, now I think it's time we went home."
"A good idea, sir."

When Hadley returned home he was in a disconsolate mood and even Alice's best efforts to cheer her husband into a better frame of mind did not succeed. Hadley knew that this investigation was going to be long and dangerous with an uncertain outcome that could prove disastrous to his career. However, after a good night's sleep, he was re-invigorated and determined to bring the case to some kind of conclusion before next Tuesday. The recovery of the diamonds would be his priority and although their theft was inextricably linked to the murders of Detrekker and Vervorde, he knew that politics and positioning were more important in this case and were of a higher priority for his superiors than bringing a murderer to justice.

As soon as Hadley arrived at the Yard, sat behind his desk and acknowledged Cooper, George came in with a newspaper and said "good morning, sir, the Chief Inspector sent this down for you to read at your earliest."
"Thank you, George" replied Hadley as the clerk placed the Times on his desk.
"I think you might need a cup of tea after you've read that, sir."
"I'm sure you're right, George" replied Hadley as he picked up the paper and read aloud the headlines from the front page.
"Second South African found murdered in zoo, police

searching for an unknown assailant who is killing foreigners at random in London Parks, police warn all foreigners that they are at risk, the editor of this newspaper advises all visitors in London to stay away from Parks and open places until the maniac is arrested and the danger is passed, but at the time of going to Press the police still remain baffled." Hadley put the paper down and looked across at Cooper and said "where do they get this nonsense from, Sergeant?"

"They make it up to sell more papers, sir."

"I'm sure you're right."

After tea they set off to the German Embassy in Belgrave Square hoping to see Herr Konigsberg before he left for Berlin. They rang the bell and waited outside for a while in the warm sunlight before the door was opened by a tall, grey haired man with side whiskers and moustache that gave him an air of superiority. Hadley introduced himself to the superior one and asked to see Herr Konigsberg, the man nodded and they were admitted into the imposing hallway and told to wait. The detectives gazed around at the portraits that ordained the walls and they both felt slightly uncomfortable under the glare of the sullen faces that stared down at them. The superior one returned with another tall, gaunt man who introduced himself as Herr Steinberg and asked if he could help.

"Yes, sir, I would like to have a few words in private with Herr Konigsberg if I may" said Hadley.

"I'm afraid that is not possible, Inspector" replied Steinberg with a curious smile.

"Why is that, sir?"

"Herr Konigsberg was called back to Berlin on urgent business and left last night, Inspector."

"Is Herr Stumpfel available?"

"No, he left with Herr Konigsberg, Inspector."

"I see" replied Hadley and he thought for a moment before he asked "do you know if Herr Konigsberg went to Sir Robert Salisbury's home at Chieveley the day before yesterday?"

"I have no idea, Inspector and of course you must appreciate that if I did know it would be improper for me to comment on Herr Konigsberg's movements" replied the German with a smile.

"Indeed, I wonder if you can confirm to me that Herr Konigsberg breeds thoroughbred horses at his schloss?"

"I believe that he has some fine horses in his stables, Inspector."

"Do you know if he…"

"Inspector, I am a very busy man and can no longer waste time answering personal questions about Herr Konigsberg, so if you will excuse me, I wish you good day!" interrupted the German and he clicked his heels before turning and striding away. Hadley called "good day, sir" after the disappearing man and the superior one showed them out into the sunshine before slamming the door shut.

"No joy there then, Sergeant."

"Very hostile, sir, do you think that Konigsberg may have the stones?"

"If he has then it will be impossible to ever recover them" replied Hadley.

"Well the Count said that his Government had bought them."

"Yes, but I do have my suspicions that someone in a high position in Berlin may be operating independently for his own financial advantage, Sergeant."

"We may never know, sir."

"Possibly, but let's not give up all hope yet of finding out!"

"Of course not, so where to now, sir?"

"Call a cab and let's get over to the Marylebone and find out what Doctor Evans has to say about our latest victim."

Doctor Evans drew back the sheet that covered the body of Vervorde and said "death was almost instantaneous because the knife slash to the throat almost severed his head."

"The attacker must have been a very strong individual to have done that" said Hadley as he peered down at Vervorde's gaping wound.

"Yes, from my observations I would say that the victim was attacked from behind by a right handed man, taller than himself by several inches and as you rightly say, very strong."

"Do you think the same person killed Detrekker?" asked Hadley.

"I'm not sure, Jim" replied the Doctor.

"Can we see his body again?"

"Yes, here it is" replied the Doctor as he went to the adjoining marble slab and uncovered the lifeless body of Detrekker. Hadley and Cooper gazed down at the once handsome, sun tanned face of the South African.

"As you can see, his throat was cut but not with so much force and the slashes across his cheeks, nose and forehead appear to be the result of a frenzied attack in an attempt to hide his identity after he was stabbed through the heart" said the Doctor.

"A maniac must have done this" said Hadley.

"Perhaps the killer was desperate to keep the police from knowing who he was."

"Well he didn't make a very good job of it" said Hadley.

"No, but have you considered that the killer may have been disturbed before he could completely disfigure his victim?"

"Good point, Doctor."

"All my points are good, Jim" replied the Doctor with a smile.

"Of course" replied Hadley.

"And when I see what members of the human race do to each other, I'm glad I've got a dog for a companion" said the Doctor and the detectives both laughed. Hadley remained silent for a few moments whilst he looked closely at the slashed face of Detrekker before he asked "have you come to any conclusions about the weapon that was used?"

"I would say that a large bladed hunting knife was used in both attacks, because the cuts are deep and broad" replied the Doctor. Hadley thanked the Doctor and then went into the adjoining room to examine the victim's clothes that had been laid out on benches by the gaunt, elderly assistant. Both sets of clothes were heavily blood stained and the contents of each man's pockets had been placed in a tray to one side. Detrekker's watch and some loose change were all that his tray contained, but in Vervorde's there were several letters and his business cards along with two guineas and some copper change. Hadley went through the letters but found nothing of particular interest except in the last one that he picked up and withdrew from its envelope. It was a short note delivered by hand to the Piccadilly Hotel from a person who just signed himself as 'Kruger.' Hadley read it aloud "Dik, come and meet me at the entrance to the zoo in Regents Park on Thursday afternoon at two o'clock and make sure that Detrekker and Boeker don't know I'm here, Kruger."

"I wonder who the devil Kruger is, sir?"

"An accomplice to a murderous crime or perhaps the murderer himself, Sergeant" replied Hadley.

"Any clues to his whereabouts, sir?"

"I'm afraid not, Sergeant, as you can see the note is on a plain piece of paper and the envelope just reads Dik Vervorde, Piccadilly Hotel and delivered by hand."

"Perhaps someone at the Hotel might remember the messenger and gives us a description" said Cooper.

"That's worth a try, Sergeant, and afterwards we'll see if Sir Robert has returned from Chieveley."

The Hansom cab hurried along to the Piccadilly Hotel where one of the receptionists remembered the person who delivered the note for Vervorde.

"I could hardly forget her, sir" said the young man.

"A lady delivered it?" asked Hadley in surprise.

"Yes, sir, she was a very beautiful young lady wearing a blue dress with a white hat and matching gloves with a parasol" replied the receptionist.

"Give me a description of her features if you would."

"She had dark hair and blue eyes, sir, she was very lovely...."

"How old do think she is?" interrupted Hadley.

"I'd say about twenty five, sir."

"When she spoke did she have an accent?"

"No, sir, she just spoke softly and very well."

"Tell me exactly what she said."

"She just asked me to give the note to Mr Vervorde as soon as possible, sir."

"And when did you do that?"

"I gave it to him when he booked out of the hotel with the other gentleman on Wednesday morning, sir."

"And when did the lady leave the note?"

"At about seven o'clock Tuesday evening, sir."

"Why didn't you give the note to him then?"

"Because he didn't arrive back until very late that night, sir and I had gone off duty" replied the receptionist.

"Why didn't the night porter give Mr Vervorde the note?"
"I don't know, sir."
"I gather by your clear recollection of the lady that you'd recognise her again" said Hadley with a smile.
"Without a shadow of doubt, sir."
"Very good, now what is your name?"
"James Burton, sir."
"Thank you Mr Burton you have been very helpful and we will be in touch again in due course" said Hadley with a smile.

As the detectives travelled to Cavendish Square in a Hansom, they discussed the latest development.
"Well I wonder who our beautiful lady messenger is, Sergeant?"
"She's certainly not Kruger sir, but who ever she is, she's made a great impression on Mr Burton."
"Hasn't she just" replied Hadley with a smile.
"Could the lady be Miss Gwendolyn, sir?"
"I wonder, Sergeant."
"I noticed that she is very attractive and has blue eyes, sir."
"Yes, so did I" replied Hadley.
"And if it is her, then Sir Robert is obviously involved somehow in the theft of the diamonds…"
"And possibly the murders, Sergeant" interrupted Hadley.
"If he is, then that will put the cat amongst the diplomatic pigeons!"
"It certainly will" replied Hadley as the cab pulled up outside number 22 Cavendish Square.

Meadows opened the door and remained aloof as he asked if he could help the detectives.
"Yes, tell me is Sir Robert at home?"
"No, sir, he has not yet returned from Chieveley" replied Meadows.
"Are Miss Gwendolyn and her fiancé still there with Sir Robert?"
"No, sir, they returned just a short while ago."
"Would you let them know that we are here and would like to speak to them?"

"Certainly, sir, please come in."

The detectives were admitted into the drawing room where Gwendolyn and Rupert were seated.

"Good day, Inspector."

"Good day Miss Gwendolyn."

"You wish to speak to us?" she asked.

"Yes…"

"What about?" she interrupted sharply and Hadley paused for a moment before he asked "did you take a note for a Mr Vervorde to the Piccadilly Hotel last Tuesday evening?"

"No, Inspector, I did not."

"Do you know Mr Vervorde?"

"No, I have never heard of the man" she replied firmly.

"Very well, Miss, do you know or have you ever heard of a Mr Kruger?" asked Hadley and noticed Rupert's concerned expression when he heard Kruger's name.

"No, Inspector, is he a friend of my father's?"

"I don't know, Miss."

"Well I suggest that after he returns from Chieveley tomorrow you can ask him" she said firmly.

"I will, Miss."

"But I would be obliged if would you leave your return visit here for another few days as I am becoming increasingly concerned about my father's health" she said.

"I'm sorry to hear that he is unwell, Miss."

"He is not at his best by any means and he needs some rest from the dreadful stress he's under at the moment."

"Yes of course."

"You must understand that after my mother died suddenly last Christmas, he has not really recovered from the shock and his health has suffered."

"I'm sorry to hear that and quite understand, Miss."

"So, if that is all, I would be obliged if you would leave us now" she said and Hadley nodded.

"Thank you for your help, Miss, and I wish you both good day."

Cooper hailed a cab and Hadley told the driver to take them to Whitechapel.

"Lunch at the Kings Head, sir?"

"Yes, then on to see if Charlie has anything for us" replied Hadley as the Hansom trotted off down Regents Street in the traffic.

The Kings Head was busy for Friday lunchtime, which was unusual because most of the drinkers arrived at the end of the day on their way home, after receiving wages for the weeks work. Vera smiled when she saw them approach the bar and asked "the usual, gents?" Hadley nodded as she pulled the pints of stout and when she had placed the foaming glasses on the beer soaked counter she asked "anything to eat?" They ordered ham and cheese with pickles then wandered off to find a table near the open door. They had finished their lunch and were just about to leave when Agnes and Florrie arrived. Cooper hurried to the bar to buy them sixpenny gins whilst Hadley asked them if they had heard anything of interest.

"Well its only rumour, Jim" said Agnes.

"Ah, Agnes, you know how I love rumours" Hadley smiled.

"You know how you asked about foreigners?"

"Yes."

"Old Nellie says that one of the girls from Clerkenwell told her that two black fellas had been asking around in the pubs there for a friend of theirs…"

"Tell me more, Agnes."

"Well they said he was easy to spot because he had a small case that was chained to his belt, I mean, what d'you make of that, Jim?"

"You've just made me a happy man, Agnes" replied Hadley.

"The chance would be a fine thing, Jim" she said with a mischievous smile as Cooper arrived back with the gins.

"Agnes has interesting news for us, Sergeant" said Hadley as Cooper sat down.

"That's good to hear, sir."

"Yes, now tell us more about these black fellas, Agnes."

"Not much else to tell, except that they said they'd give a generous reward to anybody who found their friend" she replied.

"I'm sure they would, now did Nellie say where these men could be contacted?"

"No, Jim, she said that they just kept coming round all the pubs looking for him."

"And when was that?"

"Last night, Jim."

"Thank you Agnes, we'll have to leave you now as we're in a hurry" said Hadley.

"You're always in a hurry, Jim!"

Cooper hailed a cab and they set off to Lipton Street where Charlie, after some persuasion, opened the door for them.

"Cor blimey, Jim, you've started something now and no mistake" said the old man as they followed him through the velvet curtains to his office.

"Why's that, Charlie?"

"I've had that nasty Grenville boy round here with his mate Lansbury, asking about diamonds this morning…"

"Isaacs' men?"

"Yeah, and they were asking me a lot of questions in their nasty way, threatening, I'd call it…"

"What sort of questions, Charlie?"

"I told 'em I don't know nothing, I'm just a poor old boy with plenty of debts and no friends…"

"Tell me about the questions" interrupted Hadley.

"I can't remember everything, Jim, you know me" he replied.

"Try, Charlie, it's important."

"Well they kept on about a foreigner with a case of stones and had he been to see me? So I told them that nobody came to see me these days except old men who wanted something cheap that sparkled, for their bit on the side."

"Did they say anything else?"

"Not really, except if he did turn up, I was to let them know straight away otherwise they'd take me out the back and it would be the worse for me, if you catch my drift, Jim?"

"Yes, I do, Charlie."

"They're both nasty fellas who've never given a second thought to duffing up anybody whose face doesn't fit with Isaacs."

"London is full of such ruffians I'm afraid, Charlie."

"Well you should be doing something about it, Jim."

"That's true and I will try, but in the meantime, can you

remember anything else?"

"No, but I've heard that two blacks have been round Clerkenwell looking for a foreigner with a case chained to him, so I guess he's the one with the stones" said Charlie.

"Yes, he probably is."

"So everybody is looking for him, including you Jim."

"It seems so, Charlie."

"Are you off there now?"

"Yes, Charlie, as fast as a Hansom can trot!"

The detectives called at the George and Dragon in the Clerkenwell Road first of all and the bar maid told them that two black men had been in last night asking about their lost friend.

"Have they been back today?" asked Hadley.

"No, sir" she replied.

"What about their friend?"

"No, I've never seen him in here."

The next pub they visited was The Crown, further along the road towards Hatton Garden. The response from the bar man was the same but in the Kings Arms, which was almost next door, they were told by a buxom bar maid that the men had been in the pub last night and again at lunchtime today. The detectives then made their way hurriedly to Hatton Garden where they found the two plain clothes constables on surveillance duty close to Solomon Isaacs shop. Hadley told them to leave their post and start combing all the local pubs for the black men and their friend with the case whilst he and Cooper returned to the Yard to organise a blanket search of the area.

On arriving back in the office, George told Hadley that he was to report to the Chief Inspector immediately.

"Do you know what it is about, George?"

"No, sir, Mr Jenkins came down with the message about ten minutes ago."

"Right, thank you George… now Sergeant, whilst I'm with the Chief will you go down, find the Duty Sergeant and organise some constables to help in the search for our suspects in Clerkenwell?"

"Yes, sir."

The Chief Inspector looked hard at Hadley as he entered his office and said "the Commissioner has got that Count with him and he's making complaints about you!"

"What sort of complaints, sir?"

"The very serious type, Hadley!"

"Well what about, sir?" asked Hadley in a slightly bemused tone.

"I don't know, but the Commissioner sent a message to me fifteen minutes ago saying that if you arrived back within the next half hour then he wanted to see us both immediately!"

"In that case, I've arrived just in time, sir."

"I can see you transferred to horse traffic by Christmas, Hadley!"

CHAPTER 5

Hadley and Bell entered the Commissioner's office and were confronted by the sight of Count von Rausberg and his assistant, Herr Schoender, looking gravely at the Commissioner whose side whiskers bristled more than usual. There was a few moments silence before he said in a firm tone "Chief Inspector Bell."

"Yes, sir?"

"Did you know that Inspector Hadley was going to make inquiries at the German Embassy?"

"Well, er..."

"Gott im Himmel! I told you that you were not to go there!" exclaimed the Count angrily.

"With respect, sir, you gave strict instructions that they were not to be advised of your presence in London" said Hadley calmly.

"Hadley!" exclaimed the Commissioner angrily.

"And I did not reveal that fact to anybody at the Embassy!" persisted Hadley.

"That's enough, Inspector!" exclaimed the Commissioner.

"I cannot imagine how you tolerate such insubordination, Commissioner" said the Count with venom.

"Yes, well, we are investigating two murders..."

"They are but nothing compared with what will occur between our two Governments if the diamonds are not recovered by next Tuesday!" interrupted the Count.

"I assure you that we are moving the investigation along as fast as possible, sir" said Bell.

"It's not fast enough, you Englanders are so slow at everything" said the Count.

"I regret that you feel that way, sir" said the Commissioner.

"I do have some positive news to report, if I may" said Hadley anxious to rebuff the Count's assertions that the investigation was slow.

"Yes, Inspector" said the Commissioner as he clutched at the hopeful straw.

"Two men have been seen in the Clerkenwell area searching for a man who I believe is Hans Boeker and I am certain that he has the diamonds, sir."

"There, that is good news and I presume you have men looking for Boeker?"

"Yes, sir, as we speak, two plain clothes officers are combing the area and Sergeant Cooper is organising more constables to carry out a blanket search to begin immediately" replied Hadley.

"Good, so can we expect to arrest Boeker and recover the stones within the next twenty four hours?" asked the Commissioner with a relieved smile.

"I hope so, sir" replied Hadley as he mentally crossed his fingers.

"You said that two men were looking for Boeker, do you know who they are?" asked the Count and Hadley noticed the anxious tone in his voice.

"No, sir, not yet but we will find out in due course" replied Hadley.

"Do you think that they're German by any chance?" asked the Count as he raised one eyebrow.

"No, sir, they are black men…"

"Negroes?" interrupted the Commissioner.

"Yes, sir."

"Good God, whatever are they doing looking for Boeker?"

"Possibly they know about the diamonds, sir" replied Hadley.

"Well at least they should be easy to find" said the Commissioner.

"Quite so, sir, I'm sure that Hadley will locate them quite quickly now" said Bell anxious to carry favour with the Commissioner as well as showing the Count that everything was well in hand.

"Yes, Chief Inspector, I think we can safely say that it is only a matter of time before we recover the diamonds and return them to their rightful owner" said the Commissioner with a smile and the Count gave a little nod.

"In that case, I am content to leave you gentlemen to attend to your duties and I look forward to receiving the stones before I leave London on Tuesday" said the Count before he stood up to leave.

"Before you go, sir, may I ask if you know Herr Konigsberg at the Embassy?" asked Hadley and the Count glared at him.

"I've heard of him, why?"

"Apparently he left for Berlin suddenly, sir and was unable to help with my inquiries" said Hadley.

"So what is that to do with me?" asked the Count angrily.

"It's just background information for my investigation, sir."

"You concentrate on recovering my stones, Inspector."

"I will, sir."

"Good."

"And by any chance do you know a man called Kruger?" asked Hadley and on hearing the name the Count froze and Schoender went pale.

"Questions! Questions! Must I endure all these questions?" the Count shouted at the Commissioner who looked startled and raised his eyebrows.

"Well, er, no…"

"You'd do well to instruct your subordinates to do their duty and not ask so many questions of the innocent party!" continued the angry Prussian.

"Yes, er, Hadley…"

"Commissioner, recover the diamonds that rightfully belong to the Imperial German Government and give them to me by next Tuesday or else you will suffer the consequences, good day!" exclaimed the Count before he swept from the office followed by Schoender.

"Well" the Commissioner half whispered.

"The Count appeared more than usually angry today, sir" said Bell in a sympathetic tone.

"Yes, so we'd better get a move on" replied the Commissioner.

"I'll leave immediately with the officers for Clerkenwell, sir" said Hadley.

"Good, and report back as soon as you have recovered the diamonds that's more important than arresting the killer at the moment" said the Commissioner.

"Very well, sir."

"Now tell me, Inspector, who is this fella, Kruger?" asked the Commissioner.

"I don't know, sir, but he sent a note to the latest victim telling him to meet him outside the zoo on Thursday afternoon" replied Hadley.

"So he could be the murderer" said the Commissioner.

"Possibly, sir."

"Well make sure you find him because obviously the Count knows of him and I think that this investigation might be more complicated than we think" said the Commissioner.

"Yes, sir, I'm sure you're right" said Hadley.

"Inspector, the Commissioner is always right and he doesn't need you to tell him" said Bell as he glared at Hadley.

"No, sir."

"Will you both please just get on with it!" said the great one in an irritated voice.

Hadley briefed the five constables and Sergeant Kelly in his office before they left in a police wagon to search the pubs in Clerkenwell for Boeker and the two black men. Hadley and Cooper followed on in a Hansom, which dropped them off outside the Kings Arms. The bar maid reported that the black men had not re-appeared.

"So, they may return tonight" said Hadley to Cooper.

"And we'll be in luck, sir."

"I hope so, now let's start with The Crown, then we'll try the George and Dragon before we search further afield, Sergeant."

The detectives went into each pub, looked around at the early evening drinkers and after a few words with the bar maids left quickly assuring them that would return later. As they emerged from the Unicorn in the Farringdon Road they saw Sergeant Kelly hurrying towards them.

"Sir, we've just found the body of a man and I think it's Boeker!" said Kelly.

"Oh, bloody hell!" exclaimed Hadley.

"He's in an alleyway behind the Lion, just a few hundred yards down the road" said Kelly.

"Lead on then, Sergeant" said Hadley and as they strode along at a brisk pace through the busy street he hoped that it was not Boeker because if it was, then the diamonds would be lost. They reached the narrow alley that led off the Farringdon Road by the Lion pub and there, half way along, propped up against the brick wall was the body of a man with two constables looking down at it. They stood back as the detectives approached.

"He's been badly beaten about the head, sir" said Kelly as Hadley bent down to examine the man's distorted face.

"So I see" said Hadley.

"And he reeks of drink, sir, we thought he was just drunk at first but soon realised that he was dead" said Kelly.

"What makes you think it's Boeker?" asked Hadley.

"Look at his belt, sir."

Hadley opened the dead man's coat and saw he was wearing a thick leather belt with a steel ring half torn out close to a large buckle which had a small lock, keeping it fastened about the dead man's waist.

"A security belt and whatever was attached has been ripped away" said Hadley grimly.

"Then the case with the stones is almost certainly lost, sir" said Cooper.

"Yes, Sergeant, we have to face that possibility" replied Hadley as he searched the man's pockets for some identity but he found nothing.

"Call for an ambulance and get him away to the Marylebone, Sergeant."

"It's already in hand, sir" replied Kelly.

"Good, now after he's on his way, we'll see what the barmaids in the Lion have to say for themselves before we look for our two black friends" said Hadley. The ambulance arrived and the attendants carefully laid the body on a stretcher before loading it into the ambulance and setting off to the Marylebone Hospital

In the Lion pub, the two barmaids said that they had not seen a man answering Hadley's description of the deceased; neither had they noticed any black men in the pub that day.

The detectives searched all evening and constantly returned to the pubs in the area looking for the black men, but their efforts proved fruitless. It was eleven o'clock when the police team gathered at the top of Hatton Garden where Hadley thanked them all for their efforts and told them to stand down. After the police officers had boarded the wagon and set off back to the Yard, Hadley shook his head and gazed down at the pavement.

"I fear that we are in for some difficult times, Sergeant."

"I'm sure you're right, sir, but let's call it a day and start afresh tomorrow" replied Cooper and Hadley nodded before the Sergeant hailed a passing cab.

The next morning, Hadley was in Chief Inspector Bell's office at eight thirty briefing him on the previous night's activities.

"You think this dead person is Boeker?" asked Bell anxiously.

"Yes, sir."

"Have you positively identified him?"

"Not yet, sir."

"How do you propose to that, Hadley?"

"I'll get Jack Curtis to take a photograph of him and see if the receptionist at the Piccadilly Hotel recognises him, sir."

"Well I suppose it's worth a try" replied Bell.

"I think it's my only option, sir."

"What about the diamonds?"

"It's possible that Boeker was carrying them in a case attached to a security belt which was torn apart by the assailant" replied Hadley.

"So you have no clue as to who has stolen them or where they have disappeared to?"

"No, sir."

"Tell me honestly, do you think that they ever will be recovered?"

Hadley thought carefully before he answered "I really don't know, sir, because if they are still in this country then I believe I have a chance but if they have already gone to Berlin, then the answer is 'no' I'm afraid."

"Gone to Berlin?" queried Bell.

"Yes, it is possible that Konigsberg hurried away immediately he had them" replied Hadley.

"Where did he get the diamonds from?"

"There are several possibilities, sir."

"Go on, I'm listening" said Bell anxiously.

"First of all, Sir Robert Salisbury might have received them from Detrekker before he was murdered and given them to Konigsberg when he stayed at Chieveley Manor overnight…"

"That's pure fantasy, Hadley" interrupted Bell.

"I don't think so, sir, but to continue, Solomon Isaacs was expecting Count Rausberg to bring the diamonds to him but Isaacs may have decided to acquire them before the Count had them…"

"Isaacs would have been taking an almighty risk by doing that, Hadley."

"The value of these stones after they are cut is incalculable, sir, and that's more than a strong motive to steal and kill for them!"

"This is all hypothetical, Hadley."

"And then there is Count Rausberg, sir."

"What's the matter with him?"

"I'm very suspicious of him and his assistant" replied Hadley.

"Surely you don't suspect the Count?"

"Well I ask myself why should he wish to keep this purchase and his presence in London secret from the Embassy unless he was acting either for himself or someone in the Government in Berlin?"

"It's the way the Germans like to work, they're a secretive lot by nature and along with the French they are our natural enemies, Hadley."

"Possibly, sir."

"Mark my words; we'll have trouble with them in years to come."

"I don't know about that, sir, but it concerns me when so many suspects are possibly involved with the theft and three murders."

"Quite so and what about the black men, any sign of them?"

"No, sir, they have simply disappeared."

"And what do you know about this other fella, Kruger?"

"Nothing, sir, except he sent a note to Vervorde asking him to meet him at the zoo and the Count obviously knows him."

"God, what a mess" whispered Bell.

"I'm afraid it looks that way at the moment, sir."

"What I don't understand is if the dead man is Boeker and the case is missing, how could Konigsberg have the stones, he left for Berlin days ago?"

"We're assuming that Boeker had the case on him when he was killed but perhaps it was taken from him previously or the case was empty but his assailant didn't know that, sir."

"It's getting all too complicated, Hadley."

"Yes, it is, sir."

"All I know is that if we don't find these stones by Tuesday then all hell will be let loose and I don't relish that for one moment."

"No, sir, neither do I."

"And the Commissioner certainly doesn't, I can assure you" said Bell in a resigned tone.

"I'm sure that is so, sir."

"What do you intend to do next, Hadley?"

"Identify Boeker then question Sir Robert…"

"Oh, go steady with him whatever you do!" interrupted Bell.

"I will, sir, and then I'll try to trace this man Kruger."

"Good, well get on with it and keep me posted."

"Yes, of course, sir."

When Hadley returned to his office he immediately asked Cooper to find Jack Curtis and get him to assemble all his photographic paraphernalia then follow them over to the morgue at the Marylebone Hospital.

Doctor Evans was not pleased to see the detectives so early in the day and was slightly brusque when they entered his office.

"My God, Jim, you're keeping me busy these days and I'm not used to such early starts" he said.

"I'm very sorry, Doctor, but it's the way of the world."

"Well, I don't approve" said Evans as he stood up and led the way into the cold mortuary.

"Here's your latest" he said as he uncovered the naked body.

"How did he die?"

"My preliminary examination showed the cause of death to be severe blows to the back of the head" replied the Doctor.

"What about the injuries to his face?" asked Hadley as he peered down closer to the victim.

"Possibly inflicted after he had died" replied Evans.

"Right, now I've arranged for Jack Curtis to come over and photograph him…"

"Why?"

"Because we are not sure who he is, we think he is a South African called Hans Boeker but we don't know for certain" relied Hadley.

"Well, by his complexion I'd say that he has spent much of his life outdoors in the sun" said Evans.

"That helps, Doctor."

Jack Curtis arrived soon after with his tripod and large camera case which he placed on the floor before he gazed at the body of the South African. When Hadley asked him to photograph the face of the dead man, Curtis looked for a moment and replied "you'll have to get him to sit up, sir."

"Sit up? He's dead, Jack" replied Hadley.

"I can see that, sir, but you'll have to prop him up somehow because I can't take a full face shot with him lying down" replied Curtis.

"Best thing is that we hold him up" said Evans.

"Right, Doctor" said Hadley and Curtis nodded before he opened his case. When the tripod with the camera perched on top had been placed at the foot of the marble table, Evans, assisted by two attendants, lifted the body into a sitting posture. Curtis fired off his flash illuminator and took a photo plate of the dead man.

"I need that photograph as soon as possible, Jack" said Hadley.

"Yes, sir, I'll get back straight away and I should have it ready for you about lunchtime" replied Curtis.

"Good, please bring it to my office as soon as you can."

"Very good, sir."

The detectives left the Marylebone and took a cab to Cavendish Square, where they were admitted to Sir Robert's house by Meadows who informed them that the Master had not yet arrived back from Chieveley. Hadley asked if Miss Gwendolyn was at home and Meadows nodded then announced the detectives to her in the drawing room.

"Good morning, Inspector" she smiled.

"Good morning, Miss."

"And what do you want today may I ask?" she said in a firm tone.

"When do you expect Sir Robert to return to London?"

"I'm not sure for the moment, Inspector."

"Why is that, Miss?"

"I told you quite clearly that my father was under considerable strain and I distinctly remember asking you to refrain from calling here for a few days after he returned" she replied angrily.

"So you did, Miss, but my investigations are now at a critical stage and I need to speak to Sir Robert as a matter of urgency."

"Well you can't I'm afraid" she said.

"Then I'll have to go to Chieveley, Miss."

"You'll have a wasted journey because he's not there" she said with a smile.

"Do you know where he is, Miss?"

"Yes, I do, but I'm very reluctant to tell you, Inspector."

Hadley drew a deep breath before he replied "Miss Salisbury, I must advise you that I am investigating the theft of valuable diamonds and the murders of three persons closely connected with the stolen gems, one of whom was known to your father, so if you wilfully withhold information from me which hampers my investigation, I will arrest you for obstruction, do I make myself crystal clear?" Gwendolyn went pale and she looked frightened.

"I, I don't mean to obstruct you, Inspector, I'm just very concerned for my father" she half whispered.

"That's understandable, Miss, I assure you that I will endeavour to be very gentle in my questioning of your father."

"Thank you, Inspector."

"Now where is he?"

"He's gone for a few days break with Rupert, my fiancé, to stay with his parents at their house overlooking the river at Teddington, it's very peaceful there."

"May I have the address, Miss?"

"Yes of course, Inspector."

CHAPTER 6

The detectives returned to the Yard to write reports and plan the rest of the day. Hadley decided that the best chance to recover the diamonds lay in finding Kruger, who he believed was deeply implicated in the theft. It was just before lunch that Jack Curtis brought the sepia tint photographs of Boeker to his office and Hadley was pleased at the likeness to the dead man. He and Cooper left immediately for the Piccadilly Hotel where Mr Burton the receptionist was on duty.

"Good day, Mr Burton."
"Good day, sir, can I help you?"
"Yes, may we have a word in private?"
"Yes, of course, sir, would you like to come through to our office?"

Hadley nodded and followed Burton in to a small room behind the reception where he produced the photograph and said "do you recognise this man, Mr Burton?"

"Yes I certainly do, sir."
"Tell me who it is please."
"It's Mr Kruger, sir…"
"What!" Hadley exclaimed in surprise.
"It's Mr Kruger, sir, although he does look as if he's a little the worse for wear in this photo, but it's definitely him, sir."
"It's not Hans Boeker?"
"Oh no, sir, as I say it's definitely Mr Kruger."
"Are you absolutely sure?" asked Hadley with his mind searching for an explanation.
"I am, sir."
"Tell me all you know about this man" said a surprised Hadley.
"He's a South African gentleman who arrived two days or so before the others and he was booked in for a week but he didn't stay, as I remember."
"When did he leave?"
"The day before the others arrived, sir, it'll all be in the register."
"I'd like to look at that in a moment."
"Yes of course, sir."

"Did he leave a forwarding address?"

"No, sir, but he gave me the impression that he was going abroad" replied Burton.

"Did he say where?"

"Not in so many words but if I remember rightly, he made some comment about a friend in Amsterdam who he wanted to see before going home, sir."

"That's very interesting, Mr Burton" said Hadley.

"I'm glad to have been of service, sir" beamed the young man.

"Now would you please give me an accurate description of Mr Boeker?"

"Certainly, sir, he's a tall gentleman, about your height, quite slim with fair hair and a moustache."

"Describe his clothes to me."

"He wore a dark jacket with a white shirt and a grey waistcoat, that's all I can remember, sir."

"How old do you think he is?"

"I'd say about thirty five, sir."

"Did he have any distinguishing marks at all?"

"No, sir, but he had quite a tanned face."

"Thank you, Mr Burton, now let's take a look at the register." Burton nodded then led the way back to the reception desk. The register showed that Herman Kruger from Pretoria, Transvaal had arrived last Saturday but left on the following Monday with no forwarding address. Hadley realised why Detrekker and his entourage had not seen Kruger's name in the book as Kruger's entry was only two from the bottom of the previous page and Detrekker's registration was half way down the following page. Hadley thanked Mr Burton and left the opulent hotel. Hailing a cab Cooper asked "where to, sir?"

"The Crown in the Strand, I need a drink and some time to think, Sergeant."

The pub was very busy and hot, which did not please Hadley and after ordering pints of stout as well as ploughman's lunches from the sweating, overworked barmaid. They made their way to the back of the noisy pub to find a table.

"I don't think this is the place for quiet reflection, sir."

"You're right, Sergeant, so let's finish here and sit in Hyde

Park for a while and compose ourselves" replied Hadley. After a quick lunch in silence they left the pub and whilst Cooper hailed a cab, Hadley bought The Times newspaper from a paper boy standing close by. As the Hansom trotted along the Strand towards Trafalgar Square Hadley read the front page article aloud.

"Another South African found dead, a man's body was discovered by police yesterday in an alleyway by the Lion public house in the Farringdon Road, it is believed that he is connected to the other foreign murder victims. It appears that the killer has now switched his attacks from the London Parks to alleyways near public houses and the editor of this newspaper warns all visitors to London to be on their guard as a police spokesman from Scotland Yard said they still remain baffled and an early arrest was unlikely."

"Unbelievable, sir" said Cooper as the Hansom entered the Square before turning up into the Haymarket.

"God knows we need something to break soon" said Hadley.

"It's quite a shock that the dead man is Kruger, sir."

"Yes and that means Boeker remains the main suspect for the murders and theft of the stones" replied Hadley.

"What do you think he'll do next, sir?"

"He needs to get rid of the diamonds before he ends up being caught by us or murdered, Sergeant."

"Then it's likely he'll contact Isaacs and try to sell them to him, sir."

"That's the most obvious thing to do, Sergeant, but as the stones are of such enormous value, it's hard to know what might happen next."

"As you say, sir, we need something to break in our favour."

The Hansom dropped the detectives at the Park Lane entrance to Hyde Park and they wandered in and found a seat near the gate. They sat in silence for a while and then Hadley said "Sergeant, the first thing we'll do is re-mount a surveillance team outside Isaacs place to try to catch Boeker, then we'll call upon Sir Robert at Teddington, then we'll visit Charlie to see what he's heard and finally, we'll have a drink with the ladies in the Kings Head, that is, provided we don't get diverted by unexpected events."

"Right, sir."

As soon as they arrived back at their office, George informed Hadley that the Chief Inspector wished to see him.

"Right, George... now whilst I'm up there, Sergeant, will you arrange a surveillance team to monitor Isaacs place once again and make sure they have the description of Boeker?"

"Yes, sir."

Chief Inspector Bell looked concerned as he waved Hadley to a seat and asked "have you spoken to Sir Robert today?"

"No, sir, but I intend to and I understand from his daughter that he is staying with her fiancé, Rupert Brandon-Hall at his family's home in Teddington where I plan to go to this afternoon" replied Hadley.

"That's good."

"Is it, sir?"

"Yes, now what I'm about to tell you must remain strictly confidential."

"I understand, sir."

"The Commissioner has had a highly confidential meeting this morning with the Home Secretary, Sir George West, and briefed him about the investigation so far and Sir George has told the Commissioner that he harbours certain doubts about Sir Robert..."

"Really, sir, what are they?" interrupted Hadley.

"As far as I can ascertain, nothing specific but Sir George is concerned about various meetings that Sir Robert has had at his London home as well as weekend gatherings at his place at Chieveley" replied Bell.

"Can you give me a clue, sir?"

"Not really, Hadley, it's all a bit vague I'm afraid."

"Well what sort of meetings and who goes to them?"

"I really don't know, but from what I can gather they're mostly foreigners."

"Is that improper, sir?"

"Well Sir George seems to think so bearing in mind Sir Robert's position at the Home Office."

"So in that case Sir Robert is under a cloud of suspicion, sir."

"It would seem so, Hadley."

"How do you wish me to proceed, sir?"

"With great caution and diplomacy, but try and find out what you can about these meetings and report back to me" replied Bell.

"I will, sir, now I have to tell you that there has been a surprise development in the investigation…"

"Oh?"

"The man found dead in the alleyway is not Boeker but our mystery man, Herman Kruger."

"What!"

"The receptionist at the Piccadilly Hotel recognised the photograph of the dead man instantly, sir."

"Good heavens, that means Boeker is still running around with the diamonds!"

"I believe so, sir."

"What do you plan to do next?"

"I've arranged to position plain clothes men outside Isaacs place and hope that Boeker turns up, sir."

"That's a long shot, Hadley."

"Boeker must sell the stones as soon as possible and leave the country, so I think that he would let Isaacs have them for a fraction of their value just to be rid of them, sir."

"Umm, I don't know if I would agree with that, Hadley, there are others under suspicion you know."

"I appreciate that, sir, but the man is under pressure and if he values his life then he has to get away."

"Right, keep me posted, I'll stay here until late tonight, even if it is Saturday!"

Hadley and Cooper left the Yard and hailed a cab to take them to 12 Riverside Walk at Teddington. It was mid afternoon when they arrived outside the impressive home of the Brandon-Hall family, overlooking the Thames at a very picturesque spot. Cooper paid off the cabbie and they walked up the gravel driveway to the imposing front door. Cooper rang the bell and eventually a butler opened the door. Hadley introduced them and asked if Sir Robert was there, when the butler confirmed that was so, Hadley asked to see him privately. They were admitted into the hall way and told to wait. It was obvious from the décor that the Brandon-Hall family were very wealthy and Hadley assumed that they had all the right connections in London society. One painting of many that adorned the hallway, interested Hadley because it depicted a man holding a rifle whilst striking an elegant pose with the carcass of a male lion at his feet.

"A big game hunter in Africa no less" said Hadley to himself as the butler returned.

"Would you care to wait in the study, gentlemen?"

"Thank you" replied Hadley and the detectives followed the butler through double doors into the elegant room beyond. Whilst they waited, Hadley looked around and noticed a framed certificate on the wall behind the large oak desk that proclaimed that Mr Ralph Brandon-Hall had been elected to the Governing Board of the South African Mining Consortium in 1875.

"We have another African connection, Sergeant" said Hadley as the door opened and an elegant, thick set man of about fifty with fair hair and full beard entered. Hadley recognised him as the hunter in the portrait with the fallen lion.

"Good afternoon, gentlemen, I'm Ralph Brandon-Hall, how can I be of assistance?" he asked forcefully as he strode to his desk where he sat and waved them to opposing seats.

"I wish to speak privately to Sir Robert Salisbury, who I understand from his daughter is staying here with you at the moment, sir" said Hadley.

"He is here, but I think in the circumstances it would be advisable if I answered any questions that you may have" said Brandon-Hall.

"And what exactly are the circumstances that prevent me from speaking to Sir Robert?" asked Hadley and he noticed how Brandon-Hall stiffened at that as his eyes grew narrow.

"Inspector Hadley, as you are fully aware, Sir Robert is under great strain at the moment."

"So I've been told, sir."

"And it seems to me that you are pressing him too hard, in fact to the point of harassment!"

"I'm sorry if you feel that way, sir…"

"I do, Inspector" interrupted Brandon-Hall angrily.

"But I must remind you that three men have been murdered and diamonds of incalculable value have been stolen and I'm charged by the Commissioner himself, no less, to investigate the crime whilst leaving no stone unturned, sir."

"I'm aware of your duties, Inspector."

"So, I wish to speak to Sir Robert privately for a few minutes, please ask him to see me."

"It's quite out of the question Inspector, the man is still distraught over the death of his friend Klaus Detrekker…"

"I'm certain he is and that fact surely would want him to co-operate with me to bring the killer to justice?" asked Hadley.

"Look, he's in no condition to be harassed by you with questions that he can't answer!"

"Did you know Detrekker?" asked Hadley which caught Brandon-Hall off guard.

"Well, yes, er, I knew him of course…"

"In South Africa?" interrupted Hadley.

"Well, yes, I'm on the Board of the Mining Consortium…"

"So I see. Now what about Herman Kruger, do you know him?" asked Hadley and he watched the colour drain from Brandon-Hall's face.

"Well, er, er, I've met him once or twice, he's an agent…"

"He was found dead in an alleyway last night" interrupted Hadley and he watched the man begin to sweat.

"Oh, how dreadful."

"What can you tell me about him?" asked Hadley.

"Well, he's an agent who operates for a small group of people who buy and sell precious stones, Inspector."

"Do you know who the members of this group are, sir?"

"I know some of them…"

"May I have their names and addresses please" interrupted Hadley in a firm tone.

"Well, I am glad to give you any assistance in your investigation here, Inspector, but I think that names of people I hardly know will be of much help to you."

"Nevertheless, sir, I require their names" Hadley persisted as he fixed Brandon-Hall with his penetrating blue eyes.

"Very well, Inspector" said Brandon-Hall as he opened the top drawer of his desk and took out a red leather bound book. He opened it and then thumbed through several pages before he said "perhaps you would care to take a note, Inspector." Hadley nodded as Cooper produced his note book and pencil. Brandon-Hall then read out several names and addresses of people living in Pretoria,

Johannesburg and Cape Town. None of which was of any interest to Hadley until the last name, which was Herr Victor Konigsberg.

"Do you know Herr Konigsberg well, sir?"

"I have met him several times at Sir Robert's house at Chieveley, Inspector."

"What do you know about him, sir?"

"He's a wealthy gentleman who holds an important post at the German Embassy in London and at his schloss he breeds thoroughbred horses, that's all I know, he's really a friend of Sir Robert's" replied Brandon-Hall.

"But you must have had contact with him through your position at the Mining Consortium?"

"I know of him, as I told you, but he has always remained distant and works through his agent Kruger."

"I've no more questions at the moment, sir" said Hadley.

"Good" said Brandon-Hall with relief.

"Now be kind enough to let Sir Robert know that I wish to speak to him for a few minutes" said Hadley firmly.

"Look, Inspector, I've already told you…"

"If you please, sir!" interrupted Hadley. The anxious man acquiesced and nodded before he left the room.

"This all just gets deeper and deeper, Sergeant" said Hadley quietly when they were alone.

"It certainly does, sir."

"I'm beginning to think that we'll never know the whole truth."

"You're probably right, sir, but as long as we can recover the diamonds and arrest the murderer, we've done our duty."

"Yes, that's all we can hope for and then the other skullduggery can remain secret" said Hadley as the door opened and a very attractive young woman of about twenty five with dark hair and blue eyes entered the room.

"Oh, sorry, I didn't mean to disturb you" she said.

"That's perfectly alright, Miss" said Hadley as he and Cooper stood up.

"I didn't know that Papa had visitors" she smiled.

"I'm Inspector Hadley and this is Sergeant Cooper, Miss."

"I'm pleased to meet you" she said with a sweet smile.

"May I ask who you are, Miss?"

"I'm Angelina Brandon-Hall" she replied.

"Very pleased to make your acquaintance, Miss Angelina" said Hadley. Sir Robert and Brandon-Hall entered the study just as Hadley was about to ask her if she had recently taken a letter to the Piccadilly Hotel. Her father gave Angelina a stern glance and she gave a little nod of her head before leaving the room.

"I do not appreciate your close attentions, Inspector and I'm beginning to feel somewhat harassed by you" said Sir Robert.

"I'm sorry for the intrusion, sir, I'll only keep you a moment or two" replied Hadley.

"Very well, what do you want to know?"

"We discovered the body of Herman Kruger last night, sir, did you know the gentleman?" asked Hadley and he watched as Sir Robert began to sweat.

"I knew of him, Inspector."

"Apparently he was an agent working for various persons including your friend Herr Konigsberg" said Hadley as Sir Robert looked even more anxious and sat down on a nearby sofa.

"Yes, I believe that is so."

"Did Kruger ever visit you at Chieveley, sir?"

"Look what is the point of all these unnecessary questions?" asked Sir Robert angrily.

"I think that's enough, Inspector" said Brandon-Hall. Hadley remained silent for a few moments before he said "that's all for today sir, thank you for your help."

"You're welcome, Inspector" said Sir Robert as Brandon-Hall went to the study door and opened it.

"Good afternoon, gentlemen" he said firmly and Hadley wished them the same as they left the room.

As the detectives walked down the drive from the house to the road, Hadley said "Sir Robert is a terrified man who is breaking under the strain of something imminent, Sergeant."

"Do you think he's in danger, sir?"

"Possibly, but we can do little to help him if he won't disclose what he knows" replied Hadley.

"And Miss Angelina is a prime suspect as the lovely messenger, sir."

"She certainly is, Sergeant."

"No wonder that Mr Burton was so taken by her, sir."

"Quite so, Sergeant, and if she is the lady with the letter then that ties her father to the whole bloody business!"

CHAPTER 7

On the way back Hadley decided to stop and speak to the plain clothes officers on surveillance duty near Isaacs shop in Hatton Garden, before going on to see Charlie. As the Hansom approached along Clerkenwell Road the detectives were suddenly aware of a commotion on the corner of Hatton Garden. A crowd had gathered around a fallen man and as they got closer a constable ran from the direction of Farringdon Road blowing his whistle. Several horses pulling drays were startled by this and despite the efforts of their drivers, moved sideways into each other causing havoc and the Hansom which contained the detectives was compelled to pull up sharply. Hadley leapt from the cab whilst Cooper stayed to pay the alarmed cabbie. When Hadley reached the fallen man he saw to his horror that it was one of his plain clothes officers with blood pouring from a chest wound, his colleague was kneeling beside him trying to staunch the bleeding with his handkerchief. The breathless constable arrived and said between gasps "what's going on here then?"

"This bloke's been shot!" said an onlooker.

"What?"

"Constable, I'm Inspector Hadley, please summon an ambulance!"

"Yes, right away, sir" replied the surprised constable just as Cooper arrived.

"Oh, bloody hell!" said Cooper as the officer attending to his colleague looked up and said to Hadley "thank God you're here, sir."

"What happened?"

"We spotted a man matching Boeker's description carrying a small case and making his way towards Isaacs shop, sir…"

"And then?"

"We approached him and asked if his name was Hans Boeker, then without warning, he stepped back, pulled a revolver from his coat and fired at us, sir."

"Are you alright?"

"Yes, sir, but Meredith was hit; the man then ran off down Hatton Garden towards Holborn" replied the pale young constable.

"Cooper, get to the station in Farringdon Road and tell the Duty Inspector to organise a search for Boeker immediately, he can't have got far."

"Right, sir."

"We'll have that bastard under lock and key before today is out!" exclaimed Hadley.

An ambulance arrived quickly from Saint Bart's and the wounded officer was lifted onto a stretcher and placed into the back of the ambulance and, with his colleague accompanying him, it raced away to the hospital.

Hadley went into Isaacs shop and asked to see the owner immediately. The assistant disappeared and returned soon afterwards with Mr Grenville.

"Why do you want to see, Mr Isaacs, Inspector?" asked Grenville.

"On police business, so please tell him I'm here" replied Hadley in a firm tone.

Grenville thought for a moment, smiled then nodded his head and said "follow me, Inspector."

Solomon Isaacs looked up from his desk as Hadley entered his office and Grenville closed the door then stood with his back to it.

"Ah, Inspector, to what do I owe this pleasure?" asked Isaacs with a grin.

"Hans Boeker was seen by my officers approaching this shop not twenty minutes ago and when he was challenged he shot one of my men!" said Hadley.

"And what has that got to do with me, Inspector?"

"Did you know he was coming to see you?"

"No, I don't even know the man" replied Isaacs, his hard eyes narrowing.

"He's a colleague of Detrekker" said Hadley.

"What is that to me, Inspector?"

"Boeker now has the diamonds that were brought to London by Detrekker for Count Rausberg" replied Hadley.

"Well when you catch this Mr Boeker and recover the diamonds I'm sure that the Count will be relieved and then he can call upon me for my opinion as originally arranged, Inspector" said Isaacs with a smug grin.

"If Boeker contacts you I would be obliged if you would

inform me at the Yard immediately, sir."

"Rest assured that if he comes here, you'll be the first to know, Inspector and I'll ask Mr Grenville to detain him by force if necessary until you arrive" replied Isaacs.

"Thank you, sir."

Hadley left the shop in Hatton Garden and hurried along the Clerkenwell Road then into the Farringdon Road, where he strode quickly to the police station. On his arrival at the front door he met Cooper and a Sergeant, along with several constables, coming out.

"Ah, sir, Sergeant Johnson and his men are going to search the Holborn area for Boeker" said Cooper.

"Good… Sergeant Johnson, are you armed?"

"Yes, sir" he replied.

"I'm glad to hear it, now you begin the search and we'll join you soon, and whatever you do make sure that you approach this man carefully, I don't want any more officers hurt" said Hadley.

"Right, sir" replied Johnson as he moved off quickly with his men.

"Now, Sergeant let's get back to Isaacs shop and keep an eye out for any activity there before we hurry down to Holborn."

"You think Boeker might try and come back, sir?"

"Possibly or alternatively, Isaacs knows where to find Boeker and will send his man Grenville to him!"

The detectives took up positions in an alleyway at the top of Hatton Garden from where they could see the entrance to the shop. Hadley glanced at his fob watch, it was almost five o'clock and he determined to stay there for thirty minutes before joining in the search for Boeker. They waited for about five minutes before the shop door opened and Grenville accompanied by another man, whom Hadley assumed was Lansbury, came out and looked about before setting off down the Garden towards Holborn.

"It looks like we're on our way, Sergeant" said Hadley.

"They either know where Boeker is or they're hoping to find him before we do, sir."

"Precisely, Sergeant" replied Hadley as he stepped quickly from the alleyway and strode along keeping a good distance behind the two suspects.

When they reached the end of Hatton Garden the two men turned left into Holborn towards the City. The detectives followed and kept up a brisk pace before they also turned left into Holborn. To Hadley's consternation he could only see the heavy figure of Grenville walking along in front.

"Oh, hell! Lansbury must have slipped off somewhere else, Sergeant" said Hadley as he glanced around.

"That means that they don't know where Boeker is and they're just looking for him, sir."

"Yes, I think you're right."

"What now, sir?"

"We have no alternative but to keep close to Grenville, Sergeant."

"Right, sir, and I think we should get a little closer to him."

"Yes, we don't want to lose him in the crowd."

They followed Grenville more closely along Holborn and they slowed their pace then stopped when he suddenly entered the White Horse pub.

"Shall we go in, sir?"

"No, we'll wait for him to come out, Sergeant."

"It could be a long wait, sir."

"I somehow doubt that" replied Hadley as he spotted Sergeant Johnson with a constable on the opposite side of the road.

"There's Johnson" he said to Cooper just as the Sergeant looked across the busy thoroughfare and noticed the detectives. When there was a gap in the heavy traffic, Johnson left the constable and came over to them and saluted.

"We've been unable to find him yet, sir" said Johnson.

"Well keep looking if you would" said Hadley.

"Yes, sir."

"But before you carry on, I want you to go into the White Horse pub and speak to the bar maid, tell her you're looking for a man with a small case and then as you leave, glance casually around and see what a man we've been following is up to, I'll give you a description of him."

"Very good, sir." Hadley described Grenville to Johnson who nodded and went the few yards up the road and entered the pub. The detectives waited for several minutes before Johnson re-appeared and said "he's in there, sir, sitting at a table in the corner talking to two black fellas."

"Is he by God!" exclaimed Hadley.

"Yes, sir."

"Sergeant Johnson, call over your constable, then follow us into the pub and be ready for violence!"

"Right, sir." As Johnson started to beckon his man from across Holborn, the detectives hurried into the pub and they went straight to the table where Grenville sat with the two black men. They all looked up in alarm at Hadley.

"Mr Grenville, would you like to introduce me to your two friends?"

"I don't know them, Inspector" replied Grenville as Johnson and his constable arrived. The sight of the uniformed officers caused wide eyed panic in the black men as they stood up and attempted to make their escape.

"Not so fast, my friend!" said Hadley to the taller of the two men who suddenly lashed out, catching him with a heavy blow to the side of his face. Hadley spun round and sank down as Cooper attempted to restrain the man and the constable grabbed at the second black man who hit the young officer full in the face. Pandemonium broke out and as Cooper held on grimly to the tall man's arm and Johnson drew his truncheon, the second black made his escape through the crowded pub. The tall man, with his free hand, pulled a large hunting knife from his belt and stabbed Cooper in the shoulder before he attacked Johnson who vainly tried to defend himself, hitting out with his truncheon. It was to no avail as the man was far too strong for them to overcome and he struggled free as Cooper drew his revolver, but the pub customers were so close to the melee that he dare not fire. The man made his escape leaving the police men injured and shattered by the experience. Grenville looked horrified and he attempted to assist Hadley to his feet as Johnson called for help for Cooper and his unconscious officer. Cooper sank down onto a chair with blood running from his wound as Hadley, having struggled to his feet, slumped down in a chair next to him. Johnson helped his constable up to a sitting position on the floor as the landlord and a barmaid arrived to help.

"Call an ambulance if you will" said Hadley to the pale faced landlord who nodded and hurried off. The bar maid helped Cooper take his jacket off and then tried to staunch the flow of blood from the wound with her bar cloth. Cooper looked pale and shaken as the drinkers looked on in stunned, amazed silence.

"You're under arrest, Grenville and if you try anything fancy, I'll shoot you!" said Hadley angrily as he produced his revolver from his pocket.

"What have I done for Gawds sake?" asked Grenville.

"I found you in the company of two suspicious characters…"

"I didn't know who they were!" interrupted Grenville.

"Nevertheless…"

"It's the Gawd's honest truth, when I sat down here they just came over and started asking me about London and where they should go and visit" interrupted Grenville anxiously.

"We'll sort it all out back at the Yard and until then I advise you to shut up" said Hadley. Cooper looked pale and although the bar maid was doing all she could, blood still flowed copiously from his shoulder. Hadley was very concerned for Cooper and he tried to comfort him with encouraging words. Sergeant Johnson went outside to summon his men and arrange for a police wagon to take Grenville to the Yard. Hadley told him to assemble more officers to continue the search for Boeker and the two black men. When the ambulance arrived it took Cooper and the dazed constable off to Saint Bart's and shortly afterwards the wagon arrived to take Hadley, still dazed by the blow to his head, and Grenville to Scotland Yard.

After Hadley had taken Grenville into the Yard and placed him in the tender care of the Custody Sergeant, he made his way up to his office to tell George briefly what had happened.

"Send a police messenger to Sergeant Cooper's wife, Doris, tell her that he has been wounded and taken to Saint Bart's, here is a guinea for her to take a Hansom to the hospital and tell her that I will be along later" said Hadley as he handed the coin to George.

"Right away, sir."

"Now I'm going up to report to the Chief."

"Very good, sir, may I ask if the Sergeant is badly hurt?" asked George anxiously.

"I think it looks worse than it is, George."

"What happened, sir?"

"Two black men attacked us when we approached them and one of them hit me and stabbed the Sergeant in his shoulder."

"Dear God."

Hadley knocked at Chief Inspector Bell's door and walked in without waiting for the call to enter. Bell looked up from his desk and asked "is it bad news, Hadley?"

"I'm afraid it is, sir."

"Tell me then" said Bell as he waved Hadley to a seat.

"Constable Meredith was shot by a man who I believe is Boeker, outside Isaacs' shop…"

"Good God!"

"He's been taken to Saint Bart's, sir in a serious condition."

"Have you arrested the gunman?"

"No, sir, he escaped through the crowd."

"Bloody hell, Hadley, things are getting worse!"

"Then we were attacked when we approached two black men in a pub in Holborn, I was punched to the ground and Cooper was stabbed…"

"Good God! Is he alright?"

"He's been taken to Saint Bart's but I think he's not seriously hurt" replied Hadley.

"I hope that's the case, now what about you?"

"Just a little shaken but I'll mend by the morning, sir."

"Have you got these two scoundrels under arrest?"

"No, sir, unfortunately they escaped in the pandemonium."

"What are you doing about catching them?"

"Sergeant Johnson and his men from Farringdon Road station are searching for them now, sir."

"Good, now any sign of the diamonds?"

"Not yet, sir."

"This is bad news compounded by more bad news, Hadley."

"It was ever thus, sir."

"Then put more men on the search for this man Boeker and your two blacks, it's imperative that we recover the diamonds immediately!"

"Very good, sir and I'll organise constant surveillance outside Isaacs shop."

"Good, now have you spoken to Sir Robert?"

"Yes, sir, we went to Teddington and after speaking with Mr Brandon-Hall, I had a few words with Sir Robert" replied Hadley.

"And?"

"I think that he is under some sort of pressure because he's very nervous and I'm sure he's holding back vital information, sir."

"Did you find out anything about his strange house guests?"

"Not really, sir, but I think that Brandon-Hall, Konigsberg and Kruger are all involved in something underhand…"

"And Sir Robert knows about it?" interrupted Bell.

"Without a doubt, sir."

"Well give me a report before you go, Hadley, I need something to tell the Commissioner."

"It'll be brief, sir, as I am going to the hospital to see how our injured officers are."

"Very well then, now you'll need someone to replace Cooper whilst he is indisposed."

"Yes, sir, I would like Sergeant Kelly to assist me."

"Right, I'll organise that, just let him know what's been arranged" said Bell.

"Yes, sir and I'll brief two plain clothes men for the surveillance at Isaacs."

Hadley took a Hansom to Farringdon Road police station and found Sergeant Johnson in an unhappy frame of mind as he and his men had not been able to find either Boeker or the men who attacked them. Hadley thanked the Sergeant for his efforts and then spoke to Inspector Morton requesting more men to continue the search. Morton looked perplexed until Hadley explained the seriousness of the situation and when he told the Inspector that the Commissioner himself was taking a close personal interest in the investigation, Morton showed great enthusiasm for the search. Leaving Morton in a contented frame of mind - sure that recognition for his successful arrest of the men would lead to his promotion - Hadley smiled to himself and hailed a cab to take him to Saint Bart's hospital.

The hospital was busy and nurses in starched aprons hurried about as matrons with stern features oversaw their efforts. The smell of disinfectant combined with an air of efficiency gave comfort that Cooper was being taken care of in the best possible place. Hadley made inquiries about Meredith and was told that he was in the operating theatre undergoing surgery. He was then directed to the Prince's ward where he found Cooper sitting up with his wife at the bedside.

"Evening, sir" grinned a pale faced Cooper as Hadley approached.

"Evening Sergeant… Mrs Cooper" replied Hadley with a smile as she nodded.

"Thank you for letting Doris know where I was and paying for the cab, sir" said Cooper.

"My pleasure, now how are you feeling?"

"Still a bit shaky, sir, but a lot better than when I first arrived" replied Cooper.

"That's good to hear."

"Did Johnson catch them, sir?"

"Not yet I'm afraid, Sergeant."

"Never mind, I'm sure we'll find them soon, sir."

"Yes, but in the meantime you're staying here until the Doctor says that you are fit and well."

"I'll be alright by tomorrow, sir."

"I don't think so, Sergeant."

"Well who's going to help you, sir?"

"I've asked for Sergeant Kelly to take your place for the time being."

"Well I hope he takes good care of you, sir."

"I'm sure he will."

"Make sure you tell him that I'll be back on duty by Monday at the latest" said Cooper.

"I will, Sergeant, in the meantime you rest and get better as quickly as possible" said Hadley.

"Yes, sir, you can rely on me."

"I know that, Sergeant."

"Do you know how Meredith is, sir?"

"I understand that he's in surgery at the moment."

"I hope he's alright."

"He's in good hands, Sergeant."

Hadley asked Cooper about the constable who was knocked out and was pleased to hear that he had not been seriously hurt and was discharged after a careful medical check. He then spent some time talking to them about subjects not connected with work and took every opportunity to make them smile with stories about his home life and children. Doris relaxed and when Hadley left Cooper's bedside he knew that the young couple were in a happier frame of mind. Locating the Doctor in charge of Cooper's recovery he asked for his opinion on the wounded officer.

"The stab wound was not as deep as we first expected, Inspector" said Doctor Wells.

"That's good."

"Yes, the knife point actually hit the bone in his shoulder and once we had cleaned the wound and stitched it, the bleeding stopped, to all intents and purposes, so provided he remains clear of any infection, I'm sure that he will make a good recovery and be released from hospital in a few days."

"I'm pleased to hear it, Doctor."

"We'll keep a careful eye on him but as he's a fit and strong young man, I'm sure his recovery will be quite quick, Inspector."

"Please God."

"We try to do that all the time at Saint Bart's, Inspector" said Doctor Wells with a smile before he hurried away.

Hadley arrived home and slumped down in the parlour as Alice asked if he had eaten. He did not answer her but just sat quietly as tears began to run down his cheeks.

"Whatever is the matter, Jim?" she asked in an anxious tone. He just shook his head slowly before he answered "young Meredith was shot and Cooper was stabbed today...."

"Oh, dear God!"

"I've just left them in hospital..."

"Are they alright?"

"Meredith is being operated on so we'll have to wait and see but the Doctor says Cooper will make a full recovery, but he is worried about who will look after me."

"We all do that, dear."

"I failed them all, Alice, Meredith, Cooper, Johnson and his young constable."

"Why do you say that, dear?"

"I warned them to be ready for violence but I was not prepared myself."

"Don't you blame yourself for the brutal behaviour of others, Jim Hadley" Alice said firmly.

"I should have been ready for what happened."

"Stop reproaching yourself and have something to eat" she said.

After dinner he sat contemplating the day and was very concerned at the level of violence that the case attracted, he resolved to bring the investigation to a rapid conclusion and to meet any more violence with determined and appropriate force.

CHAPTER 8

Although it was Sunday, Hadley left home as usual and took a Hansom to Scotland Yard. Once in his office he began to study all the reports that he had written since the investigation began. He knew that time was against him if he was to recover the diamonds before Tuesday and he thought that given the current circumstances it was unlikely. He had just finished reading his notes when there was a knock at the door and Sergeant Kelly entered.

"Ah, good morning, Sergeant."

"Good morning, sir" replied Kelly with a smile.

"Now, your attachment to me will only be until Cooper has recovered and is fit for duty again."

"Yes, sir, I understand, how is the Sergeant?"

"Well he was better than I expected when I saw him in hospital last night" replied Hadley.

"That's good news, sir."

"It is. As this is the first time you been on duty in plain clothes you'll have to mind your 'P' and 'Q's."

"Yes, I'll do that, sir."

"We're involved in a very difficult investigation which might become even more dangerous than we have already experienced."

"I understand, sir."

"And everything about this case must remain absolutely confidential, do you understand?"

"Oh, yes, sir."

"Good, now we're going to call at Farringdon Road station first of all and then we're going to call on two gentlemen who are staying at the Savoy Hotel."

"Very good, sir."

"Have you some cash on you to pay for the cab?"

"Yes, I think so, sir."

"Let's be off then."

At Farringdon Road police station Inspector Morton reported that neither Boeker nor the two men had been apprehended although the search area had been widened. Cheap lodging houses as well as hotels in the vicinity had been circulated with the descriptions of all three men and Morton felt that if they were still in the area they would be caught. Hadley thanked him for all his efforts and promised he would report his actions to Chief Inspector Bell who would undoubtedly inform the Commissioner. Morton smiled broadly as he confirmed that he would keep up the tempo of the search for the suspects.

Arriving at the Savoy Hotel Hadley asked to see Count von Rausberg. The receptionist sent a messenger to the Count's room to advise him accordingly and Hadley waited impatiently for the messenger to return. The boy arrived back and told the receptionist that the Count would see the detectives in his room at eleven o'clock. Hadley glanced at his pocket watch and noted that it was just after half past ten.

"We'll wait in the lounge and perhaps you would organise some tea for us" said Hadley to the receptionist who nodded.

Whilst they waited and sipped their tea, Hadley kept a close eye on all who entered the hotel lobby. Just before eleven o'clock, he noticed the well built figure of Herr Schoender enter and stride quickly across the lobby then up the stairs to the rooms above.

"That's very interesting, Sergeant, and I wonder where he has been?"

"Who, sir?"

"The man who has just gone upstairs is the assistant to the Count and he appeared to be in a hurry!"

At a few minutes to eleven a bell boy escorted the detectives to the Count's room and knocked before entering and announcing them. Von Rausberg was lounging on a sofa, dressed in a black silk dressing gown and smoking a cigar, whilst Schoender stood by the large window overlooking The Strand. As Hadley glanced at him he appeared anxious and looked out of the window again.

"Good morning Inspector, have you brought me my diamonds?" asked the Count with a sly grin.

"I'm afraid not, sir."

"You continue to disappoint me, Inspector."

"I'm sorry about that, sir."

"So why are you disturbing me on a Sunday?"

"There's been a development, sir."

"And what is that may I ask?"

"The last time we met in the Commissioner's office, I asked you if you knew a man called Herman Kruger…"

"More questions! Your duty is to find my diamonds not to ask me questions!" interrupted the Count angrily. Hadley waited for a few moments before he continued.

"You didn't tell me if you knew him, sir, and with respect, you still don't answer my question" said Hadley.

"It's none of your business who I know and who I don't know, Inspector."

"Well, you may say that, sir, but I warn you that withholding information from my investigation will lead to your prosecution for obstruction" said Hadley calmly as he watched the Count go red in the face.

"You are an insolent devil!" he exclaimed.

"That's your opinion, sir, but I'll ask you again, do you know Herman Kruger?"

The Count looked about him as if wrestling with a difficult decision before he replied "I may have met him some while ago, why do you ask?"

"Because Kruger was found murdered in an alleyway off the Farringdon Road…"

"Gott im Himmel!" exclaimed the Count before he looked hard at Schoender who paled and gave a slight shrug of his shoulders.

"And I need to trace the movements of the deceased and anybody who knew him" continued Hadley as the Count remained visibly shocked.

"Well all I know is that he was an agent for a consortium who bought and sold diamonds" said the Count.

"When did you last see him, sir?"

"Some time ago, I don't remember when exactly" replied the Count.

"And what about you, Herr Schoender, when did you last see Kruger?" asked Hadley.

"Probably at the same as the Count, Inspector" replied Schoender hesitantly.

"Do you recall when that was, sir?"

"No, I cannot remember."

"Did either of you know that Kruger was in London?" asked

Hadley.

"No, Inspector" replied the Count as Schoender shook his head.

"Sir, have you ever visited Sir Robert Salisbury at his house at Chieveley?" asked Hadley as he fixed his gaze back on the Count who was taken aback by the question.

"I have met Sir Robert, Inspector."

"At Chieveley, sir?"

"Yes, on occasions, but what has that got to do with the murder of Herr Kruger?"

"I'm just gathering background information, sir" replied Hadley.

"I hope that you are as thorough in recovering my diamonds" said the Count.

"I believe that the theft of your stones is the motive for the three murders and it seems to me that there is a wide conspiracy surrounding these diamonds and you are wittingly or unwittingly part of it all, sir."

"That's a monstrous accusation!" exclaimed the Count.

"Nevertheless, the facts speak for themselves, I have an officer shot by a man I believe is Hans Boeker who now has the diamonds…"

"Boeker has the stones?" interrupted the Count wide eyed with amazement.

"Yes, do you know him?"

"He's one of Detrekker's men" replied the Count.

"But do you know him?"

"I've met him once or twice" replied the Count.

"I believe that he has the stones and when he was confronted by my officers outside Solomon Isaacs shop in Hatton Garden, he shot one of them before making off" said Hadley and he watched the Count's reaction to the news. Von Rausberg looked about once again as he tried to gather his thoughts before he said almost inaudibly "we must find him then."

"That is what I intend to do, sir, and if either of you have any information that would assist my investigation, then please let me know at the Yard."

"Yes, of course, Inspector."

"And by the way, two black fellas are also looking for Boeker, and they seemed desperate to avoid questioning because when we confronted them, they stabbed Sergeant Cooper and knocked me to the ground."

"Mein Gott!"

"So any information you have might stop another murder, sir."

"Yes, Inspector" said the Count in an anxious tone.

Hadley and Kelly left the Savoy and took a Hansom to Saint Bart's hospital where, upon enquiring about the condition of Meredith, they were told by the duty Doctor that the officer had not survived long after the operation to remove the bullet and was pronounced dead in the early hours. Hadley was stunned and sat down in a chair with the tears streaming down his face at the loss of a bright, enthusiastic young constable. When he had composed himself he vowed to arrest Boeker and see him hang for the crime he had committed. Kelly was silent after hearing the tragic news and looked down at the floor in reflective contemplation. Hadley did not speak and went alone to the Prince's ward to see how Cooper was faring.

"Morning, sir" said the Sergeant brightly as Hadley approached his bed.

"Morning. How are you feeling today?"

"Much better thank you, sir, and the Doctor said that all being well I can go home on Tuesday" replied Cooper.

"That's good to hear."

"So I'll be back on duty on Wednesday, sir."

"There's no rush, Sergeant, a few days off to fully recuperate is my good advice."

"But sir, we need to arrest Boeker and the blacks…"

"I realise that, Sergeant and I promise you that I will not rest until they are all under lock and key" said Hadley.

"What about the diamonds, sir?"

"When we find Boeker I'm sure we'll find them" replied Hadley.

"Do you know how Meredith is getting on, sir, I have asked the nurses but they say they don't know."

"The Doctor has just told me that unfortunately he died during the night, Sergeant."

"Oh dear God" whispered Cooper.

"I'm desperately sad about his tragic death, he was a fine young officer."

"We'll find Boeker and see him hang for that!" said Cooper.

"Indeed we will, so you rest and get fit as soon as possible, I need you with me, Sergeant."

"Yes, sir."

Hadley and Kelly left the hospital in grim mood and took a cab to the Farringdon Road station where Hadley spoke to Inspector Morton in his office. After Hadley told him about the death of Meredith and the recovery of Cooper, he asked "how goes the search for these three villains?"

"I've got men combing the area, checking all the hotels, pubs and lodgings again for them, but at the minute I've had no positive reports" replied Morton.

"Right, I'll send a telegraph message to all London stations requesting assistance" said Hadley. When he had sent out a full description of the three wanted men, he thanked Morton for his help and then checked with his plain clothes officers outside Isaacs shop before he hurried back to the Yard to question Grenville.

The man was morose and after being brought from his cell, sat at the table in the interview room waiting for Hadley to arrive. He looked up when the Inspector and Kelly entered and sat opposite him.

"How long are you going to keep me here, for Gawd's sake?" Grenville asked angrily.

"Tell me what you know about those two blacks you were sitting with in the pub" said Hadley ignoring Grenville's question.

"I've already told you, I don't know them."

"That's not good enough."

"Well it's the Gawd's honest truth" replied Grenville.

"Let me help clarify your thinking with the facts my friend…"

"Go on then" he grinned.

"As you know, they attacked my Sergeant Cooper, Sergeant Johnson, a constable and me before making off."

"I know that" said Grenville.

"But what you don't know is that the officer who was shot by Boeker outside Isaacs shop has died!" When he heard that, Grenville's face drained of all colour.

"That's nothing to do with me" he said angrily.

"You are involved up to your neck in some sort of conspiracy and so are the black fellas, but I promise you that by the time I'm finished, some of you will dangle at the end of a hangman's rope whilst others will spend the rest of their miserable lives in Dartmoor" said Hadley with deadly menace.

"I've done nothing and you can't prove I have, so there!"

"Tell me exactly what those men said to you before we arrived in the pub."

"They just came over and asked if I was a local bloke and did I know where they could go to stay somewhere cheap whilst they looked around London."

"And what did you tell them?"

"I told them that I knew an old girl in Whitechapel who'd look after 'em, cheap like" Grenville replied.

"Where about in Whitechapel?"

"In Fieldgate Street."

"The number?"

"Fourteen."

"And the woman's name is?"

"Mary Taylor, she's a widow."

"How do you know of her?"

"She's a friend of my aunt's" replied Grenville. Hadley remained silent whilst Kelly made a note of the address.

"When you and Lansbury left the shop yesterday, you walked down Hatton Garden then turned into Holborn" said Hadley.

"Yes, so what?"

"Where did Lansbury go to?"

"He went home and I went to the pub" replied Grenville.

"Where does he live?"

"He's got lodgings in Fetter Lane."

"What's the number?"

"I dunno for sure, ten, I think."

"Right, that's all for the time being" said Hadley.

"Can I go now?" asked Grenville.

"No, certainly not."

"You can't hold me here" wailed Grenville.

"Oh yes I can, my friend" replied Hadley as he stood up.

"How long have I got to stay banged up then?"

"Until I say you can go!"

"You'll be in trouble with Mr Isaacs if I don't turn up for work tomorrow!"

"Considering the mood I'm in, Grenville, I positively look forward to it!"

Hadley arranged for two constables to accompany him and Kelly to Fieldgate Street in a police wagon to arrests the black men. On the high speed journey along London's cobbled streets, Hadley prayed that Grenville had told him the truth and that the arrest of the men was imminent. He hoped that their capture would unlock the case and help in the search for Boeker.

They arrived outside number fourteen and Kelly hammered on the door as Hadley drew his revolver and the constables prepared themselves. An elderly woman opened the door and looked at them in bewilderment.

"Yes?"

"Mrs Taylor?" asked Hadley.

"Yes, I am."

"We're police officers…"

"I can see that dear" she interrupted.

"Do you have two lodgers in this house?"

"I did have until this morning" she replied.

"Were they black South Africans?"

"Yes, they were black but I dunno where they're from, dear."

"You say that you did have so are they gone now?"

"Yes, they left first thing with their bags" she replied.

"Do you know where they've gone?"

"No, dear, they just paid me for the one night and I never ask questions, I mean, you don't know where that can lead or what you're getting into these days" she said with a shake of her head.

"Yes quite so, but please think again, did they give any clue as to where they were going" said Hadley in desperation.

"No, I don't remember them saying much at all, other than that Charlie Grenville sent them, I know his aunt Mrs Balcombe you know, so they just paid me and kept themselves to themselves in their room until this morning" she replied.

"Thank you, Mrs Taylor."

"Shall I call a Bobby if they come back?" she asked.

"Yes, please do, but somehow I doubt if you will ever see them again" replied Hadley.

"Oh, that's a shame, dear, they seemed quite nice" she said before she closed the door.

Hadley sent the constables back to the Yard and he and Kelly walked up Fieldgate Street, passed the small terraced houses, to the Whitechapel Road and along to the Kings Head. The pub was busy and they struggled to get to the bar where Hadley ordered pints of stout from a harassed Vera.

"Where's your other young fella?" she asked as she pulled the pints.

"In hospital, Vera."

"What's wrong with him?"

"He was stabbed…"

"Oh my Gawd! No one's safe these days, I blame all these bloody foreigners" she said.

"You're right in this case, Vera."

"I knew it, I knew it, I said to my old man only last night…"

"Vera, we're looking for two black South Africans, have you seen them in here?" asked Hadley.

"Can't say that I have, but I'll ask around" she replied.

"They were staying with a Mrs Taylor in Fieldgate Street until this morning so they might still be somewhere in the vicinity."

"Right, I'll keep me eyes peeled, now anything to eat, gents?"

"Yes, I'll have a ploughman's lunch and what will you have, Sergeant?"

"I'll have the same, sir, if that's alright."

"It is, so pay Vera whilst I find somewhere to sit."

Hadley found a small table and squeezed in on the bench seat between the lunchtime drinkers. Kelly joined him and they sat quietly sipping their drinks before a bar girl appeared with their lunches. They had just started to eat when Agnes and Florrie arrived.

"Hello, Jim."

"Hello Agnes… Florrie"

"Well who's this young fella then?" asked Agnes with a smile.

"Sergeant Kelly."

"Hello Sergeant" said Agnes.

"Sergeant, this is Miss Agnes Cartwright and her constant companion, Miss Florrie Dean" said Hadley.

"Please to meet you I'm sure" said Kelly.

"Now the ladies always have sixpenny gins, so if you wouldn't mind Sergeant" said Hadley and Kelly nodded and pushed his way back to the bar.

"He's a nice looking fella, you training him up, Jim?" asked Agnes.

"Not really, he's already well trained but he's helping me whilst Cooper recovers…"

"Is he ill?" interrupted Florrie anxiously.

"He's been stabbed…"

"Oh my God no!" exclaimed Florrie.

"But he's recovering well, so don't worry, he'll be back on duty by the end of the week" said Hadley.

"Thank God for that" whispered Florrie.

"Now listen, we're looking for two South African blacks, the one who stabbed Cooper is about my height and the other one, he's a short fella, knocked a constable down before they escaped."

"Bloody foreigners" said Florrie.

"They stayed in lodgings in Fieldgate Street last night but left this morning and I'm sure that they are still hereabouts".

"We'll look out for them, Jim" said Agnes.

"Thank you Agnes, and tell all the other girls down the lane."

"Yes, I will Jim" said Agnes as Kelly arrived back with the gins.

After finishing their lunch the detectives made their way to Mile End police station and Hadley gave details of the suspects to Inspector Bromwich. He immediately instigated a search of the area by his men and promised to telegraph Hadley at the Yard as soon as he had any news.

Back at his office, Hadley and Kelly spent the rest of the afternoon going through all the notes and reports surrounding the investigation. Hadley did not come to any startling conclusions and when he left for home he was very disconsolate knowing that he had only one more day to recover the diamonds and capture Boeker.

CHAPTER 9

The Monday morning traffic was heavier than usual and Hadley arrived at the Yard later than he anticipated. This did not please him and other than a cursory 'morning' to Kelly and George, he hurried up to Bell's office. He knocked and entered as Bell looked up from his desk and said "I hope you've some good news for me today, Hadley."

"Not really, sir."

"It's a damned tragedy that young Meredith has died."

"It is, sir."

"The Commissioner wants an immediate arrest and has given his permission to use all the manpower required to catch this bloody man, Boeker!"

"I think we're doing all we can, sir."

"Well it's not good enough, the Press are going mad and we need to catch this bloody bugger and hang him as soon as possible" said Bell angrily.

"I'm sure we will, sir."

"And as he's got the diamonds you've only got today to find him before the Count wanders off to Amsterdam on Tuesday, otherwise we've a serious diplomatic situation on our hands!"

"It never rains but it pours, sir."

"Quite so, anything else?"

"I tracked the black fellas down to a house in Whitechapel but when I arrived they had left the place, sir."

"Damn! What have you done to find them?"

"I contacted Mile End station and alerted them there to search the area as I think they are constantly on the move, staying for one night only in cheap lodgings, they know we're after them, sir."

"Well, organise more men from here if you need to, Hadley."

"Very good, sir."

"How's Cooper?"

"Much better and recovering well, thank you, sir."

"I'm pleased to hear it, when do you expect him back on duty?"

"The Doctor told him that he could go home on Tuesday…"

"He'll back on Wednesday then" interrupted Bell.

"I think that's a bit soon, sir."

"We are in a very difficult situation, Hadley and we need all the good men we can get on this investigation" said Bell firmly.

"Of course, sir and that's why I'd like to keep Sergeant Kelly with me for the time being…"

"Why?"

"He can work with Cooper, sir and I'm sure that with the two of them helping me on the case, we'll have results in double quick time" replied Hadley.

"Very well then, get to it and keep me informed."

Hadley returned to his office and over a pot of tea told Kelly that he would be staying with him for a while after Cooper returned to duty. Kelly was delighted and Hadley was pleased to have the keen young man with him. When they were ready they set off to contact the plain clothes officers on surveillance outside Isaacs shop to find out if anything unusual had occurred. The Hansom stopped and waited for them in the Clerkenwell Road as they walked down Hatton Garden to have words with the officers standing back in the alleyway opposite the shop. To Hadley's disappointment, the officers had nothing to report other than two distinguished looking men calling at the shop as soon as it opened and leaving about half an hour later. This gave Hadley food for thought as the detectives returned to the waiting Hansom and continued on to the Farringdon Road police station. There was no sign of the three suspects and nothing to report so Hadley left the station a disappointed man. The Hansom took them to the Mile End police station where once again, the search had proved fruitless so far and Hadley wondered where these men were hiding. The detectives returned to the Yard in sombre mood and as soon as they entered the office, George told Hadley that he was to go to Chief Inspector Bell's office immediately.

Hadley knocked and entered as Bell looked up.

"Glad you're back, Hadley, any news of these blackguards?"

"I'm afraid not, sir, they all seem to have vanished into thin air" he replied.

"Well things do look bad and I think they may get worse before they get better."

"Why do you say that, sir?"

"Waiting in the Commissioner's office are two Germans from the Embassy…"

"Do you know their names, sir?" interrupted Hadley.

"Yes, I'm told they are Herr Konigsberg and his assistant Herr Stumpfel" replied Bell.

"So they've returned from Berlin."

"Apparently so, Hadley."

"You say they're waiting, sir?"

"Yes, they've called without an appointment to see the Commissioner on an urgent matter."

"This will be interesting, sir."

"He is at the Home Office at present but is expected to return within the next ten minutes or so and he has sent word that we are to attend him" said Bell.

"Very good, sir."

"I only hope that you've got some answers for the questions that we'll be asked, Hadley."

"I agree, sir."

They did not have to wait long before the Commissioner's clerk arrived to tell them that he had returned.

On entering the grand office they were introduced to Konigsberg and Stumpfel before being waved to a seat. Hadley studied the two men carefully. Konigsberg was exactly what he had expected, the man was about fifty, tall with piercing black eyes, iron grey hair and side whiskers. He had an aristocratic face that almost hid the sneer as he looked down at the lesser mortals that surrounded him. Stumpfel was about forty, short, thick set with black hair and a large moustache that looked slightly comical on his hard face.

"Gentlemen, I've called Chief Inspector Bell and Inspector Hadley in to this meeting because I believe that they may be able to help" said the Commissioner with a smile of re-assurance.

"I hope you're right, Commissioner, because this serious matter is highly confidential and normally I would not discuss it in front of such low ranking men" replied Konigsberg.

"I assure you, Herr Konigsberg that their rank has nothing to do with their competence!" exclaimed the Commissioner and Hadley felt quite proud as Bell smiled.

"Is that so" said Konigsberg in a cold and haughty tone.

"It is and I'll have you know that they have been involved with many cases that they have brought to successful conclusions and their efforts have been praised by the highest in the land" said the Commissioner and Hadley felt that he was gilding the lily a little too much, but very comforting to know, none the less.

"Very well, now what I am about to tell you must remain totally secret" said Konigsberg and he raised his index finger in front of his face and looked quickly at each of them.

"We understand, Herr Konigsberg" said the Commissioner as Hadley and Bell nodded.

"This is good and as it should be. Now my Government has secretly purchased four precious diamonds from the Transvaal Mining Company and has paid an agreed sum into the Swiss Bank account of that Company…"

"We already know that, Herr Konigsberg" interrupted the Commissioner and the German looked stunned.

"How could you know that?" he asked.

"We've been informed by Count von Rausberg" replied the Commissioner with a smile.

"Who?" asked the wide eyed German and Hadley groaned silently as Bell looked totally bemused.

"Count von Rausberg, he was here a few days ago telling us that your Government had purchased the diamonds and he was here to collect them from a man called Detrekker before having them valued in London and then taking them to Amsterdam for cutting" said the Commissioner. Konigsberg looked shattered before he whispered "Gott im Himmel."

"When did you arrive back from Berlin, Herr Konigsberg?" asked the Commissioner as the German's jaw dropped in total surprise.

"Mein Gott! This morning, but how do you know all this?" he half whispered then glanced at Stumpfel who had gone quite pale and wide eyed.

"I'm afraid since you left London last Thursday evening after your visit to Sir Robert Salisbury's country house at Chieveley there have been some unpleasant developments" said the Commissioner.

"This is all a great shock to me, my secretary at the Embassy told me this morning that Detrekker had been found murdered in Hyde Park" said Konigsberg as he mopped his forehead with his handkerchief.

"I'm sure it is, sir" said the Commissioner.

"And who is this Count von Rausberg?" asked Konigsberg.

"A fellow countryman of yours, sir, I do believe."

"I do not know him and I assure you that he has nothing to do with the purchase of these stones which I have come to report are now missing!" exclaimed Konigsberg.

"Oh dear, that's unfortunate, tell me how did he know about this transaction?"

"I have no idea, but I will find out!"

"Well, we will give you every possible assistance in the matter, sir" said the Commissioner with a confident smile.

"I'm glad to hear it, because if these stones are lost then my Government will hold you responsible, Commissioner."

"We understand that, sir, it's usual for the Metropolitan Police to be held responsible for everything these days."

"Do you know who murdered Detrekker?" asked Konigsberg anxiously.

"I'm afraid we don't know for sure, sir, but we do have several suspects."

"Mein Gott, this is a catastrophe, he was supposed to bring the stones to the Embassy last Thursday by appointment and give them personally to our Ambassador, Count von Hollenhoff" said the shocked German.

"I'm sorry to hear that, sir."

"Do you have any idea where the diamonds are now?" asked Konigsberg in an anxious tone.

"We're sure that a man called Boeker has them sir, and we are at this moment searching for him" said Hadley. Konigsberg gave the Commissioner a hard look and his eyes narrowed as he asked "what chance have you got of finding this man soon?"

"We are hopeful that he will be under arrest within twenty four hours, sir" said Bell in a positive tone and the Commissioner smiled.

"As you see, sir, we are taking steps to recover the diamonds and I'm sure that they will be returned to your Government quite soon, but I must insist that we bring them to your Embassy and give them in person to Count von Hollenhoff" said the Commissioner.

"That will be the outcome I pray for, Commissioner" said Konigsberg.

"May I ask why your Government agreed for the stones to come to London, sir and not go straight to Berlin?" asked Hadley. Konigsberg fixed him with a hard look and replied "my Government wanted an appraisal of the diamonds from an expert in Hatton Garden before they were taken to Antwerp by me for cutting, Inspector."

"Not Amsterdam, sir?" persisted Hadley.

"Nien! Antwerp is the centre for diamond cutting in Europe, Inspector" replied Konigsberg firmly.

"Why did your Ambassador, Count von Hollenhoff, not notify us when Detrekker failed to materialise and then was found murdered, sir?" asked the Commissioner. Konigsberg glared at him and replied "as I told you all the arrangements surrounding this purchase were most secret and the Ambassador preferred them to remain so."

"Have you got men searching for these diamonds, sir?" asked Hadley.

"I will not answer any more of these questions!" exclaimed Konigsberg.

"We understand, sir, so if there is nothing else you wish to discuss, we'll not detain you any longer" said the Commissioner with a smile.

"This is a grave situation, Commissioner and I will report to my Ambassador that, in my opinion, you are not taking it seriously!"

"Oh I am, sir, you can be very sure of that and you may inform Count von Hollenhoff from me that at the moment I have one police officer who has been shot and killed, another recuperating in hospital after being stabbed, not to mention Inspector Hadley and other officers attacked in the course of investigating crimes of murder and theft carried out by foreign persons, involved in secret and clandestine deals to purchase diamonds from South Africa!" exclaimed the Commissioner angrily and Konigsberg was taken aback whilst Hadley wanted to shout out 'bravo!' Before the German could reply, the Commissioner continued "and I regard the murder and attacks on my officers as very serious and your Government is central to this whole underhand affair, Herr Konigsberg, so please bear that in mind when you're busy complaining to von Hollenhoff about our shortcomings!" The German went pale with shock then red with indignation before he stood up and shouted at the Commissioner "you are insolent, sir! I will report exactly what you have said to our Ambassador and you may expect serious political repercussions from your unwarranted outburst and your failing duty to protect innocent people going about their lawful business!"

The Commissioner remained silent for a few moments and then said very calmly "good day, Herr Konigsberg, Herr Stumpfel" before he returned his gaze to the paperwork on his desk. The Germans glared at Hadley and Bell before they stormed out of the office, leaving the door wide open.

The Commissioner looked up and said "gentlemen, I fear that we've not heard the last of this and we must expect difficult times from now on."

"Yes, sir" they replied in chorus and Hadley was pleased that the Commissioner had made his feelings known to the arrogant German.

"Now I want you to plan carefully what needs to be done to catch this man Boeker and recover these diamonds, use whatever means necessary and ensure that you are armed at all times" said the Commissioner.

"Very good, sir" said Bell and Hadley nodded.

"First of all, I want this Count von Rausberg and his man brought in for questioning, please see to it immediately and report back to me."

"Yes, sir."

Hadley ensured that Sergeant Kelly was armed before they set off to the Savoy Hotel to arrest von Rausberg and Herr Schoender. After they arrived at the Savoy, they hurried up the stairs to the Count's suite and were surprised to find the door open. Hadley entered the room with Kelly close behind and they were confronted by a maid with an anxious look on her face and a feather duster in her hand. She bobbed a curtsy and waited for

Hadley to speak.

"Where are the gentlemen who were staying here?" he asked.

"They left this morning, sir" she replied.

"Damn!" exclaimed Hadley before he rushed out of the room and headed for the reception. Hadley questioned the nervous receptionist quite aggressively but the young man was unable to give him any indication of the whereabouts of the Count and his assistant. The detectives went outside, hailed a cab, telling the driver to 'whip up' and take them to Hatton Garden with all speed. The Hansom clattered along through the busy London streets and made good time to the Clerkenwell Road, it was just about to turn down into the Garden when Hadley saw the two black men that had attacked Cooper and him, walking along the busy street. He shouted "Stop the cab!" and the driver pulled up sharply as Hadley and Kelley leapt from the Hansom and drawing their revolvers. Hadley rushed towards the men who suddenly stopped when they saw his fast approach and turned to run back towards the Farringdon Road. Hadley shouted "stop those men!" repeatedly but the people on the pavement looked bemused and as they were uncertain what was happening, took no action. The two men could run very fast and in desperation, as Hadley became breathless, he fired two rounds up into the air in the hope that would cause them to stop. However, this made all the people close by, duck down and some of the women screamed, whilst horses in the road shied and panicked with fright at the sound then tramped sideways causing collisions amongst the traffic, but the black men carried on running and then turned right when they reached the corner of Farringdon Road. By now Kelly was alongside Hadley and called out "don't worry, sir, I'll catch them!"

"Be careful, Sergeant" gasped Hadley as he slowed down and watched Kelly forging ahead. The Sergeant reached the corner and turned right after the men and when Hadley eventually arrived in the Farringdon Road he could not see Kelly or the two black men in the busy street. He hurried on, breathless and frustrated at his failure to catch the criminals, then, as he passed the entrance to a narrow alleyway he glanced along it and saw to his horror Kelly struggling with the two men, one of whom was repeatedly stabbing at the Sergeant with a large knife. Hadley did not hesitate but fired his revolver at the man and missed. Running down the alleyway towards the melee, he fired again, but he missed once more and at that moment the men broke off their attack and ran down the alleyway leaving Kelly slumped against the wall covered in blood.

"Good God Almighty" said Hadley between gasps as he bent down to assist Kelly.

"I'm alright, sir, I think it looks worse than it is, you get after them" said Kelly bravely as a police whistle sounded.

"I'm staying right here, Sergeant, those bastards won't get far now!" replied Hadley as he examined the worst cut which was in Kelly's neck. He placed his handkerchief over the wound as he heard someone running towards him from the Farringdon Road. Hadley glanced up to see a police constable followed by another hurrying towards him.

"Thank God you're here, constable!"

"I was close by and came when I heard the gun shots, sir."

"Good, I'm Inspector Hadley, send for an ambulance then get back to the station and organise a search party for two black men who've just attacked Sergeant Kelly!"

"Right, sir" said the first constable.

"Can I stay and help, sir?" asked the second constable as the first officer ran off.

"Thank you, constable, help me attend to Sergeant Kelly until the ambulance arrives" replied Hadley with a heavy heart.

CHAPTER 10

Hadley and the constable applied pressure to the worst stab wounds in Kelly's neck and shoulder and waited patiently for the ambulance to arrive. Hadley breathed a sigh of relief when he heard it clatter to a halt at the end of the alleyway and then two attendants pushed their way hurriedly through the crowd that had gathered. Soon the wounded policeman was on his way to Saint Bart's whilst Hadley strode purposefully along to the Farringdon Road police station. Inspector Morton had already deployed his officers in the area and each Sergeant was armed with a revolver.

"This is a terrible situation for you, Hadley" said Morton after he waved the distressed Inspector to a seat in his office.

"It's a damned sight worse for Meredith, Cooper and now Kelly" replied Hadley.

"That's true, I think you'd better sit and rest for a while, you do look all in" said Morton.

"I'll be alright after a cup of tea and a sandwich" replied Hadley with a faint smile and Morton nodded then called for his clerk. They discussed the search operation in detail whilst drinking tea and eating cheese sandwiches. When Morton asked for extra men, Hadley telegraphed Bell with news of the attack on Kelly and requested that a suitable number of armed officers should be sent to Farringdon Road as soon as possible. Within an hour, twelve constables with two Sergeants arrived in a police wagon and presented themselves to Hadley. Morton was impressed and set out the present search cordon to the Sergeants' before they were sent to broaden the area.

Hadley left the station and took a cab to Saint Bart's where he made inquiries about Kelly. He was told that his wounds were serious but not life threatening and he would be leaving surgery soon. Hadley was relieved to hear that news and made his way to the Prince's ward to see Cooper.

"Hello, sir, I didn't expect to see you today" said Cooper brightly as Hadley approached his bed.

"To tell the truth, I hadn't planned to call but they've just brought Kelly in…"

"Kelly, sir?"

"Yes, I'm afraid he's been attacked by the same man who stabbed you, Sergeant."

"Oh good God, is he alright, sir?" asked Cooper.

"Yes, the Doctor says he'll make a full recovery" replied Hadley.

"What happened, sir?"

Hadley told him the events of the day in detail and when he had finished, Cooper said "I think I'd better get out of here damned quick and be back on duty to protect you, sir."

"Not so fast, Sergeant, I think you'd better wait until the Doctor says you can leave" said Hadley with a smile.

"But sir…"

"I'll be alright, Sergeant, don't you worry" interrupted Hadley.

"Well don't take any risks until I'm with you, sir."

"I promise, Sergeant" said Hadley with a smile.

They discussed the case and tried to predict what was likely to happen next, which helped Hadley gather his thoughts. Eventually when he said 'goodbye' to Cooper, he was feeling somewhat uplifted by their conversation and left the hospital in a better frame of mind.

Returning to Farringdon Road station, Inspector Morton told Hadley that there had been no sighting of the two men and he thanked him for all his support before taking a cab back to the Yard.

Once back in his office, Hadley telegraphed all London stations and the Dover Harbour Police with the descriptions of Rausberg and Schoender, requesting their immediate arrest. He then briefed George on the events of the day and enjoyed a few moments of peace with a pot of tea before going to report to Chief Inspector Bell.

Hadley explained to Bell what had happened in the alleyway and the Chief looked stunned when he heard the full detail of the attack.

"Why didn't you shoot the bastard?" Bell asked angrily.

"I did fire at him, sir, but unfortunately I missed" replied Hadley.

"Damned unfortunate if you ask me Hadley, and as soon as this investigation is over you're to go on a firearms course and learn to shoot straight!"

"Yes, sir…"

"And that's an order, Hadley!"

"Yes, sir."

"And now I suppose you need another Sergeant to assist you?"

"Yes, please, sir."

"God if this keeps up we'll have the whole of the Yard in Saint Bart's or the Marylebone!"

"I hope not, sir…"

"So do I Hadley. Now, I suggest that you have Sergeant Talbot with you until Cooper is back on duty."

"I don't know him that well, sir, and I'd prefer…"

"Listen Hadley, I think you need an ex-army man with you, someone who's used to shooting at the Fuzzy Wuzzy's" interrupted Bell.

"I think they're black South Africans, sir…"

"I don't care where they come from, Hadley as far as I'm concerned everyone south of Calais is either a Johnny Foreigner or a Fuzzy Wuzzy!" exclaimed Bell.

"Yes, sir…"

"And there's far too many of them here in London for my liking!"

"Quite so, sir."

"You heard what the Commissioner said to that pompous German fella, Konigsberg, it's his damned Government's fault that we're involved in this violent crime spree on our streets, if they want to do secret deals and kill one another, then let them do it in Berlin!"

"I agree, sir."

"Now, have you arrested that other fella, Count Rausberg and his man?"

"No, sir, I'm afraid that they left the Savoy first thing this morning…"

"Good God Hadley!"

"I've telegraphed all the London stations with their description…"

"I don't think we'll have much luck finding them!"

"I was on my way to Isaacs shop to question him about

Rausberg when I saw the black men, sir."

"You think that the Germans might have gone there?"

"Yes, my surveillance officers saw two smartly dressed men go into the shop this morning, sir."

"Were they able to identify them?"

"I'm afraid not, sir."

"Pity, well with those two now wandering around London along with Boeker and the blacks, it seems to me that you've got your work cut out for the moment, Hadley."

"I have indeed, sir."

"Well, get Talbot out of uniform and into plain clothes, then get on with it."

"Yes, sir."

"And make sure you're both well armed and don't hesitate to shoot anybody who resists arrest!"

"Very good, sir."

"The Commissioner wants quick results and we can't waste time on any suspects who get in the way of that."

"No, sir."

Sergeant Talbot was a ruddy faced, well built man of about forty, who was delighted to be taken out of uniform and into plain clothes to assist Hadley. They left the Yard and hailed a cab to take them to Hatton Garden. On the way, Hadley briefed Talbot on what had happened so far in the investigation and warned him to be ready for anything.

"Don't worry about me, sir, I'd as soon as shoot them as look at 'em!" said Talbot.

"In this case you may have to, Sergeant."

"I'm used to it sir, I saw action in Afghanistan as well as Egypt with the 4th Fusiliers."

"I'm glad to hear it Sergeant, your experience in the army may prove to be invaluable" said Hadley with confidence.

After the Hansom dropped the detectives off in the Clerkenwell Road, they walked down Hatton Garden to where the surveillance officers were still on duty. They reported that they had seen nothing untoward since this morning and Hadley thanked them for their efforts before crossing the street. He and Talbot entered

Isaacs shop and when the assistant saw them he said "good day, gentlemen, I expect you wish to see Mr Isaacs again?"

"Yes, please" replied Hadley.

"I'll let him know you're here, sir, I won't be a moment."

After the assistant disappeared through the door behind the counter, Talbot looked about the shop and his eyes widened at the glittering array of jewellery on display.

"My word, sir, this lot is worth a pretty penny."

"It certainly is, Sergeant."

Talbot peered closer at the sparkling diamonds on display behind the glass counter and gave a low whistle every so often. Suddenly the door opened and the assistant returned followed by Lansbury.

"Mr Isaacs will see you now, follow me" said Lansbury in an abrupt tone. They followed him upstairs to Isaacs' office where he waved them to seats after wishing them 'good day.'

"So what is it now, Inspector?" asked Isaacs in a firm tone.

"Did Count Rausberg and Herr Schoender call to see you today?"

"Yes, they did and what of it, Inspector?"

"I'm trying to contact them regarding the missing diamonds but they have un-expectedly checked out of the Savoy, where they were originally staying until tomorrow morning" said Hadley.

"Is that so, Inspector?"

"It is, sir. Did Count Rausberg say where they were staying before they leave for Amsterdam tomorrow?"

"No, Inspector, and talking of where people are staying, is my man Grenville still in custody at the Yard?"

"He is, sir."

"On what charge are you holding him?"

"He's helping us with our inquiries at the moment, sir."

"Inquiries in to what?" asked Isaacs angrily.

"I'm investigating four murders, two violent stabbings, diamond theft, threatening behaviour and possibly perverting the course of justice, sir."

"If you think Grenville had anything to do with all of that, you're mad, Inspector!"

"So people say, but one of those murders was of a police officer on duty and that makes me very mad!"

"So it seems."

"And as I have already told Grenville, everybody connected with these crimes I'll see hanged from a rope or spending the rest of their miserable life in Dartmoor!"

"I see" said Isaacs as he narrowed his eyes.

"With no exceptions, no matter what their rank or who they know, I do hope I make myself abundantly clear, sir" said Hadley in a firm tone.

"You do indeed, Inspector, now as I've told you everything I know concerning Count Rausberg, you will excuse me as I am a very busy man, Mr Lansbury will show you out…"

"Why did Rausberg come here and what did you discuss with him?" asked Hadley.

"That's none of your business, Inspector" replied Isaacs angrily.

"It is if it's connected to the whereabouts of the diamonds!" exclaimed Hadley and at that Lansbury moved close to him in a menacing way. Talbot stood up and faced the man as a knock came at the door.

"Yes?" shouted Isaacs. The assistant entered and said in an anxious tone "I'm sorry to disturb you, sir, but there's a Mr Brandon-Hall downstairs who wants to see you urgently." Isaacs looked surprised and Hadley said "how very interesting."

"Tell him I've got Inspector Hadley with me at the moment and he'll have to wait" said Isaacs.

"Please feel free to invite him up, sir, I'd like to hear what you have to say to each other" said Hadley with a grin.

"It's none of your business!" exclaimed Isaacs.

"On the contrary it is if it's connected to the missing diamonds, sir" Hadley persisted.

"I've nothing more to say to you and I will not be questioned in this manner when I'm trying to carry out legitimate business with a customer, Inspector" said Isaacs firmly. Hadley thought for a few moments before he said "then I'll leave you now, sir, but I'll be back in due course as I have more questions for you and the net tightens on my list of suspects."

"Good day to you, Inspector" said Isaacs through clenched teeth. Hadley followed Lansbury down to the shop where he smiled and wished a surprised Mr Brandon-Hall 'good day' before leaving and striding up towards the Clerkenwell Road. Hadley stopped and briefed the surveillance officers regarding Mr Brandon-Hall, he wanted a report on the time he left the shop and the direction he headed.

The detectives walked briskly to the police station in the Farringdon Road where they were shown into Inspector Morton's office.
"No luck yet, Inspector" said Morton as Hadley sat down opposite him.
"These people could not have just disappeared, someone must have seen them" said Hadley.
"You say that, but London is getting more crowded by the day with folk coming in from the country looking for work, not to mention the mass of foreigners arriving" said Morton.
"I realise that but it seems as if Boeker and the black men have disappeared into thin air" said Hadley in an exasperated tone.
"With so many people on the streets it's hard to find suspects and I think someone may be hiding them" said Morton.
"Well, we'll have to keep searching, the Commissioner wants quick results" said Hadley.
"I'm sure we'll find them" said Morton.
"Please God that we do and soon" replied Hadley. They discussed the operation in detail and it was late when Hadley and Talbot left to return to the Yard.

On arrival at his office Hadley asked George if there had been any telegraph messages regarding the searches for the suspects.
"I'm afraid not, sir."
"We need something to break for us, George" said Hadley in a disappointed tone.
"We certainly do, sir."
"There's no more to be done today so let's see what tomorrow brings" said Hadley and he wished George and Talbot 'good night'.

Alice did her best to comfort her husband but it was to no avail. After dinner she left him sitting in the parlour deep in thought. Even his children were unable to rouse a smile from him, which was most unusual and when they had gone up to bed Alice tried once again.

"You mustn't let it get on top of you, dear" she said firmly as she sat with him.

"I suppose not."

"You cannot give of your best if you remain so down hearted and you owe it to Cooper and Kelly as well the officer who was shot, to rise above it all and concentrate on catching these killers" she said and Hadley gazed at his wife then smiled and gave her a kiss on her cheek.

"You're right as usual, dear, and I always wonder what I'd do without you" whispered Hadley.

"So do I Jim, now I think it's time for bed, because you need a good night's rest!"

CHAPTER 11

The ride to the Yard in the sunshine on the Tuesday morning did much to improve Hadley's outlook in general and he was even happier to discover Cooper at his desk.

"Good morning, Sergeant."

"Good morning, sir."

"And what are you doing here may I ask?"

"I'm reporting for duty, sir" replied Cooper.

"I thought you had to remain in hospital until tomorrow" said Hadley.

"The Doctor said I was well enough to leave this morning, sir, so I came straight here."

"I think he meant that you were to go home and rest, Sergeant."

"He may have done, but I can't sit at home twiddling my thumbs sir, when you need me" replied Cooper.

"I always need you, Sergeant, but I need you fit and well, not recovering from a knife attack."

"I'm alright, sir" said Cooper as Talbot came into the office.

"Good morning, sir, and Sergeant Cooper, I didn't expect to see you today" said Talbot with a smile.

"I didn't either" replied Hadley as George came in from his office and after wishing them all 'good morning' and remarking on Cooper's hasty return to duty, suggested that a pot of tea could get the day off to a good start, to which Hadley agreed. Over tea, Hadley laid out his plans and he started by telling Cooper that he should stay in the office and collate all the reports into the murders as well as monitoring the telegraph messages from the stations and advising him of any development. Meanwhile, Hadley and Talbot would call on Sir Robert's home and then Brandon-Hall's riverside house at Teddington. Before he left the office, Hadley checked the report from the surveillance officers outside Isaacs shop, which informed him that Mr Brandon-Hall had left the shop twenty minutes after he went in and proceeded down Hatton Garden where he turned left into Holborn and promptly disappeared. The officers presumed he had hailed a cab.

Hadley and Talbot hailed a cab and went to number 22 Cavendish

Square. Meadows opened the door and when Hadley enquired if Sir Robert was at home, the butler replied "no, sir, but Miss Gwendolyn is here, would you like to speak to her?"

"Yes, please" replied Hadley. Meadows opened the door wider and stood back for them to enter and wait in the hall whilst he went into the drawing room to advise Miss Gwendolyn of their arrival. He came back quickly and led them into the room before announcing them. Hadley was pleased to see the young woman and wished her 'good morning' before he introduced Talbot.

"Good morning, Inspector, Sergeant Talbot, how can I help you today?" she smiled

"Can you tell me where your father is at the moment, Miss?"

"He's gone down to Chieveley, Inspector."

"Do you know when he left Mr Brandon-Hall's house at Teddington?"

"Yesterday or possibly this morning, Inspector, and I understand that my fiancé Rupert has accompanied him to Chieveley" she replied.

"I see" said Hadley thoughtfully before he asked "when do you expect your father to return to London, Miss?"

"I really don't know, Inspector."

"May I ask why, Miss?"

"I've told you repeatedly that my father is under great strain at the moment and on his Doctor's advice he has retired to Chieveley for some rest until his health improves" she replied.

"I'm sorry to hear that he is unwell, Miss."

"And I would be much obliged if you did not trouble him at Chieveley and left any questions you may have until he returns to London, Inspector" she said firmly.

"I'm afraid I can't promise that, Miss."

"In that case if you go to Chieveley I shall report you to your superiors for harassment of my father!" she said with her eyes blazing.

"You may do so, Miss, but I'm investigating four murders and the theft of valuable diamonds in which your father is implicated, so I expect any complaint from you will have to wait until the case is closed" replied Hadley firmly. Gwendolyn fixed him with an icy stare for a few moments before she said "then there is nothing more to discuss, Inspector, so I wish you good day."

"Good day, Miss."

They hailed a cab and the horse trotted quickly through the London traffic to 12, Riverside Walk in Teddington where the door was opened by the butler. When asked if Mr Brandon-Hall was at home he replied haughtily "he is not here sir."

"Do you know where he has gone?"

"I am led to believe that the Master and Mr Rupert have accompanied Sir Robert Salisbury to his country estate for the time being, sir."

"When do you expect Mr Brandon-Hall back here?"

"I couldn't say, sir, I am not privy to the Master's travelling arrangements."

"Is Miss Angelina at home?" asked Hadley.

"She is, but she is not receiving visitors today, sir."

"We're not visitors, we're police officers investigating murders and theft, so please inform her that we wished to speak to her right now" said Hadley firmly. The butler went pale and said "please come in and wait in the hall whilst I announce your arrival, sir."

"Thank you." The butler strode off through double doors and returned moments later, nodded at Hadley, who followed him into the drawing room. Angelina smiled and stood up as the detectives entered the room. Hadley introduced Talbot and Angelina smiled at him then asked "where's the other young officer?"

"He's back at the Yard, Miss whilst he recovers from a knife attack sustained during investigations into this case" replied Hadley.

"Oh, dear, I am sorry to hear that, do please give him my kind regards."

"I will, Miss."

"Now how can I help you, Inspector?"

"I understand that your father and brother have gone down to Chieveley with Sir Robert, can you confirm that, Miss?"

"Yes, Inspector, they left first thing this morning" she replied.

"Do you know when they are expected to return?"

"Not for certain, Inspector, but usually my father comes home from Chieveley after just a few days down there" she said sweetly.

"Does your father often go there?"

"Yes quite often, Inspector."

"May I ask if your mother accompanies him?"

"My mother is not here, in fact she is never here Inspector, she prefers to live at our home in Pretoria" she replied in a firm tone and Hadley sensed the underlying hostility towards her mother.

"I understand, Miss."

"I'm glad you do because it's a total mystery to me why she should wish to remain in Africa and miss out on London society with everything it has to offer" said Angelina forcefully.

"Yes, I'm sure she is socially the poorer for it, Miss" said Hadley as diplomatically as he could.

"Well that's what I tell her but it's her loss I'm afraid."

"Quite so. Now, I'm anxious to trace some other gentlemen who may be friends or associates of your father and I would be obliged if you recognise any of their names, Miss."

"Well I don't know many of Papa's friends but if you tell me the names I'll try and help you."

"Thank you, Miss, now do you know a Mr Hans Boeker?"

"I haven't met him but I have heard Papa mention his name" she replied.

"What about Count Rausberg?"

"No, I've never heard of him."

"Mr Solomon Isaacs?"

"Again I haven't met him but Papa and Sir Robert did mention him in conversation at dinner last night."

"Do you remember what they said, Miss?"

"Not really I'm afraid, I wasn't paying much attention but if I remember correctly, I think Papa had been to see him yesterday about some diamonds that Mr Isaacs hoped to have soon, but I'm not really sure, Inspector."

"Thank you, Miss Angelina, you have been most helpful" said Hadley with a smile.

"Oh, good" she smiled.

"One final question if I may."

"Yes, what is it, Inspector?"

"Did you recently take a note addressed to a Mr Vervorde and deliver it to the Piccadilly Hotel, Miss?"

"Yes, my father asked me to drop it in whilst I was out shopping, Inspector" she replied with a smile.

"Thank you once again."

"Not at all, Inspector."

"We'll leave you now, Miss."

"Very well and remember me to your wounded Sergeant" she said with a twinkle in her eyes.

"You may rest assured that I will do so, Miss."

Talbot hailed a cab outside the house and Hadley told the driver to 'whip up' and get them back to Scotland Yard as fast as possible. When they arrived, Cooper had some good news for them.

"Sir, Inspector Morton's men have arrested one of the black men!"

"Good!" exclaimed Hadley with excitement.

"They're bringing him here now, sir."

"This is good news indeed, gentlemen" said Hadley as his Sergeants beamed.

"Is a celebration pot of tea in order, sir?" asked Cooper.

"Without doubt, please summon George and ask him to organise some sandwiches for us all for lunch" replied Hadley.

Over tea and cheese sandwiches Hadley told Cooper what had transpired so far that morning and he had just finished when Sergeant Johnson came up to the office and announced that the arrested man was in custody down stairs and waiting for Hadley to interview him.

"Thank you, Sergeant, now gentlemen, let's get to it and hope that we have answers to some of the outstanding questions!"

"Yes, sir" they smiled.

"George, bring your pens, ink and plenty of paper!" Hadley called as he led the way out of the office and downstairs to custody.

The arresting officer was Sergeant Browne and he gave them the details of the arrest.

"We first saw the two suspects in Fetter Lane, sir and then we followed them towards Holborn and challenged them just as they reached the end of the Lane."

"Then what happened?"

"They put up a struggle and one of them produced a knife and started to slash at my men before he ran off, two constables gave chase but eventually lost him in the crowd, sir, but we managed to overpower and arrest the other one" said Browne.

"Very well done, Sergeant, please thank your constables. I will be writing to Inspector Morton to thank him and I will bring your swift, brave actions to the notice of the Commissioner" said Hadley with a smile.

"Thank you very much, sir" replied Browne with a broad grin.

"Do we know this man's name, Sergeant?"

"He says he's called Setsi Nkumo and he claims to be the son of a native chief, sir" replied Browne.

"Very good, I'll read your full report later after I have had a few words with our friend from Africa" said Hadley.

Setsi Nkumo looked up as Hadley, the two Sergeants and George entered the interview room. Hadley waited until they were all seated at the table and George had all his writing utensils ready before he said to the anxious, frightened man "I'm Inspector Hadley and these officers are assisting me with my inquiries now tell me your name."

"I am called Setsi Nkumo and I am the son of chief Mangalawi" he replied.

"Where are you from?"

"Beeste-Kraal in the Transvaal."

"Who was the man with you when you were arrested?" asked Hadley.

"He is called Tousi Mombesi..."

"Where is he now?"

"I don't know where he is because he ran off somewhere."

"Why are you here in London?"

"I can't tell you that."

"Why not?"

"Because it is a secret."

"Not any more it's not, my friend, because you and your colleague are facing a hanging or a long jail sentence and if you want to avoid those dreadful possibilities then you must tell me everything you know" said Hadley in a determined tone with his hard blue eyes glinting.

"You have to catch Tousi first and he is a great warrior, he can run so fast that even the Springbok's are afraid of him!" replied

Setsi proudly.

"Well we're not Springboks and we are not afraid."

"You will never catch him."

"And you make the mistake of underestimating us, my friend" replied Hadley.

"We are not afraid of the white man or what you think you can do to us!"

"I repeat, why are you in London?" asked Hadley.

"On business."

"Diamond business?"

"It's a secret."

"Do you know a man called Hans Boeker?" asked Hadley.

"No."

"Do you know a man called Solomon Isaacs?"

"No." Hadley then waited for a few moments before he asked "will you tell me why you are here?"

"I have told you, it's a secret…"

"Right, Mr Nkumo I am charging you with the murder of Klaus Detrekker in Hyde Park, the murder of Dik Vervorde at the Regents Park zoo, the attempted murder of Sergeant Cooper and the attempted murder of Sergeant Kelly…"

"I didn't kill anybody" interrupted Nkumo, his eyes wide with fear.

"Who killed Detrekker and Vervorde?"

"Tousi did it" he half whispered.

"Why did he murder them?"

"I can't say…"

"When we catch him we'll find out, then he'll hang for certain and you'll probably hang as an accessory to murder" said Hadley with menace.

"I do not want to die here…" wailed Nkumo.

"You should have thought of that before you came to London on your secret mission and started killing innocent people and attacking police officers!" Hadley shouted.

"My father is the chief of our tribe and when he hears what you have done to me he will send warriors to kill you!"

"They can try!"

"You will die…"

"One day I will but I'm sure it will be of old age. Now,

Sergeant Talbot..."

"Yes, sir?"

"Would you please ask the Custody Sergeant to bring Mr Grenville in here?"

"Right away, sir."

They waited in silence for Grenville to arrive and when entered the room he looked hard at Nkumo.

"Mr Grenville, do you recognise this man?" asked Hadley.

"I've seen him before" replied Grenville.

"Where and when?"

"He was in the pub with that other fella when they attacked you" replied Grenville.

"Had you ever seen him before then?"

"No."

"Be sure about this" said Hadley.

"I'm sure."

"Thank you, that will be all for now" said Hadley.

"Can I go home now?" asked Grenville.

"Certainly not, I've got to make up the charges against you" replied Hadley.

"What charges?"

"All in good time, you can take him back to his cell now, Sergeant."

"Right, sir, come along you..."

"You can't keep me here!"

"Oh yes I can."

"Mr Isaacs will have you over for this, its wrongful arrest and imprisonment..."

"He can try, meanwhile, go back to your cell" said Hadley.

Nkumo was charged with accessory to murder and then removed to a cell. Hadley and his men returned to the office where they discussed the interview before Hadley set off to brief Chief Inspector Bell.

He knocked and entered then told his chief briefly what had happened.

"Morton's men have done well to arrest one of these black fellas" said Bell with a smile.

"Yes, sir, and they put themselves in some danger tackling

them in the street" said Hadley.

"No one was hurt I trust?"

"No sir, the one that escaped slashed at the constables with his knife but fortunately he did not injure them."

"Thank God for that, Hadley."

"The man in custody has accused this other black of killing Detrekker and Vervorde, sir."

"That's good, something positive to report to the Commissioner" said Bell.

"Yes, sir."

"Now all we've got to do is catch him and then hang him, case closed!"

"Indeed, sir."

"All that leaves is the recovery of the diamonds, Hadley."

"Yes, sir."

"Any further clues as to where they might be?"

"I'm sure that Boeker still has them, sir."

"But where is he?"

"I'm not certain, but I want to go down to Chieveley, sir."

"Whatever for?"

"I found out this morning that Sir Robert has gone there with Brandon-Hall and his son."

"No Hadley, it'll be another wild goose chase, stay here until this fella Boeker is arrested."

"I have a suspicion that Boeker may have already gone down to Chieveley, sir."

"What makes you think that?"

"Because despite our best efforts, he remains at large and I'm sure that if he was still in London we would have found him by now" replied Hadley.

"It could be that he is in the German Embassy under lock and key, have you considered that possibility?"

"It did cross my mind but I dismissed it as our German friends are anxious to keep everything secret, but they told us about the disappearance of the diamonds and if they have Boeker, they have the stones and we wouldn't have known anything about the loss, sir."

"But what if they have Boeker but he hasn't got the diamonds?"

"You mean he's given them to someone else?"

"Possibly or he's been murdered and his killer has them now" said Bell.

"I really don't know what to think at the moment, sir."

"Very well, Hadley, but in the meantime, whilst you're thinking, writes a report for me, so I have something to give the Commissioner."

"Yes, sir."

"And tell me, how is Cooper?"

"He's been released from hospital and is back on duty, sir."

"Good man, what about Kelly?"

"I plan to send a messenger to the hospital later today to find how he is, sir."

"Let me know, Hadley."

"Very well, sir."

"And have you told the black man in custody that British justice will see him hang after he's had a fair trial?"

"I told him that he would probably face execution, sir."

"Well done, Hadley, because it's good to know where we all stand in these situations and the criminals need to have the comfort of certainty about their future fate."

"If you say so, sir."

"Yes and I find that the shadow of the noose helps concentrate minds wonderfully well in these occasions."

"I'm sure you're right, sir."

"Indeed I am and that's why I'm a Chief Inspector" he beamed.

Hadley left Bell's office worried and confused by events whilst wondering what action he should take next to recover the missing diamonds.

CHAPTER 12

It was late afternoon when Hadley and Talbot left Cooper writing notes at the Yard and hailed a cab to Hatton Garden. The surveillance officers had nothing to report other than the fact that they had not seen Mr Isaacs arrive at his shop first thing that morning as usual. Hadley kept that in mind as they walked along to the Farringdon Road station. Inspector Morton had nothing positive to tell Hadley about the continuing fruitless search for the black knifeman and Hans Boeker, so they hailed a cab to take them to Mile End station where once again they were told that there had been no sightings or reports of the two men. On the return journey to the Yard Hadley decided to take action and once he had arrived in his office he told Cooper and Talbot what he had planned.

"Gentlemen, I think that we should pay a lightning visit to Chieveley tomorrow."

"Good idea, sir" said Cooper enthusiastically.

"I'm glad you think so, Sergeant but do you feel up to it?"

"Yes of course, sir" replied Cooper.

"And you can count me in, sir" said Talbot.

"I did that without any hesitation, Sergeant" said Hadley.

"Thank you, sir" said Talbot with a grin.

"I admire your enthusiasm gentlemen but I must warn you that we're stepping over the line because when I asked the Chief Inspector if we could visit Chieveley he told me to stay here in London until Boeker and the black man were arrested" said Hadley.

"Had he considered that Boeker may have gone to Chieveley, sir?" asked Cooper.

"The Chief Inspector thought it was more likely that Boeker was still in London" replied Hadley.

"But where, sir?"

"He suggested that he might be at the German Embassy."

"If he was then they would have the diamonds now, sir" said Cooper.

"That was precisely my point, Sergeant."

"So it's off to Chieveley tomorrow first thing then, sir?" said

Talbot.

"Yes, meet me at the Paddington ticket kiosk at eight thirty and we'll catch the first available train to Newbury. I plan to return in the afternoon" said Hadley.

"We'll be there, sir" said Talbot.

"Good and make sure you're armed because we may face difficult and dangerous situations" said Hadley.

"We will be, sir" said Cooper.

"We must keep this little jaunt between ourselves, gentlemen, so I will tell George that we are conducting a far reaching search tomorrow in case the Chief asks him where we are" said Hadley.

"A good idea, sir, we wouldn't want George to mislead the Chief" said Cooper with a smile.

"Exactly, all George needs to know is that we'll be back in the afternoon and I'll see the Chief then and give him my report".

Hadley summoned George and asked him to send a messenger to Saint Bart's inquiring about Sergeant Kelly's condition and then make a pot of tea.

"Very good, sir."

"And tomorrow, George, for your information and should anybody ask, I am planning sweeping searches of places that I believe that Boeker and our black assailant may be hiding" said Hadley.

"I understand completely sir."

"Good."

"You don't want anybody to know where you're going" said George with a smile.

"Exactly so, George."

"And when can I expect you back from this sweeping search, sir, just in case anybody asks?"

"I will be back here by late afternoon, George."

"Very good, sir, I'll make a careful note."

Discussing the investigation and reviewing their notes as they sipped tea, it was about an hour later that the messenger returned with the good news that Sergeant Kelly was making a speedy recovery and hoped to be discharged from hospital within the next two days.

Hadley returned home in a buoyant mood, which delighted

Alice and the children. After a good meal and a pint of stout, he relaxed for the evening and put the difficult investigation out of his mind. He slept soundly and awoke refreshed and ready for the day ahead.

Cooper and Talbot were waiting by the ticket kiosk at Paddington station when Hadley arrived and they caught the nine o'clock express to Bristol, the train only stopped at Reading, Newbury and Bath. Hadley felt a tingle of optimistic anticipation as he stepped down from the train at Newbury station in the warm morning sun. Hiring a trap they set off for Chieveley Manor in high spirits as they hoped that this visit might bring a much needed breakthrough in the investigation. The chestnut mare trotted out of Newbury on the Oxford road and the detectives sat quietly enjoying the sunlit view over the rolling green Berkshire countryside.

"This is very pleasant" said Talbot.

"It is indeed, Sergeant."

"Shame we're on duty, sir."

"Never mind, treat this as a welcome break that we all deserve" said Hadley with a smile.

"Yes and I can tell you that this is much better than hospital" said Cooper and Hadley smiled at him and replied "I'm sure it is, Sergeant and I must say that this ride in the country must be doing you some good because you are looking better by the minute, you'll soon be your old self!"

"Does that mean I'll have to pay for lunch as usual, sir?" asked Cooper and the other two laughed.

"I might let you off this time as it's your first day out after your stay at Saint Bart's" Hadley replied as the trap reached the outskirts of Chieveley village. In the centre of the village stood The Lamb public house, a thatched and oak beamed, whitewashed building that looked welcoming, cool and comfortable in the sun.

"That's a promising pub for local ale and good food" said Hadley.

"An early lunch then, sir?" asked Cooper with a smile.

"Most definitely, Sergeant, I don't want to get back late to the office" replied Hadley and the Sergeants' smiled.

Soon afterwards the trap turned off the road and into the grounds of Chieveley Manor. As it came into view, Talbot was impressed by the Georgian house nestling amongst the trees with its perfect lawns sloping gently away from the building down to the ornate lake, which was surrounded by weeping willows.

"My word, this is just the place to hide away from the world and all its troubles" said Talbot.

"Indeed it is, Sergeant and that very fact makes me think we shall find something or someone of interest here" said Hadley as the trap approached the turning circle in front of the steps. Cooper paid the driver whilst Hadley and Talbot surveyed the front of the imposing house. All three ascended the steps, passed through the pillars and up to the large front door. Cooper rang the bell and they waited for some moments before Wilson opened the door. His face became pale and dropped visibly when he saw the detectives.

"Yes, gentlemen?"

"Good morning, Mr Wilson, please inform Sir Robert that we have arrived and wish to see him now" said Hadley with a smile.

"I'll see if the master is in, sir" replied Wilson with a slight nod of his head.

"I know that he's here alright, so that will save you the bother of looking for him" said Hadley. Wilson fixed them with an icy stare before he said "please come in and wait in the hall."

"Thank you" said Hadley with a smile as they stepped through the doorway. Wilson disappeared through double doors into the drawing room and Hadley could hear raised voices before the butler returned and said "the master will see you now, sir." The detectives followed Wilson into the spacious room where he announced them in a dismissive tone.

"The police, sir."

"Thank you, Wilson" said Sir Robert who looked pale and anxious. Ralph Brandon-Hall and his son were seated opposite each other and Sir Robert was standing with his back to the fireplace. They all stared at the detectives and there was an uneasy silence before Hadley wished them 'good morning' and introduced Talbot.

"Well what do you want now, Inspector?" asked Sir Robert testily.

"I'd like to put some questions to you, sir that will assist me in my investigations" replied Hadley.

"I'd be obliged if you would be quick about it as I'm expecting guests" said Sir Robert.

"I'll do my best to be brief, sir."

"I'm glad to hear it."

"Do you have any idea where Hans Boeker is?" asked Hadley. Sir Robert glanced nervously at Ralph Brandon-Hall before he replied "no I don't know where he is, Inspector."

"I expect he's in London where you should be" said Brandon-Hall firmly.

"I somehow doubt that, sir."

"Well where do you think he is then?" asked Brandon-Hall.

"In a police investigation it is customary for me to ask the questions, sir and the suspects answer them" said Hadley in a determined tone.

"You've got a damned nerve coming here and accusing us of being suspects!" said Brandon-Hall indignantly.

"Your actions are questionable" said Hadley.

"When I return to London, Inspector, I shall report you to the Commissioner and recommend that you be removed from your duties for that grave insult!" said Sir Robert.

"Listen to me gentlemen and pay close attention, I'm investigating four murders, one of which was of a police constable and the theft of precious diamonds that could lead to a serious diplomatic situation between Germany and Britain!"

"And how are we to blame for all that?" asked Brandon-Hall as Sir Robert, looking pale, sat down on a nearby chair.

"All three of you are implicated or have knowledge of the murder victims" replied Hadley as the front door bell rang. They all listened for any sound emanating from the hall before they heard footsteps then Wilson entered the room and announced "Mr Isaacs, sir." When Isaacs followed Wilson in he was smiling but when he saw Hadley his jaw dropped visibly and he stopped dead in his tracks, so much so that Lansbury walking behind him, almost collided with his employer.

"Good God, what are you doing here, Inspector?" asked Isaacs.

"Making discreet inquiries into murder and theft, sir, so tell me, why you are here?"

"You impudent fellow!" shouted Brandon-Hall as he stood up.

"I'll see you back in uniform pounding the London streets for that impertinence, Inspector" said Isaacs as his hard black eyes narrowed.

"Oh really sir?"

"Yes, Inspector!" exclaimed Isaacs.

"Well it may be your wish to see me back in uniform but until it happens I'm in charge of a murder investigation so I'll ask you again, why are you here?"

"I know many people in high places that will destroy you if you persist in this line of questioning of me and the harassment of these gentlemen who are my friends" said Isaacs.

"I also know people in high places who are determined to see murderer's hanged and a serious diplomatic situation with Germany avoided at all costs" replied Hadley as the sound of the front door bell being rung again interrupted the heated conversation. Within moments Wilson entered and announced "Count Rausberg and Herr Schoender, sir." Hadley smiled and whispered "the gathering of the clans no less." He then glanced at Sir Robert who now looked even paler and was sweating slightly.

Rausberg strode into the room and stopped dead when he saw Hadley then pointing his silver topped walking stick at him said "Gott im Himmel! What is he doing here?"

"Following up my investigations into murder and theft, Count Rausberg" replied Hadley before any of the others could answer the angry German.

"There is nothing of interest for you here, Inspector and you'd do better to return immediately to London to search for the diamonds" said Rausberg.

"On the contrary, sir, there is much to rouse my curiosity at Chieveley" replied Hadley.

"Gott! Must we endure this upstart!" exclaimed the Count.

"I'm afraid you must, sir, and I will not stop asking questions until I have the killers behind bars and the recovered diamonds back safely in the hands of the German Ambassador" said Hadley.

"I told you to keep this matter secret, I knew that you were not to be trusted!" said the Count.

"I must inform you that Herr Konigsberg came from the Embassy to see the Commissioner and in my presence told him that you have no right to the stones and they were to be delivered to Count Hollenhoff personally when they are recovered, so that means that you, sir are actively engaged in fraud and deception, or worse!" said Hadley and on hearing that the Count went white with rage and his lips quivered.

"You lie Englander, you lie!" exclaimed the Count angrily. Hadley made no reply and there followed a few moments of complete silence before Brandon-Hall asked "Count Rausberg, Mr Isaacs, will you join me for a private discussion in the library?" They all looked at one another before Isaacs replied "yes" and the Count nodded.

"Will you excuse us for a few minutes, gentlemen?" said Brandon-Hall before he led the way out of the drawing room. Hadley was suspicious of their motives for a meeting but decided to say nothing and wait. He looked at the limp figure of Sir Robert as he sat slumped in his chair and the anxious face of Rupert Brandon-Hall. He knew that the situation was becoming very tense and the glowering looks from Schoender and Lansbury did nothing to lift the atmosphere.

"You have a very fine house here, Sir Robert" said Hadley.

"Yes, I suppose I do" replied the disconsolate Knight. Hadley felt some sympathy for the man who, he was beginning to believe, was caught up in a nightmare situation which was not of his making.

"I'm surprised that your daughter is not down here with you" said Hadley.

"Well, she prefers to stay in London these days" replied Sir Robert. Hadley decided to say nothing more for the moment but gave a knowing look to Cooper and Talbot to be ready for action if needed. Talbot moved towards Schoender who was standing close to the window staring out over the neat lawns towards the lake. Cooper stood closer to Hadley and prepared himself for any situation. They did not have to wait long before the door opened and the three men entered quickly. Brandon-Hall held a revolver and pointed it at Hadley whilst Isaacs signalled to Lansbury, who drew a pistol from his pocket and Schoender pulled a short barrelled revolver from his belt. Before Cooper, Talbot or Hadley could respond, Brandon-Hall shouted "hands up Inspector! And you as well!" he nodded at Cooper and Talbot.

"Oh my God!" exclaimed Sir Robert.

"Whatever you're planning will not succeed" said Hadley as he slowly raised his hands.

"That's what you think, you meddling fool!" said Brandon-Hall.

"Have a care, Ralph and stop this nonsense before it goes too far" pleaded Sir Robert.

"It's too late Robert, the die is cast and there is no going back for any of us now" replied Brandon-Hall.

"Listen to Sir Robert…" Hadley began.

"We're tired of listening, Inspector, its action we need now!" interrupted Isaacs.

"It will lead to your inevitable arrest and…"

"Let me assure you, little Englander, that we will be back in Germany with the diamonds before you can do anything to stop us" interrupted the Count.

"Search them for weapons, Lansbury" said Isaacs and the revolvers that the detectives carried were quickly taken from them by Isaacs' thug.

"And what do you propose to do now?" asked Hadley.

"Put you safely away whilst we get on" replied Brandon-Hall.

"I think you have been reading too many lurid novels" said Hadley with a smile.

"You're pathetic, Inspector and you have no idea of what you have stumbled into" said Brandon-Hall with a sneer.

"I've not stumbled into anything but murder, theft and now threatening behaviour by you and your accomplices and if you think for a single moment that you can avoid the might of the police force descending upon your heads then you are sadly mistaken!" said Hadley.

"Enough of this nonsense take them away and lock them up" said Isaacs. When he heard that Sir Robert looked positively shaken and asked "what are you going to do with them?"

"Lock them up in your extensive wine cellar, Robert" replied Bandon-Hall.

"But you can't do that, they're police officers, don't you realise what you are doing?" pleaded Sir Robert.

"It's far too late for sentiment, the stakes and rewards are so high that we must be bold and take decisive steps from now on" said Isaacs.

"But that means we'll all be ruined when we are caught" said Sir Robert.

"How very true" said Hadley with a smile.

"We will not be caught you weak fool" said the Count and Isaacs nodded.

"Come on you lot" said Brandon-Hall as he waved his revolver at the detectives.

"And now you cross the line" said Hadley.

"Lead the way, Robert and let's get these meddling fools out of the way" said Brandon-Hall.

Sir Robert led the way down to his cellar followed by the detectives, Lansbury, Schoender and Brandon-Hall. Hadley suspected that Sir Robert was a reluctant participant in the scheme and he tried to think of ways of escape. They came to a stout door at the end of the cellar and Sir Robert opened it to reveal a small room with several racks of bottles and a table.

"In you go" said Brandon-Hall. The detectives entered the room and looked about in the gloom before the door slammed shut behind them and they heard the sound of bolts being snapped home. The only light was from a small dusty cobwebbed window which was set high up in the wall. Cooper looked at Hadley and said "well we won't be having an early lunch at the village pub, sir."

"That is true" replied Hadley.

"And it's unlikely that we'll be back at the Yard for afternoon tea" said Talbot.

"Again that's true, but we must not become downhearted by the situation."

"No, sir" said Cooper.

"We must rise to the occasion and do our duty" said Hadley.

"Do you mind telling us how, sir?" asked Talbot.

"A good question, Sergeant, I'm giving it my undivided attention right now!"

CHAPTER 13

Hadley sat on the table in the gloomy room whilst Cooper and Talbot searched for something suitable for them to sit on. They found three small empty wine casks and some sacking which they draped over the casks to form relatively comfortable seats.

"Now we know who is who in this monstrous charade, we can begin to make some plans" said Hadley.

"Do you think that they have the diamonds, sir?" asked Cooper.

"No, I'm sure that Boeker still has them and the misfits upstairs don't know where he is" replied Hadley.

"That's why they are meeting here to discuss what they do next, sir" said Talbot.

"Exactly so, Sergeant, and I suspect they also wanted to get Sir Robert away from London, anybody can see that the man is cracking up" said Hadley.

"He's a liability to them without doubt, sir" said Cooper.

"Indeed he his; I hope that they don't consider him to be a danger to their plans otherwise I'm sure that they will not hesitate to kill him" said Hadley.

"You think that they are that desperate, sir?" asked Talbot.

"Without doubt, you heard what Isaacs said about the rewards being so great, well if what Rausberg told us originally is true, these diamonds are of incalculable value, we are talking millions of pounds if not tens of millions, certainly enough money to kill for again and again if necessary" said Hadley.

"Where do you think Boeker is, sir?" asked Cooper.

"I really have no idea, I half expected him to be down here, Sergeant."

"Is it possible that Konigsberg knows where he is, sir?" asked Cooper.

"No I don't think so but I'm sure that he has men out looking for him in London" replied Hadley.

"We have to get out of here quickly, sir any ideas?" asked Talbot.

"Not at the moment, Sergeant, I think we are at the mercy of someone who will unbolt the door and they need to be here, because unfortunately nobody at the Yard knows where we are" said Hadley.

"Do you think that George might guess, sir?" asked Cooper.

"I'm sure he will but he won't raise the alarm until tomorrow morning at the earliest" replied Hadley.

"So we could be facing a long and uncomfortable night, sir" said Cooper.

"I'm afraid so."

"Never mind, we've got plenty to drink in here" said Talbot and Hadley smiled which hid his deep concern for their predicament.

Discussing the investigation Hadley said he surmised that Detrekker had in fact sold the diamonds to the Germans but had planned, for some unknown reason, to sell them again to Rausberg and that Isaacs was implicated in that underhand transaction. Matters were complicated when Detrekker was murdered unexpectedly by the black African, presumably for the diamonds, then things began to spiral out of control. Hadley thought that the situation was now very volatile with no clear outcome in prospect. The over- riding priority was to find Boeker and recover the diamonds so that spurred them on to try and escape from the gloomy room. The stout door had a small barred opening for air to circulate but it was not large enough to get more than a man's hand through the bars, however, it did allow them to look out along the wine cellar to the door at the far end. Hadley wondered if they could find something in the room that they could use to locate the bolts and pull them back. They began to search for any long thin implement and they were so engrossed that they were unaware of Wilson looking through the small opening until he coughed. Hadley whirled round to see the pale face of the butler and his heart leapt with anticipation of release.

"Ah, Mr Wilson, the very man, unbolt the door quickly if you please" said Hadley.

"I'm afraid I can't do that, sir."

"Why not?"

"The Master has given me strict instructions that I am only to bring you food, sir" replied Wilson.

"I must tell you that you are aiding and abetting a very serious criminal offence, Mr Wilson" said Hadley firmly.

"Possibly I am, sir, but I have my orders, so I have brought you some sandwiches for your lunch, sir."

"Thank you" said Hadley as Wilson offered up a large plate of sandwiches to the barred opening. Hadley squeezed his hand through and took a sandwich and the others did the same. They repeated the process until all the sandwiches had been passed through to them.

"I will return later with something else to eat, sir" said Wilson and he gave a nod and disappeared from view.

"I think he is our only hope of getting out of here, gentlemen" said Hadley before he took a bite out of a chicken sandwich.

"But can he be persuaded to unbolt the door, sir?" asked Talbot.

"I don't know but I'll try very hard" replied Hadley.

"These sandwiches are simply delicious, sir" said Cooper.

"They are and that proves that there's always a silver lining to every black cloud, Sergeant."

After finishing their sandwiches they began to search once again for any implement that could be used to reach the bolts. To Hadley's delight, Cooper found an iron bar, about eighteen inches long that had fallen behind the rack containing bottles of brandy.

"That might just do the trick, Sergeant" said Hadley as Cooper raised the bar in triumph.

"I hope it's long enough" said Cooper.

"As the Bishop said to the actress" grinned Talbot and they all laughed.

"I can tell you were in the army, Sergeant" said Hadley.

"Does it show that much, sir?"

"Yes" replied Hadley as Cooper approached the door and fed the bar slowly through the aperture. They all held their breath as he tried to manipulate the bar up to the top bolt. He made contact with it and their hopes were raised by the sound. Cooper tried hard to shift the bolt but he was unable to do it and as he swung the bar down to try and reach the bottom bolt it slipped from his grasp and clattered to the flagstone floor. Their hearts collectively sank at the loss of the bar.

"I'm very sorry, sir" said Cooper.

"It couldn't be helped, Sergeant it was a risky manoeuvre at best" said Hadley.

"Let's see if there is anything else we could use" said Talbot, as they began to search once more, Hadley thought he heard the door open and close at the far end of the cellar. He stepped up to the barred aperture and saw to his delight a young woman in a maids outfit wearing a mop cap. She was looking at the wine in the racks and moving closer to him, he waited until she was just a few feet away from him before he called to her "Miss! Over here Miss!"

"Oh my Gawd!" she shrieked as she glanced up at him and clutched her hands to her chest.

"I'm sorry, Miss, I didn't mean to frighten you" said Hadley.

"Well you did and no mistake…"

"I'm sorry, would you please…"

"What are you doing in there?" she interrupted.

"Look, just unbolt the door will you?" asked Hadley.

"Who are you and does cook know you're in there?"

"No she doesn't" replied Hadley testily.

"When she finds out she won't be best pleased and you'll be for the high jump, Mister" she said in a serious tone whilst nodding her head.

"I'm a policeman…"

"A poacher more like" she interrupted.

"I assure you that I'm a policeman from London…"

"I think that you're one of the poachers that Mr Drake caught down at Flitton Wood and he's bunged you in there until the constable from Newbury comes to take you away" she said firmly. Cooper now joined Hadley at the aperture and said "listen to me…"

"My Gawd there's another one!" she interrupted.

"Will you please unbolt..."

"How many of you are in there?" she asked.

"Three" replied Hadley.

"Three! A gang of poachers, well I can tell you Misters you'll all be for it when you're up before the magistrate, you'll get six months each and a hefty fine I shouldn't wonder" she said with authority.

"Yes we probably will" said Hadley.

"And you deserve it" she said as she nodded her head.

"Will you go and tell cook that we're here…" Hadley began.

"No, she's too busy serving up lunch for the guests, and she wouldn't be bothered with the likes of you anyway" she interrupted.

"Well after she's served up lunch, ask her to come down here and talk to me" said Hadley.

"After lunch we'll have to clear away and wash up, cook won't ever leave the kitchen until everything is clean, inspected and put back in its place" she replied defiantly.

"Good for her, so kindly ask her to come down then" said Hadley firmly.

"I'll see if I've a mind to."

"It is very important that we speak to your Master's guests…"

"That's not bloomin' likely, they're important gentlemen from overseas" she interrupted.

"Well then it might be a good idea not to trouble cook as she's very busy, so if I gave you a guinea would you unbolt this door?" asked Hadley as calmly as he could.

"A guinea?"

"Yes, I'll give you a guinea if you do as I say and it will be our little secret."

"You'd give me that much money for just opening the door?"

"Yes I would."

"You must be desperate to escape Mister, so I think you best keep your guinea and stay there until the constable comes for you!"

"Please, please help us" said Hadley.

"It's no good you going on so, you'll just have to stay there because you've been put there for a reason and I'm sure it won't be long before the constable arrives with Mr Drake, then he can unbolt the door" she said finally before she turned and walked away. Hadley watched her leave the wine cellar with utter dismay.

"You stupid girl!" shouted Cooper as the door at the far end of the cellar closed behind her.

"She's not to blame, Sergeant."

"She is, sir."

"No, just think for a moment and put yourself in her position, if you were a kitchen maid and came down to a wine cellar for a bottle of wine and you found three men locked up who claimed to be policemen, wouldn't you be suspicious and leave well alone?"

"Probably, sir, now I come to think of it" replied Cooper.

"Exactly" and just as Hadley said that the door opened again and the girl re-appeared. She smiled at Hadley and said "I clean forgot the wine."

"Miss, Miss, before you go, would you take a note to cook for me?"

"What sort of note?" she asked in a curious tone.

"We're very hungry and haven't eaten for some while so the note will ask her for something to eat" Hadley lied.

"You needn't write a note I can tell her" she said.

"Oh, would you?"

"Yes."

"Then tell her that the three poachers in the wine cellar would like some sandwiches for lunch" said Hadley with a smile.

"Very well, but I'm still not letting you out, Mister."

"Quite right, we'll just have to wait for the constable and Mr Drake" said Hadley.

"Yes you will."

"And make sure you tell cook that we're waiting patiently for the constable from Newbury but if he doesn't arrive by tea time can she send us some cake and biscuits at four o'clock?" said Hadley.

"I'll tell her, make no mistake" she said firmly before she looked for a bottle of wine. She selected one and then left the cellar.

"Now that should arouse cook's curiosity" said Hadley.

"Hopefully, sir, but why would the girl come down for a single bottle of wine?" asked Cooper.

"For use in cooking something tasty for the guest's dinner tonight, Sergeant" replied Hadley.

"If cook or Mr Drake don't come down to find out about the poachers in the cellar, we're in for a long cold night, sir" said Talbot.

"Indeed we are, Sergeant."

They searched the room again for something that might make their escape possible but found nothing of any material use. Sitting down, they opened a bottle of brandy and enjoyed a nip each as they made plans to implement once they were released. It was almost three o'clock when Hadley looked at his pocket watch and said to his two companions "gentlemen, it seems to me that cook's curiosity has not been aroused by our presence."

"The girl might not have told her, sir" said Cooper.

"Or if she did, cook didn't believe her" said Talbot.

"Possibly, and I must admit it is a bit of a tall tale to swallow" said Hadley with a sigh.

"Yes, three poachers locked up in the wine cellar, does seem a little fanciful" said Cooper and Hadley gave a little chuckle then nodded.

"Somebody will turn up eventually and let us out" said Hadley confidently.

"Or the misfits will decide to kill us, sir" said Cooper.

"No, that won't happen, Sergeant, all our friends upstairs are worried about is retrieving the diamonds and getting away" said Hadley.

"I'm not so sure, sir" replied Cooper.

"Have another tot of Sir Robert's brandy to cheer yourself up" said Talbot as he offered the bottle to Cooper.

"Thanks, I think I will."

It was just after five o'clock when Wilson appeared once again carrying a large plate of cakes and biscuits.

"Here you are gentlemen, something to keep you going until dinner this evening" said the butler as he offered the plate up to the aperture.

"Thank you, Mr Wilson" said Hadley as he took a piece of fruit cake and several biscuits. The others followed suite and before Wilson turned to leave Hadley said "as I have already told you, Mr Wilson, you are an accomplice to the crime of unlawfully imprisoning police officers…"

"I'm fully aware of that, sir, but I have my orders from my Master and I must obey him, right or wrong" interrupted the butler.

"It will go badly for you when we get out and this affair is finally over" said Hadley.

"I know that, sir and I will face whatever punishment is metered out to me" Wilson replied.

"You could mitigate your sentence by letting us out now" said Hadley.

"I'm afraid I can't do that, sir."

"I think you may have misguided loyalty, Mr Wilson."

"I may have, sir, but as you say, I am loyal" replied Wilson as he gave a little nod and then left the cellar.

"Well it seems we're going to have dinner tonight, gentlemen" said Hadley.

"And it will be something tasty, cooked in wine no doubt" said Talbot.

"Yes, and I'm curious to know if the maid told cook about us" said Cooper.

"We'll find out all in good time" said Hadley.

The next three frustrating hours were spent trying to think of a way to escape. They climbed up and examined the small window, which did not open and every other idea they had was dismissed by Hadley as impractical or just not possible. As the evening drew in the room became quite dark and they were relieved when Wilson arrived with a candelabra containing three lit candles and placed it on a shelf close to the door of the brandy store. The flickering light was a comfort to the hungry detectives.

"I will serve dinner to you soon, gentlemen" said Wilson.

"May I ask what it is?" asked Hadley.

"Roast beef served in a red wine sauce, sir, with a selection of seasonal vegetables" replied Wilson.

"That sounds very nice but how are you going to serve us without opening this door?" asked Hadley.

"It will be simplicity itself, sir as you will see in due course" replied Wilson as he gave a little nod and left the cellar.

"I'll be interested to see how he does that, sir" said Cooper.

"So will I" nodded Talbot.

Before long the butler returned carrying a large tray with plates and dishes with silver covers. He placed the tray on the shelf with the candelabra and then carried three warm dinner plates to the door and passed them vertically through the bars.

"Now Inspector, if would kindly stand close with your plate, I will now serve you with dinner" said Wilson. Hadley did as he was asked and Wilson removed a silver cover from a dish to reveal slices of beef in red wine. He then served the meat through the bars with a serving spoon and asked Hadley when he had enough. The vegetables were served in the same manner and when Hadley had a good plate full he thanked Wilson, then stepped back to allow Cooper to be served, Talbot followed before knives and forks were passed through to the detectives.

"I will not be returning again, so I wish you all goodnight, sir" said Wilson before he gave a little bow and then departed with the tray.

"Well at least the food smells good" said Talbot.

"Yes, Sergeant, we won't go to bed hungry tonight" said Hadley as they sat at the small table with their dinners. They did not speak until they had all finished eating.

"I must say that Sir Robert employs a very good cook" said Hadley.

"He does indeed, sir and I hope that he also employs a talkative maid, because I don't fancy sleeping on the floor in here tonight" said Cooper.

"Yes and I want Mr Drake to know that we're here as well as cook!" said Talbot.

"So do I Sergeant but all we can do now is wait and hope" replied Hadley.

"And have another nip of brandy whilst we're waiting" said Talbot and the others smiled.

Unfortunately nobody came to see them and the detectives spent a very uncomfortable night sleeping on sacks that they laid on the stone floor. A few extra nips of brandy kept them warm and they were pleased to see the first glimmer of daylight as it permeated through the small dusty window. Hadley got up and used one of the empty wine casks to relieve himself, Talbot arose and also made use of the receptacle whilst Cooper remained blissfully asleep.

"I wonder what's for breakfast, sir" said Talbot.

"Hopefully something hot and delicious" replied Hadley as Cooper stirred himself. Hadley knew that they could not stay imprisoned much longer and desperate measures would have to be used if Wilson could not be persuaded to release them. It was just after eight o'clock that the butler appeared with a large tray and wished them 'good morning' as he placed it on the shelf. Breakfast consisted of scrambled eggs on toast, served in the same manner as dinner last night, followed by more toast and marmalade. Wilson informed them that he would serve luncheon at one o'clock and as he turned to leave, Hadley said "Mr Wilson, thank you for all you have done for us, but I must ask you to unbolt this door and release us…"

"I have already told you that I cannot do that, sir" interrupted Wilson.

"I know that, and although your loyalty to Sir Robert is to be commended, it is gravely misplaced, I believe that your Master is in danger from his guests and by keeping us imprisoned, you endanger his life" said Hadley firmly.

"I have my orders, sir and will obey them" replied Wilson.

"Then you will have the probable murder of Sir Robert on your conscience for the rest of your life!" exclaimed Hadley. Wilson stared at him through the bars for a moment and then said "I will see you at one o'clock, sir." The butler left the cellar and slammed the door after him.

"We'll wait until then, gentlemen, in the hope that Mr Drake or some other will come down but after lunch we'll take drastic measures to escape!"

It was just mid morning when Wilson hurriedly entered the cellar and to Hadley's surprise and relief, unbolted the door. He stood back as the detectives filed out of the brandy store.

"What changed your mind, Mr Wilson?" asked Hadley.

"Sir Robert left the house with his guests after breakfast, sir and gave me strict instructions to release you and to give you this letter" replied Wilson as he handed a sealed envelope to Hadley. He read the letter aloud "*Dear Inspector, I am now caught up in a serious situation through my own naivety and foolishness. My associates have insisted that I return with them to an unknown destination in London and I am being escorted there under duress. Please do not hold Wilson responsible for my wrong doing and I hope your forced imprisonment was not too uncomfortable. Please follow on as fast as you can and save me from the actions of unscrupulous, violent men. Yours, Sir Robert Salisbury.*"

"Oh God" whispered the butler.

"So, Mr Wilson, let it be a lesson to you that obeying the law is always the right thing to do and following orders is never an acceptable excuse for breaking it!" exclaimed Hadley angrily.

"Sir Robert is now in danger!" wailed the butler.

"Indeed he is, now go and arrange transport to get us to Newbury station at the gallop!"

"Yes, sir" Wilson nodded and he hurried off.

"Right gentlemen, its back to London as fast as possible to recover the diamonds and save a foolish man!" exclaimed Hadley as he strode towards the wine cellar door.

CHAPTER 14

It was just after one o'clock when the detectives arrived back at Scotland Yard after a hectic journey from Chieveley. When Hadley entered his office he was met by his concerned clerk, George.

"Thank heavens you're back, sir, the Chief has been going mad!"

"I'm sure he has, George, I'll go up to see him immediately. First tell me, have there been any telegraph messages for me?"

"No, sir."

"Right... Sergeants!"

"Yes, sir" they chorused.

"Please go to the armoury and draw three revolvers and 36 rounds of ammunition..." said Hadley.

"Very good, sir" replied Cooper and Talbot nodded.

"...then go to custody and ask the Duty Sergeant to put Charlie Grenville in an interview room."

"Right, sir" said Cooper.

"And stay with him until I arrive, tell him that I'm in a particularly unpleasant mood at the moment and will want some truthful answers from him when I get down there!"

"Yes, sir."

"I'm off to see the Chief and when I have finished with him and Grenville, be ready to go!"

Chief Inspector Bell looked up from his desk when Hadley knocked and entered his office. The two men stared at one another for a few moments before Bell waved Hadley to a seat.

"Where the devil have you been, Hadley?" he asked angrily.

"Chieveley, sir."

"Why?"

"Because I suspected that something untoward..."

"I told you not to bloody well go there!" shouted Bell.

"I know, sir, but..."

"You disobeyed my strict instructions yet again, Inspector or should I say 'constable'!"

"Am I to be demoted, sir?" asked Hadley anxiously.

"If I had my way!"

"There have been developments that I think you should know about…"

"And whilst you and your men were swanning about in Berkshire there have been serious developments here!"

"Really, sir?"

"Yes dammit; you should have been here to support the Commissioner and me in these difficult hours!"

"I'm sorry, sir."

"You will be! The Commissioner is beside himself with anger" said Bell.

"I'm very sorry to hear that, sir."

"You disappeared with two Sergeants and told nobody where you were going, anything could have happened to you! You might have been killed or kidnapped and we'd never have known!"

"We were kidnapped, sir."

"What?"

"We were kidnapped and imprisoned in the wine cellar at Chieveley, sir."

"Trust you to end up where there was plenty of drink available" said Bell.

"The most important fact is that Count Rausberg and Schoender were there along with Brandon-Hall and his son then Isaacs arrived with Lansbury" said Hadley.

"Why were they all there?"

"I don't know, sir, but I suspect they had gathered for a meeting to plan the recovery of the diamonds" replied Hadley.

"And what of Sir Robert?" asked Bell.

"He left with them to return to London and after our release by his butler, I was given this note, sir" said Hadley as he produced the envelope from his pocket and handed it to Bell. The Chief read it quickly and gasped "we must do something immediately to save him, Hadley."

"I agree, sir."

"Have you any idea where Sir Robert might be?"

"I have the feeling that Isaacs is probably the person who is most likely to have somewhere safe to keep Sir Robert, sir" replied Hadley.

"And how are you going to find that out?"

"I've still got his man Grenville in custody and I'm going to question him now, sir."

"That's good, Hadley, you see I was right about keeping suspects in custody until they can provide useful information, even if we have to beat it out of them" said Bell with a broad grin.

"Indeed, you're quite right as always, sir" Hadley said with a smile.

"Of course I'm right, now get on with it and keep me posted" said Bell.

"Very good, sir."

"And don't go wandering off anywhere without telling me first."

"No, sir."

"And on no account go to the German Embassy" said Bell firmly.

"Why is that, sir?"

"Whilst you were imprisoned in a convenient wine cellar, Count Hollenhoff, the Ambassador, called to see the Commissioner and he complained forcefully about our lack of progress in recovering the diamonds, Hadley."

"Oh, dear."

"Oh dear indeed, the Commissioner and I were both quite shaken and afterwards he left for an early lunch at his club to settle his nerves."

"I'm sorry to hear that, sir."

"So keep away from the Embassy, the Commissioner could not endure any more complaints from the Ambassador at the moment" said Bell.

"I'll keep well away in that case, sir."

"Good, now try and find Sir Robert before the end of the day, I don't want the Commissioner to have another sleepless night after I've told him that Sir Robert's been kidnapped."

"I'll do my best, sir."

"And I'll try and keep the news of the kidnap from the Home Office and the Press until you've found Sir Robert, so be as quick as you can" said Bell.

"I will, sir."

Hadley left the Chief's office and went straight down to the interview room where Charlie Grenville sat at a table with Cooper and Talbot.

"Now let me be rightly understood, Mr Grenville, I've very little time to spend going round in un-necessary circles with you…" Hadley began.

"When are you going to let me out of here?" interrupted Grenville.

"If you answer my questions truthfully and assist me then you might be on your way home this very afternoon" replied Hadley and Grenville smiled.

"Now you're talking!"

"Tell me where Mr Isaacs has workshops where he cuts diamonds and makes his jewellery."

"Oh, I can't do that" replied Grenville.

"Is that because you don't know or won't tell?"

"Won't tell, Mr Isaacs swore us to secrecy when he took us on and he told us that he would kill us if ever we said where he does his work" replied Grenville.

"Is that so?"

"Yes, it is."

"And that's your final word?"

"It is."

"Then let me help clarify your thinking, Sir Robert Salisbury has been kidnapped by Mr Isaacs and brought to London today under duress, Chief Inspector Bell has just given me instructions to beat the truth out of you in order to find out where he is, and if you survive, you're to be charged with aiding and abetting the kidnap of a Minister of the Crown and possibly his subsequent murder!" said Hadley.

"Oh my Gawd!" exclaimed Grenville as he began to shake visibly.

"That means that you will not be going home this afternoon or ever, if Sir Robert is killed before we find him" said Hadley.

"Oh, no" whispered Grenville.

"Or alternatively, you may become another unfortunate suspect who has died in police custody, and that would certainly save the cost of a trial" said Hadley in an offhand tone.

"I don't know what to do" wailed Grenville.

"Always do the right thing - tell the truth to shame the devil" said Hadley.

"He'll kill me!"

"And we'll probably kill you if you don't tell us what we want to know, and as we have you here, we have a head start on Isaacs!"

"Oh Gawd, I should never have got mixed up with Isaacs, everyone told me he was a bad lot" he whimpered.

"How right they were, now tell me where his places are and save yourself" said Hadley. Grenville hesitated for a few moments and then said "alright, but for Gawd's sake protect me from him."

"We'll do our best."

"He's got a place in Clapham, near the common and another house at Gravesend" said Grenville.

"Give us the addresses" said Hadley, his eyes glinting with anticipation.

After Cooper had written down the addresses of Isaacs secret workshops, Grenville was returned to his cell, still shaking. Twenty minutes later the detectives and four constables were in a police wagon which was at the gallop on its way to Clapham.

The wagon pulled up outside the address that Grenville had given them. The house was a large detached property set back from the road and the officers leapt out onto the pavement in readiness to begin the search.

"Sergeant Talbot, you go round the back and take two constables with you!"

"Right, sir."

"And don't hesitate to shoot if you meet any armed resistance" said Hadley.

"I won't, sir, don't you worry!"

"Now Sergeant, we'll see if our friends are here with Sir Robert."

"Yes, sir" replied Cooper as he followed Hadley up the gravel drive with the other two constables bringing up the rear. They climbed the four steps up to the door and Cooper rang the bell. They heard some movement and Hadley reached into his pocket for his revolver as the door was opened slightly to reveal an old man.

"What do you want?" he asked angrily.

"We're police officers, open this door and let us in!" exclaimed Hadley.

"Why?"

"We're looking for Solomon Isaacs…"

"He's not here" interrupted the old man hurriedly.

"Open up, we're searching the place!" replied Hadley.

"You can't come in, this is private property!"

"Oh yes we can!" exclaimed Hadley as he put all his strength into forcing the door open and he pushed the old man out of the way. Cooper and the constables followed him into the dark hallway.

"I tell you Mr Isaacs is not here and when he finds out about this you'll be in big trouble" said the old man.

"Not as much trouble that Isaacs will be in when we find him!" said Hadley.

"You are making a big mistake whoever you are" said the old man.

"I'm Inspector Hadley and this is Sergeant Cooper."

"I shall remember your names when I tell Mr Isaacs" said the old man.

"Sergeant, start searching these rooms and be careful" said Hadley ignoring the old man.

"Right, sir" said Cooper as he drew his revolver and entered the room to the left of the hall.

"One of you go and let Sergeant Talbot and the others in through the back door" said Hadley to the Constables.

"Yes, sir" replied one young constable before he hurried off.

"Now then, what's your name?" asked Hadley.

"Ronald Briggs, and I'm Mr Isaacs' house manager here" he replied.

"Very good Mr Briggs, you'll come with us and give us a full tour of this property" said Hadley as Cooper re-appeared from the room.

"Empty, sir and no sign that anybody has been there recently" said Cooper.

"Indeed that is true because Mr Isaacs has not stayed here for several weeks now" said Briggs.

"Are these all empty rooms?" asked Hadley as Talbot and his constables arrived.

"Yes" replied Briggs.

"Where do you do the work then?"

"What work?"

"You know what work, Briggs" said Hadley.

"I don't know what you're talking about" replied Briggs.

"Isaacs work, the cutting of diamonds for making expensive jewellery" said Hadley impatiently.

"I can't say" stammered Briggs.

"Right men, we'll search room by room, Sergeant Talbot, take your constables and begin upstairs" said Hadley.

"Right, sir" nodded Talbot as he set off.

"Now Mr Briggs, you'll show us into every room downstairs and then the cellar" said Hadley as he drew his revolver menacingly.

"Very well, Inspector" stammered Briggs.

All the rooms on the ground floor of the large house were carefully searched and revealed nothing of interest. The house was well furnished and obviously Isaacs sometimes stayed there. They found a cook in the kitchen and a maid, who looked very frightened by the gun carrying police officers. Then on Hadley's insistence they were taken to the locked door to the cellar.

"I must tell you that Mr Isaacs is a well respected business man with many friends in high places" said Briggs.

"So he keeps telling me, open this door immediately, Briggs" said Hadley angrily.

"His business is totally legitimate, Inspector."

"Open the door!"

"I must protest…"

"Sergeant, shoot the lock off!"

"No, no! I'll open it" said Briggs as he fumbled in his pocket for a key ring. He selected the largest key on the cluttered ring and unlocked the stout cellar door. Hadley swung it wide open to reveal stone steps that were poorly lit. He descended carefully holding his revolver tightly and was ready for anything untoward. He heard muffled voices and he prepared himself to face Isaacs and the others. When he reached the bottom of the steps he was confronted by another stout door. He opened it carefully to reveal a well lit workshop with four men sat at benches with glittering arrays of diamonds before them, which sparkled in the light of the gas lamps.

"Who the bloody hell are you?" shouted the old man sitting closest to the door as two others stood up looking anxious.

"I'm Inspector Hadley and this is Sergeant Cooper of Scotland Yard…"

"No one is allowed in here, no one!" said the man.

"Just calm down if you please, I'm looking for Mr Isaacs, have any of you seen him?" asked Hadley.

"You're looking for him holding a gun?" asked the man.

"It's more like you're thieves and you're here to steal the diamonds" shouted a young man as he drew a revolver from a drawer and pointed it at Hadley.

"I'm a Police Inspector, now put that gun down!"

"I will if you put yours away" replied the young man.

"Very well" said Hadley as he pocketed his revolver and he watched the man reluctantly replace his revolver in the drawer.

"You can't be too careful these days and thieves are everywhere" said the old man.

"True enough, now we do not wish to disturb your work but we need to find Mr Isaacs as soon as possible, so do any of you know where he might be?"

"If he's not at his shop in Hatton Garden he'll be at his home in Gravesend" said the old man.

"Thank you" said Hadley.

"Have you his address?" asked the old man.

"Yes, we have it."

As Sergeant Talbot and his men found nothing of any note upstairs, Hadley decided to leave the house and return to the Yard. The detectives had a brief meeting in the office whilst George made a pot of tea and procured some sandwiches to keep them going. Hadley asked his clerk to look up the times of the trains to Gravesend whilst he went upstairs to report to Chief Inspector Bell.

Bell listened to Hadley's report on the fruitless search of the house at Clapham and his suspicions regarding the house at Gravesend before he asked "do you really think Isaacs has taken Sir Robert there, Hadley?"

"It is a distinct possibility, sir."

"Well in that case you'd better go down there" said Bell anxiously.

"Yes, sir."

"And telegraph the police there and arrange enough armed officers to accompany you" said Bell.

"I will, sir."

"Confrontation with these desperate men could be dangerous in the extreme, Hadley."

"I fully realise that, sir."

"Good and don't hesitate to shoot first and ask questions afterwards!"

"No, sir."

"Because of this bloody diamond affair we've already had one constable killed and I don't want any more, Hadley."

"I quite understand, sir."

"Now get going and bring Sir Robert back safely if you will!"

CHAPTER 15

The detectives hurried to Waterloo Station after telegraphing the Gravesend police that they were on their way and required armed assistance. They arrived at Gravesend at four o'clock and went straight to the police station where Inspector Huntley invited them into his office. Huntley said "this must be damned serious business to bring you down from Scotland Yard then."

"It certainly is, Inspector" replied Hadley before he went on to brief Huntley.

"Well I've two Sergeants and four constables available to assist you, is that enough men?" asked Huntley.

"Indeed it is, will you please arm the Sergeants?"

"Yes, of course."

When the officers were armed and the constables were ready to go, Hadley briefed them all in the office.

"We are here to arrest a man called Solomon Isaacs, his associate, Edward Lansbury, Ralph Brandon-Hall and his son Rupert, a German Count called von Rausberg and his man Schoender. Now, they are armed and dangerous and we know that they have kidnapped Sir Robert Salisbury, I believe that they are holding him captive in Isaacs house here in Gravesend" said Hadley as he glanced at the anxious faces of the officers.

"As this is very serious situation I will be attending but Inspector Hadley and his two Sergeants, Cooper and Talbot, will be in overall charge" said Huntley and his men nodded.

"Thank you, Inspector" said Hadley.

"Now I suggest that Sergeant Mills and two men accompany Inspector Hadley and his men whilst Sergeant Croft and his men accompany me" said Huntley and the Sergeants nodded and murmured 'sir'.

"Right, we intend to surround the property in the London Road and then go in with force" said Hadley.

"Very good, sir" said Sergeant Mills.

"Be ready to expect armed resistance, I have orders from the Commissioner himself to meet force with lethal force if necessary to save the life of any officer who may be in danger from these desperate suspects" said Hadley.

"That's good to know, sir" said Mills.

"Indeed and I assure you all that I, or my two Sergeants, will not hesitate for one second to shoot these desperados down" said Hadley with conviction.

"Right, if we are all ready, let's go and see if we can bring these men to book and save Sir Robert" said Huntley.

They set off in two police wagons for 58, London Road where Hadley hoped that he would find all the miscreants together and arrest them before releasing Sir Robert from his captivity. The wagons pulled up outside a large detached house set back from the road and surrounded by high walls. The officers disembarked quietly. Inspector Huntley and his men filed through the wrought iron gate and made their way to the back of the house whilst Hadley and his men went up to the large front door. Hadley, Cooper and Talbot drew their revolvers before Cooper rang the bell. They heard someone approach the door then a man's voice called out "who is it?"

"Telegraph messenger, sir, with an urgent message for Mr Isaacs" said Hadley with a grin. The door opened slightly and without waiting for a moment, Hadley barged the door wide open and rushed in followed by the others. The man who had opened the door was knocked to the floor by the force of the entry and sat looking pale and totally amazed at the armed officers surrounding him.

"Who are you?" he asked with a gasp.

"Police, now where's Isaacs?" demanded Hadley.

"He's not here" replied the shaken man.

"Search the place men, and if necessary tear it apart!" shouted Hadley. Cooper and Talbot set off with Mills and his constables whilst Hadley hauled the man to his feet and asked "what's your name?"

"I'm Mr Mellors."

"And what do you do?"

"I'm Mr Isaacs butler."

"You say he's not here."

"No, he left with his guests after lunch today, sir" said Mellors.

"Where have they gone to?"

"I have no idea, perhaps Mr Lansbury can help you, sir."

"Lansbury! Is he here?"

"Yes, sir, he's upstairs with the other gentleman" replied Mellors.

"Sergeants!" shouted Hadley and Cooper followed by Talbot appeared from the room they were searching.

"Yes, sir?" asked Cooper.

"Lansbury is upstairs, he must have heard us so we'll go up very carefully!"

"Right, sir."

"Sergeant Mills, please send one of your constables to let Inspector Huntley in from the back of the house" said Hadley.

"Yes, sir" nodded Mills.

"Now let's see if we can find Lansbury" said Hadley as he began to climb the stairs with the others following. When Hadley reached the landing he cautiously looked both ways and decided to turn left.

"You come with me, Sergeant" he said to Cooper and he continued "Talbot, you and Mills look in the rooms down there." Talbot nodded and set off down the corridor as Hadley led the way to the first door on his left. He swung the door open and rushed into the well furnished bedroom which was empty. They tried the next room which was also empty but in the third bedroom they found Lansbury. He was standing motionless by the window and was pointing his gun at the detectives.

"Put it down, Lansbury, it's all over now!" said Hadley.

"You get out of here!" he said.

"Lansbury, put the gun down!"

"You heard me" Lansbury shouted.

"I have orders to shoot you if you resist arrest" said Hadley as a cry of 'help!' came from a dressing room beyond. Lansbury glanced quickly at the door to the room and Cooper seized the opportunity to lunge at him, knocking him off balance. As Lansbury fell with Cooper on top of him, he fired his gun and the muzzle flash illuminated the room whilst the sound reverberated around the house. Hadley feared for Cooper and rushed forward to help him with Mills close behind. Cooper had grabbed Lansbury's wrist as they fell and the gun slid away from the two men as they crashed to the floor. Hadley bent down then swung his fist and caught Lansbury full in the face with such force that the man went limp and ceased struggling. They hauled him to his feet and pushed him down onto a chair where he sat dazed and bemused.

"Are you alright, Sergeant?" asked Hadley.

"I'm fine, sir" replied Cooper with a grin.

"Good. Well done, Sergeant" said Hadley before he crossed the room and tried to open the door to the dressing room but it was locked. He called out "who's in there?"

"Is that you Hadley?" came the voice of Sir Robert.

"It is, Sir Robert" replied Hadley.

"Thank God you're here!"

"I'll be with you in a moment, Sir Robert" said Hadley before he went over to Lansbury and held out his hand and just said "key!" Lansbury produced the key and gave it to Hadley. When he unlocked the door and entered the room, Sir Robert was sitting on a chair looking pale but relieved.

"Are you alright, sir?"

"I am now that you're here, Inspector" replied Sir Robert with a smile.

"We'll get you out of here and back to London straight away, sir."

"Thank you, Inspector."

"Do you know where Isaacs and the others have gone, sir?"

"I think that they have probably split up and are searching for Boeker, Inspector."

"You can tell me everything when we get back to the Yard, sir."

"Of course, but I am very concerned about the safety of my daughter can you protect her from these men?"

"Yes sir, we'll take her into protective custody immediately and keep her safe until we have arrested everybody concerned" replied Hadley.

"Thank you, Inspector."

By now all the officers, having heard the gunshot, arrived in the bedroom and when Hadley came out of the dressing room, Lansbury was handcuffed and being led away by two constables.

"Are you all alright, Inspector?" asked Huntley in a concerned tone.

"Yes, thank you" replied Hadley.

"Thank heavens for that, I dread to think of the paperwork if any of you Scotland Yard fellows had been injured here" said Huntley and they all laughed.

"Quite so, now we'll search the house thoroughly before we go and I'll interview Lansbury back at the station before we leave for London" said Hadley.

"Very good, Inspector" said Huntley with a nod.

The house was searched from the attic to the cellar and nothing untoward was found except a large lever lock safe built into the cellar wall where Hadley assumed that Isaacs kept his stock of diamonds. Other than a table with a spirit lamp on it and a chair, nothing else was in the cellar. Hadley had expected to find men working at benches as in the house in Clapham but there was no sign of any such activity here. The house in Gravesend was nothing more than a large comfortable residence for a wealthy gentleman.

Returning to the police station, Hadley discussed the successful operation with Huntley over a pot of tea, whilst Sir Robert rested in an adjoining room. Hadley telegraphed all the news to Bell and requested he ordered an immediate search for Isaacs and his conspirators in London as well as the protective custody of Sir Robert's daughter. Lansbury was brought from his cell into an interview room and Inspector Huntley joined Hadley, Cooper and Talbot at the table, where a shocked and pale faced man sat opposite them.

"Mr Lansbury, you have been arrested for a number of serious crimes which you will be formally charged with when we have you in custody at Scotland Yard, meanwhile, you can be in no doubt as to the seriousness of your situation" said Hadley.

"No, sir" mumbled Lansbury.

"Good, I'm glad that you understand your predicament."

"I do, sir."

"Now as I am anxious to return to London, I'll be brief and you will answer my questions truthfully."

"Yes, sir."

"Do you know where Isaacs and the others have gone?"

"They went to London to look for Boeker because he has the diamonds" replied Lansbury.

"Whereabouts in London?"

"I don't know but I heard Mr Isaacs say that it was best if they all split up and met back at Waterloo station by six o'clock tomorrow night."

"So are they're all coming back here tomorrow?" asked Hadley.

"I don't know for sure but I think so, because Isaacs told me to meet Mr De Haas when he arrived on the Packet steamer from Calais tomorrow morning" replied Lansbury.

"What?" asked Hadley in a surprised tone.

"Mr Isaacs said he was due in on the eleven o'clock steamer and I was to be at the dock to meet him and bring him to the house" said Lansbury.

"How very interesting" said Hadley.

"Do you want us to arrest this man De Haas when he arrives?" asked Huntley.

"Yes please, I am sure that he will be able to give us some useful information" replied Hadley.

"Right, I'll organise that and telegraph you at the Yard when we've got him here" said Huntley.

"Thanks, I'll come immediately when I hear from you. Meanwhile I'd be obliged if you would place Isaacs house under twenty four hour surveillance and arrest everyone who goes there" said Hadley.

"Consider it done" replied Huntley.

"Now, Mr Lansbury, I want you think very carefully and tell me if you have any idea where Hans Boeker is in London" said Hadley.

"I don't know and that's the God's honest truth so help me" replied Lansbury.

"Then tell me what you know about Hans Boeker" said Hadley.

"I know nothing, I've never met the fella but I've heard Isaacs and the others talk about him" said Lansbury.

"What did they say?"

"Isaacs kept on about how he must have the stones and somebody was hiding the bastard, because the police and the German fellas from the Embassy couldn't find him" replied Lansbury.

"Do you know the names of the men from the Embassy?"

"No, Isaacs never said any names."

"Did Isaacs or the others ever say who they thought might be hiding Boeker?"

"No, it seemed a mystery to them all because he simply disappeared after shooting the Bobby outside the shop" replied Lansbury and Hadley remained silent for a few moments whilst he gave some thought to what he had been told.

"Does Isaacs have any other houses in London?" asked Hadley.

"He has a place near Clapham Common."

"We know about that and have already been there" said Hadley.

"The only other place he has is the shop in Hatton Garden" said Lansbury.

"Are you sure?"

"I think so" replied the anxious man.

"Do you know of any relatives who live in London?"

"I think he has a brother somewhere Shoreditch way, but I don't know where he lives" replied Lansbury.

"Did Isaacs or the others ever talk about two black men?"

"Yes, Isaacs seemed anxious about them because he kept saying that they had come over from Africa for the diamonds and they would kill anybody to get them" replied Lansbury.

"Anything else?"

"Brandon-Hall said he'd shoot the black fellas down like dogs if they ever came near him" replied Lansbury. Hadley remained silent for a few moments and then said "that's all for now, we'll carry on this interview after we've got back to the Yard."

Within half an hour Hadley had thanked Inspector Huntley for his assistance and was on the train back to London with his Sergeants, Sir Robert and Lansbury. The detectives remained silent for the comparatively short journey back to Waterloo and when they arrived, Cooper arranged a trap to take them to the Yard. Lansbury was placed in Custody whilst Hadley escorted Sir Robert up to Chief Inspector Bell's office, where the Chief was all smiles when they entered without knocking.

"I'm glad to see you safe, Sir Robert" said Bell as he waved him to a seat.

"Well it's all due to Hadley's prompt intervention" replied Sir Robert.

"Good I'm pleased to hear it" said Bell.

"I regarded Isaacs and the others as friends but I really thought that they might do me some harm in the end" said Sir Robert.

"Yes, we feared that too and the Commissioner and I ordered Hadley to rescue you at all costs" said Bell.

"I appreciate that, Chief Inspector."

"We're only doing our duty to protect innocent citizens from desperate criminals, sir" said Bell.

"You and your men are a credit to the force" said Sir Robert.

"Thank you, sir."

"I am concerned about my daughter's safety…"

"You need not worry for a single second, because as soon as I received Hadley's telegraph message, she was invited here for her personal safety and is at this moment comfortably settled in rooms that have been set aside for both of you. We keep these rooms at the Yard for such eventualities" interrupted Bell.

"That's wonderful and a great load of my mind" said Sir Robert.

"Not at all, sir, it's our pleasure, now if you would like to see the Commissioner, I'll arrange it immediately" said Bell.

"That would be most agreeable, Chief Inspector, and I shall make a point of telling him how much I appreciate all you have done for me and my daughter."

"Thank you, sir, a little praise from a very important person like your good self, helps oil the complex and intricate wheels of management in this organisation" said Bell with a smile and Hadley winced.

After handshakes and warm gestures, Sir Robert was conducted upstairs by Bell to see the Commissioner, whilst Hadley was told to wait. Bell arrived back in the office within ten minutes and was all smiles.

"That went very well, don't you think, Hadley?"

"Very well indeed, sir."

"I think I handled that situation to our best advantage"

"Absolutely right, sir."

"I'm glad you agree."

"When will I get the chance to interview Sir Robert, sir?"

"Interview Sir Robert?"

"Yes, sir."

"Now he is safe that is out of the question, Hadley."

"But sir…"

"Hadley, Sir Robert is above any questions that you may have for him" interrupted Bell.

"I must point out with all due respect, sir, that he is implicated in these murders and the theft of the diamonds" said Hadley.

"And I must point out that Sir Robert is a Minister of the Crown and our paymaster, let's not forget that, Hadley."

"But he is not above the law…"

"Hadley, you have done your duty and rescued him from a terrible fate" interrupted Bell.

"I must protest…"

"Protest all you like but it will do you no good, no good at all, in fact it might cause your career to falter somewhat" interrupted Bell again, much to Hadley's annoyance.

"I think you should carefully consider what you have said, sir."

"Hadley! How dare you challenge my decision!"

"I have only asked you to consider my questioning of Sir Robert as a material witness, sir." Bell gave it a moment's thought before he said "I'll have a discreet word with the Commissioner tomorrow morning and be guided by him."

"Very good, sir."

"Now that we have Sir Robert and his daughter safe all you have to do is clear up the investigation, arrest the miscreants and recover the diamonds, Hadley."

"Yes, sir."

"That shouldn't be too difficult as they all seem to be in London now."

"I hope you're right, sir."

"And try and get everything tidied up fairly soon before the German Embassy gets angry once again. The Commissioner does not want another unpleasant visit from the Ambassador."

"I'll try, sir."

"It's getting late now, so I suggest you go home and have a good night's rest and think of how you're going to clear everything up quickly."

"Thank you, sir, I will."

"And let me have a full report first thing in the morning" said Bell, as he waved Hadley to leave.

CHAPTER 16

After a restless night and a hurried breakfast, Hadley kissed Alice 'goodbye' and told her that he had no idea when he would be home again. Alice was concerned for her husband's health as he looked tired and worried when he left the house to hail a cab. The bright sunny morning helped improve his outlook on the journey to the Yard and he put his concerns about the investigation to the back of his mind as the cab made its way down to Marylebone High. When he arrived in his office, Cooper and Talbot were already there and George had just brewed a pot of tea in anticipation of his arrival.

"Morning, gentlemen."

"Morning, sir" they all chorused.

"I hope and expect a good day today" said Hadley as he settled down behind his desk.

"I'm sure it will be, sir" said Cooper as George appeared with the tea tray. As they sipped the golden reviver, Hadley started to outline his plans for the arrest of the suspects and the recovery of the diamonds.

"When do you plan to interview Sir Robert, sir, he may hold the key to our success" said Cooper.

"That's uncertain at the moment, Sergeant."

"Why sir?"

"Because Chief Inspector Bell has asked me to hold off until he has had words with the Commissioner about Sir Robert" replied Hadley.

"Why is that, sir?"

"The Chief Inspector thinks it's a delicate and political situation, Sergeant."

"A delicate and political situation, what old fanny that is!" exclaimed Talbot. Hadley laughed and said "I have to agree with you, Sergeant, but the Chief thinks he knows best and all we can hope is that the Commissioner will allow me to question Sir Robert in due course."

"Well he should do because the man's up to his neck in all this" said Cooper.

"Yes he is, although I do think that he has been incredibly

naïve to be led down this dangerous path by the others" said Hadley.

"To say the least, sir" said Cooper with feeling.

"Well they say rank has its privileges" said Talbot with faintly disguised sneer.

"So it seems" said Cooper.

"Never mind all that, gentlemen, let's concentrate on the matter in hand" said Hadley.

"Yes, sir" they chorused.

"The first thing I want to organise is constant surveillance outside Isaacs house in Clapham and Brandon-Hall's home at Teddington, then I want to see if…" Hadley was suddenly interrupted by a messenger from the telegraph office who burst in and held out a brown envelope.

"Inspector Hadley sir, this very urgent message just came in for you, sir" said the young man breathlessly. Hadley opened the envelope and read the message out aloud "Inspector Hadley, Black South African murder suspect found by constables in lodgings at 14, Albert Road, Whitechapel, attempted arrest ended in a violent struggle with one officer injured, suspect is now barricaded in his room with a woman hostage, I will attend with more officers and suggest you do the same, regards, Inspector Palmer, Whitechapel Police Station."

They all remained silent for a few moments as the news sank in then Hadley said "gentlemen, I think the tide of events is now beginning to turn in our favour!"

"Thank heavens for that!" exclaimed Cooper.

"At last" murmured Talbot.

Climbing aboard a police four wheeler, Hadley said to the driver "whip up and don't spare the horses!"

"Right sir" replied the driver as he slapped the reins and the two chestnut mares raced out of the Yard then galloped up the Embankment towards the City and Shoreditch. As the speeding carriage swung about, the detectives could hear the driver calling out above the sound of the clanging bell, "make way ahead there!" and "Police! Pull back and give way!" as the wheels clattered loudly over the cobbles. The other traffic did their best to allow the carriage through and other than the occasional bump of wheels against Hansoms and drays accompanied by curses from their driver's, the carriage arrived in record time outside 14, Albert Road, Whitechapel.

Inspector Palmer was already there with two Sergeants and six constables. Neighbours and onlookers milled around in the narrow street all trying hard to find out what was going on.

"Glad you're here, Hadley" said Palmer.

"Yes, thanks for letting me know that you'd found him, what do we know so far?" asked Hadley.

"My constables, whilst making routine house to house inquiries were suddenly confronted by the suspect, who drew a knife and stabbed one of my men…"

"Is he badly hurt?" interrupted Hadley.

"I don't think so, he's been taken to Saint Bart's with a shoulder wound which I'm told looks worse than it is" replied Palmer.

"Thank God for that" said Hadley.

"After the struggle, the suspect grabbed the householder, a Mrs Mildred Johnson, and whilst holding a knife to her throat managed to get her to his room upstairs where he has barricaded himself in."

"The poor woman must be demented with fear" said Hadley.

"I'm sure she is."

"I think I'll try and reason with him before we use force" said Hadley.

"Very good" nodded Palmer.

Hadley entered the small terraced house followed by Palmer, Cooper, Talbot and a Sergeant. They climbed the stairs to the narrow landing and Hadley stopped outside the only closed door then called out "I'm Inspector Hadley of Scotland Yard and I know that you are Mombesi because I have your friend Setsi Nkumo in custody and he has told me all about you." Hadley waited for some kind of reply but he heard nothing except the sound of a woman crying.

"Mombesi, you cannot possibly escape, so I want you to calmly open this door and let Mrs Johnson go free, do you understand?"

"You keep away otherwise I'll kill her!" shouted Mombesi.

"That would be very foolish thing to do" said Hadley calmly.

"You will never catch me because I can run faster than a Springbok!"

"So Nkumo has told me, but you can never escape the law no matter how fast you run" said Hadley.

"You'll see."

"Let Mrs Johnson go" said Hadley more firmly.

"I'll kill her now" shouted Mombesi and then the woman screamed a hideous spine chilling scream. Hadley pushed at the door with all his might, immediately helped by Palmer and Cooper. The door was locked but it began to creak at its hinges and Hadley said "hold up for a moment!" then they stood back whilst he fired all six rounds from his revolver into the lock. The wood work splintered and they all pushed once again at the door, which began to slowly open. Mombesi had barricaded some furniture behind the door which suddenly gave way under the pressure from the determined officers. When the door was open enough to get through, they rushed into the room as Mombesi climbed out of the window.

"Get him!" shouted Hadley to Cooper and Talbot as he knelt down by Mrs Johnson. She had a knife slash across her throat and was bleeding profusely but was still conscious. Palmer called to his Sergeant "quick get an ambulance!" He nodded and ran down the stairs.

"You'll be alright, Mrs Johnson, an ambulance is on its way" said Hadley calmly as he tried to staunch the gaping wound with his handkerchief. The pale faced woman managed to give him a brave smile before she closed her eyes.

"My God, I hope we haven't lost her" whispered Palmer.

"So do I" said Hadley as he glanced up at Cooper who had climbed out of the window and was standing on the sill with Talbot holding his legs.

"The bugger has climbed onto the roof, sir!" said Talbot.

"Right, get Cooper back in and we'll catch him outside!" shouted Hadley as he rushed from the room leaving Palmer to attend to the injured woman. By the time they had all got downstairs and into the street, Mombesi was running at a fast pace along the top of the terraced houses towards the end of the road. Hadley and the others raced along the pavement but failed to keep up with the man running on the ridge tiles.

"When he jumps down we'll shoot him if he resists arrest!" gasped Hadley.

"Right, sir" said Cooper who was now running in front of Hadley with Talbot following. As they reached the last house in Albert Road, they saw Mombesi prepare to jump to the pavement from the highest part of the roof.

"If he jumps it'll probably kill him" said Cooper.

"And if it doesn't then we will, Sergeant!" exclaimed Hadley. They ran around the corner of the house as Mombesi launched himself from the roof and his body accelerated downwards until it landed on the pavement with a sickening thud followed by his scream of agony. The detectives rushed up to Mombesi as he lay motionless and wide eyed with pain.

"You're under arrest, my friend" said Hadley as other police officers arrived on the scene. Cooper instructed one of them to summon an ambulance as Hadley removed the large hunting knife from the injured man's belt. Mombesi's legs were splayed out at unnatural angles and Hadley assumed that he had broken both legs in several places. He looked into the face of the desperate man and said "you damned fool." By now a large crowd had gathered and Hadley was glad that there were so many constables on hand to keep them back from the injured man. There were shouts from the crowd of "hang him!" and "bloody blacks!" from neighbours who had learned of the attack on Mrs Johnson. It was not long before the first ambulance arrived from Saint Bart's to take Mrs Johnson away. As soon as that hurried off with the injured woman, Palmer joined Hadley at the end of the road.

"He'll hang for all that he's done" said Palmer.

"That is for certain" replied Hadley as the second ambulance arrived.

"Will you detail two of your men to go with him to hospital whilst I get back to the Yard?" asked Hadley.

"Yes, of course" replied Palmer.

"Thank you. I'll send some of my men to relieve them after lunch" said Hadley.

"Will you want to question him then?" asked Palmer.

"Looking at him at the moment, I don't think he'll be in any fit state to answer questions for a while" replied Hadley and Palmer nodded as the attendants lifted Mombesi onto a stretcher.

When the detectives arrived back at the Yard, Hadley went straight up to Chief Inspector Bell's office to report and then request an interview with Sir Robert.

Hadley finished detailing the events of the morning to Bell and asked "has the Commissioner given his permission for me to interview Sir Robert, sir?" Bell cleared his throat before he answered.

"The Commissioner has decided that Sir Robert should remain untroubled for the time being, Hadley."

"How long will that be, sir?"

"I just told you, for the time being, Hadley" replied Bell firmly.

"Sir Robert could help my investigation to move quickly forward if…"

"Hadley, you're not listening" interrupted Bell.

"I am, sir, but I just don't understand why he's being shielded when he is so involved with the diamond theft" said Hadley.

"Careful now, Inspector, you're over stepping the mark!"

"I'm just trying to do my duty, sir, without fear or favour" replied Hadley.

"I appreciate that, but higher authority has come into play and you must obey orders that come from the Commissioner, as I do" said Bell.

"It is most unsatisfactory, sir."

"Yes, but it is the fact so put it to one side and proceed with the investigation" said Bell.

"Very well, sir."

"Now, what next, Hadley?"

"I'm waiting to hear from Inspector Huntley at Gravesend, sir."

"What about?"

"The Dutchman, De Haas is expected to arrive at the Gravesend dock from Calais aboard the Packet steamer this morning and I've asked Huntley to arrest him, sir."

"That's good to hear, I feel that we are at last making some progress" said Bell.

"I think so too, sir."

"Are you going down to Gravesend?"

"I've decided to stay in London for the time being, sir."

"I think that is wise, in the meantime tell Huntley to keep our Dutch friend comfortable until you're ready to question him."

"I'll do that, sir."

"Tell me about these others who are busy searching for Boeker and the diamonds."

"I will be at Waterloo station before six o'clock with Cooper and Talbot in the hope of arresting them all, sir" replied Hadley.

"How many constables do want to assist you?"

"I think at least twenty, sir."

"That many?"

"Well if all the suspects arrive together then we're talking about five men, some of whom are armed, sir" replied Hadley.

"Very well, make the arrangements with the duty officers and I'll sanction it" said Bell.

"Thank you, sir."

"Go to it then, Hadley and leave no stone unturned to arrest that foreign lot at Waterloo and recover the diamonds" said Bell firmly.

"I will, sir" replied Hadley with a smile as he left the office. He paused for a few moments on the landing outside Bell's office before he turned and made his way up the next flight of stairs which led to the Commissioner's office and the private suite of rooms beyond. There was a constable sitting on a chair by the door of the suite. As Hadley approached, the young constable looked up and, recognising the Inspector, smiled at him.

"Morning, constable, I've just come to have a quick word with Sir Robert if I may."

"Oh, sir, I've been given strict instructions that no one is officially allowed in there" said the constable as he stood up.

"That's perfectly alright, constable, my visit is strictly un-official, I just wish to give Sir Robert a message from his friend Count von Rausberg" said Hadley hoping that the constable would be impressed enough to let him pass.

"Well as long as you're quick, sir, otherwise I'll be in deep trouble" said the constable.

"Oh I will be" said Hadley as the constable smiled and then knocked gently at the door. Hadley heard Gwendoline call out "come in." The constable opened the door then went in and announced "Inspector Hadley is here to see Sir Robert, Miss."

Hadley strode into the room and smiled at Gwendoline.

"Good morning, Miss."

"Good morning, Inspector, to what do we owe this pleasure?" she asked with a sullen look.

"I'm here just to have a very quick word with your father, Miss."

"I was told by your Chief Inspector Bell that we would not be disturbed by anyone and that includes you Inspector."

"I'm aware of that, Miss, but events have overtaken us somewhat and I wish to just have a few minutes alone with Sir Robert" said Hadley.

"He's resting at the moment and as I have repeatedly told you, he is under great strain" she said firmly.

"We all are under strain, Miss, but as soon as we have an end to this mayhem, then we will all be much better in ourselves" replied Hadley. She looked at him defiantly for a few moments and then said "I'll go and see if he is prepared to talk to you." Hadley nodded as she turned away and made for the bedroom door. She tapped gently at it and then went quickly through into the room beyond closing the door behind her. A few minutes later she returned and holding the door open said "my father will see you now." Hadley smiled and stepped in to the spacious bedroom where Sir Robert was resting on a comfortable day bed by the window overlooking the Embankment and the fast flowing Thames.

"Good morning, Sir Robert and thank you for seeing me."

"Good morning, Inspector, I will always help in any way I can but I would ask you to be brief, in deference to my condition" said Sir Robert.

"Yes of course, sir, now I have some news for you and then just one question."

"Please continue."

"We expect to arrest all the suspects at Waterloo station this evening, sir."

"That is good news" smiled Sir Robert.

"And my question is the following, do you have any idea where Boeker may be hiding in London, sir?"

"No, Inspector."

"Do you know if he or the others, Detrekker or Vervorde have any friends or relatives that might assist Boeker, sir?"

"No, Inspector."

"Please give this your careful consideration, sir, did any of them ever speak of someone, anybody at all, that they knew in London?" Sir Robert then gazed out of the window at a steam tug pulling several barges loaded with coal as it made its way up river. Hadley was becoming impatient at the man's seemingly disinterest in his question and was just about to press him again when suddenly Sir Robert, with a gleam in his eye said "Vervorde has a sister living here, I remember Detrekker telling me about her, I can't recall where she lives but I think she's a matron or something important at one of our hospitals."

"Oh, thank you, Sir Robert, you've been most helpful" smiled Hadley.

. "Not at all, Inspector" smiled Sir Robert. Hadley thanked him again before he hurried from the room stopping only for a brief moment to thank Gwendoline and then the constable sitting outside in the hallway. He was just passing the Commissioner's office when the great man came out and stopped in his tracks when he saw Hadley.

"What are you doing up here, Inspector?" he asked in a firm tone.

"I'm just about to follow up some very useful information, sir" replied Hadley.

"Inspector, I did not ask you what you were about to do, but what were you doing up here?"

"I've just been to see Sir Robert, sir" Hadley admitted.

"You have seen fit to go against my strict instructions that he should not be troubled by anyone, Inspector Hadley?"

"I'm afraid so, sir."

"Then kindly explain your disobedience before I decide whether to reprimand you or punish you more severely!"

"Sir Robert has provided me with a vital clue as to the probable whereabouts of Hans Boeker and the diamonds, sir."

"Do you think that the information is truly valid?"

"Yes, I do, sir."

"Very well then, you may proceed immediately and inform Chief Inspector Bell of the outcome."

"Yes, sir, I will."

"Meanwhile, consider yourself severely reprimanded, Inspector."

"Yes, sir."

"I am very serious about this, Hadley."

"I am sure you are, sir."

"Sometimes Hadley, I think you're a trifle too cavalier for your own good."

"I hope not, sir."

"And if this cavalier trend continues in your behaviour, which has been noticed, you will likely remain an Inspector until you retire."

"I shall be very careful in the future and mindful of my position, sir."

At that the Commissioner raised his head and looked down his nose at Hadley before he replied with a slight twinkle in his eye "only results matter in the end and good ones may yet save your career, Hadley."

"I shall remember that, sir."

Hadley returned to his office where he found a telegraph message on his desk from Inspector Huntley, he read it aloud to Cooper and Talbot.

"Inspector Hadley, on your instructions I have arrested Mr Van De Haas this morning at Gravesend dock, he is now in custody and I await your further instructions, regards, Inspector Huntley."

"Another one in the bag, sir" said Cooper.

"Yes indeed, now only five more to go, plus Hans Boeker" said Hadley.

"And his whereabouts are a complete bloody mystery" said Talbot.

"That may not be so, Sergeant" said Hadley with a grin.

"You've a clue, sir?" asked Cooper.

"Yes, I've been up to see Sir Robert…"

"Blimey sir, you're for it if the Commissioner ever finds out!" interrupted Cooper.

"I'm afraid he knows because he caught me up there" said Hadley as his Sergeants looked at each other open mouthed.

"Well what did he say?" asked Talbot.

"The Commissioner or Sir Robert?" asked Hadley with a smile.

"Both!" exclaimed Cooper.

"Well, Sir Robert told me that Vervorde has a sister living in London and he thinks she's a matron at one of our hospitals, so she should be easy to find" said Hadley.

"And you think she's hiding Boeker, sir?" asked Talbot.

"I think it's most likely."

"What did the Commissioner say to you, sir?" asked Cooper in an anxious tone.

"He gave me a severe reprimand, Sergeant."

"Thank God for that, I couldn't bear to see you demoted and on horse traffic duties, sir" said Cooper.

"Neither could I, Sergeant. Now gentlemen, let's get cracking and see if we can find Matron Vervorde before we rush off to Waterloo this evening!"

CHAPTER 17

Hadley sent a telegraph message to Inspector Huntley asking him to hold De Haas until tomorrow when he anticipated sending Talbot to collect him and bring him to Scotland Yard. Whilst he was engaged in this George produced a map of London with all the hospitals marked on it. The detectives studied the map then Hadley wrote down the ten major hospitals that he planned to visit.

"To carry out this search as quickly as possible we'll each take a Hansom" said Hadley.

"Right, sir, where would you like us to start?" asked Cooper.

"You go to Saint Bart's first, then the London Hospital in Mile End and finally the Brompton" said Hadley.

"Very good, sir" said Cooper.

"And you, Sergeant, start at the Hammersmith then Saint Stephen's and then the Westminster."

"Right you are, sir" said Talbot.

"And I'll go to the Marylebone, then Great Ormond Street then University Hospital and lastly, the Royal Free" said Hadley.

"Do you want us to arrest her if we find her, sir?" asked Cooper.

"No, just get her address from the records department, I want to surprise Hans Boeker if he is hiding at her home" replied Hadley.

"Yes and what a surprise it will be for him, sir" said Talbot.

"Indeed it will be; of course she may be married so you'll have to ask each hospital if they've a South African matron or senior ward sister if they don't recognise her name, use your initiative on each occasion" said Hadley.

"We will, sir, don't you worry" said Cooper.

"Good, so let's get under way and see if we can find Vervorde's sister before we rush off to Waterloo!"

The detectives set off with high hopes clutching their lists of hospitals to visit. Hadley's first call was at the Marylebone where he found the clerk in the records department helpful but a little slow. The hospital had no one named Vervorde, neither did they have any South African nursing staff. It was the same answer at

Great Ormond Street and at University Hospital but at the Royal Free, Hadley's hopes were raised when he was told that they had a matron by the name of Mrs Taylor who came from South Africa but he was disappointed when it was revealed that her maiden name was Barnes. Hadley returned to the Yard in a gloomy mood hoping that his two Sergeants had better luck. When he arrived in his office he was met by a grinning Cooper.

"I've found her at the London Hospital in Mile End, sir!"
"Bloody good show, Sergeant!"
"Yes, her name is Miss Hannah Vervorde and she is a ward sister…"
"And her address?" interrupted Hadley.
"84, Turner Street, sir, its right by the hospital" replied Cooper.
"Excellent, we'll just wait for Talbot to get back and have a quick bite to eat before we go!" said Hadley with a smile.
"Very good, sir."
"George…"
"Yes, sir?" the clerk replied from his adjacent office.
"After this good news I think we're ready for some refreshment."
"A nice pot of tea then, sir?"
"Yes please George and some sandwiches to keep us going, we've a very busy afternoon ahead of us" said Hadley.

By the time George had made the tea and gone down to the canteen for sandwiches, Talbot had arrived back with a look of disappointment but that changed to a big grin when Cooper told him the news. Immediately they had finished their lunch they set off in a two horse trap for Turner Street. The driver went along to the Mile End Road and then turned right down by the London Hospital and made his way to the bottom of the street looking at the house numbers.

"Here we are, sir" said the driver. Hadley asked him to pull up beyond number 84 so the detectives could walk back and survey the house without attracting undue attention.

"Very good, sir" replied the driver.
"And please wait for us" said Hadley.
"Right you are, sir."
As the detectives climbed down from the trap, Hadley said "if

Boeker is in there we've got to try and arrest him without bloodshed."

"Right, sir" said Cooper and Talbot nodded.

"We know he's a very desperate man who has already killed young Meredith and I'm sure he won't hesitate to shoot at us" said Hadley as the three of them slowly wandered passed number 84. All the curtains were drawn across the upstairs windows which made the house look secretive, sombre and forbidding. The detectives walked up to the terrace end and then turned into the next street before they stopped by the entrance to the narrow alleyway that ran along the back of the houses.

"Sergeant Talbot, you make your way down to the back of 84 and watch for our suspect should he attempt to slip away, Cooper and I will try the front door."

"Right sir, and if he does run out and resists arrest can I shoot him?"

"Yes, you certainly can, Sergeant" replied Hadley.

"That's good to know, sir" smiled Talbot.

"Take no chances, Sergeant, it's the diamonds we want and if Boeker is fool enough to make a fight of it and resist arrest, then he'll be the loser!"

"Yes, sir" said Talbot.

"Now let's go and see if the gentleman is at home and ready to receive unwanted visitors!" said Hadley and Cooper smiled then nodded.

Cooper knocked hard on the front door then waited patiently. They heard movement before the door was opened by an attractive middle aged lady.

"Yes, what do you want?" she asked.

"Miss Vervorde?" asked Hadley with a smile.

"No, I'm Mrs Wainwright, Miss Vervorde lives upstairs" she replied.

"Would you kindly call her?"

"She's not here I'm afraid."

"Do you know where she is?"

"Yes, she's gone down to Gravesend with her brother…"

"Her brother?" interrupted Hadley.

"Yes, you've only just missed them, they left about an hour

ago" replied Mrs Wainwright.

"Good grief" whispered Hadley.

"Is it something important?" she asked.

"Yes, very" replied Hadley.

"Are you gentlemen from the Hospital?" she asked.

"No, I'm Inspector Hadley and we're police officers from Scotland Yard" replied Hadley.

"Oh dear, it must be serious then" she said.

"Tell me about her brother" said Hadley.

"Not much to tell, sir, he has stayed with her ever since he arrived from Africa, they're both from the Transvaal, you know" she said helpfully.

"When did he arrive?"

"About a week or so ago" she replied.

"Did Miss Vervorde seem surprised when he arrived or was she expecting him?" asked Hadley.

"Well, funny you should say that, I mentioned it to Mr Wainwright at the time, she seemed anxious when she saw him, because when I opened the door to him and then called her down, she didn't seem to recognise him at first, but after they went upstairs she seemed alright" she replied.

"Did you notice if he had a small case chained to his wrist?"

"I didn't notice to be honest, sir, I think he was carrying two cases but I was too busy looking at Miss Vervorde to remember what size they were, although one was bigger than the other, if that helps."

"Yes it does, thank you, now did she say where they were going to in Gravesend?" asked Hadley.

"She said it was a surprise visit to see a friend who was coming over from Amsterdam to see another family friend and I must admit, because I said to Mr Wainwright at the time, it's quite remarkable that these foreigners seem to have so many friends all over the place, don't you agree?"

"Oh I do, Mrs Wainwright, do you happen to know the name of this friend who lives at Gravesend?"

"No, she never said his name."

"Thank you, Mrs Wainwright you've been most helpful" said Hadley with a smile.

"You're welcome, I'm sure, and I do hope that she is not in any trouble, she's such a nice person, very quiet and she keeps herself to herself, if you know what I mean."

"Yes, I do, but no, she's not in any trouble and we just want to speak to her brother about something, which is important."

"Oh that's good to know."

"But if in the meantime they arrive back from Gravesend don't tell them we've been here" said Hadley.

"Very well, sir."

"If they do come back, would you call in at Whitechapel police station and tell them that they have returned and I'll leave a message at the station to contact me if they hear from you" said Hadley.

"Yes of course, sir."

"Thank you, good afternoon, Mrs Wainwright."

"Good afternoon, sir" she replied with a smile before closing the door. Hadley looked at Cooper and said "the bird has flown again but the net gets ever tighter, Sergeant."

"It certainly does, sir."

"Give Talbot a shout then and we'll be off."

"Yes sir."

"We'll call at Whitechapel station on the way to the Yard and brief Inspector Palmer."

The first thing Hadley did after he returned to the office was telegraph Inspector Huntley with all the information regarding the expected arrival at Isaacs house of Boeker and Miss Vervorde. He advised that Boeker was armed and very dangerous but must be apprehended at all costs as he was carrying the diamonds. Hadley confirmed that he, along with Cooper and Talbot, would be arriving later that night and requesting that lodgings should be arranged for them all.

Hadley and his Sergeants then planned the operation to arrest the five suspects at Waterloo station. The detectives went down to the duty officer and made arrangements for twenty constables to assist them. The officers were assembled in the watch room and Hadley briefed them in detail whilst explaining the importance of a successful outcome to the planned arrest of the suspects. The constables were to be hidden from view around the concourse of the station and would assist immediately when Hadley gave the signal by raising his hat and Cooper blowing his whistle. Hadley instructed them to be at the station by five o'clock when he and his Sergeants would oversee their deployment in the concourse.

It was just before five o'clock when the detectives were about to leave for Waterloo station when a telegraph message arrived from Inspector Palmer at Whitechapel. Hadley read it out aloud *"Inspector Hadley, Mrs Wainwright of 84, Turner Street, has just reported that three unsavoury men called at her address seeking Miss Vervorde's brother and when she explained that he was not at home, the men forced their way in and searched the house before leaving abruptly, which has caused Mrs Wainwright considerable distress and she has requested that you should be informed of the incident, regards, Inspector Palmer."* When he had finished reading the message he looked at his Sergeants.

"Could it have been the Germans, sir?" queried Cooper.

"Possibly, or any of the others, but obviously whoever it was, knows the whereabouts of Miss Vervorde and Boeker" replied Hadley.

"The next few hours should reveal all" said Talbot.

"You're quite right, Sergeant, so gentlemen if you're armed and ready to go, let's make a move!"

At Waterloo, whilst Hadley and Cooper surveyed the concourse for suitable hiding places for the constables, Talbot remained outside the station to meet the officers. They arrived promptly and were deployed by the detectives in places hidden from the view of the general public. Hadley bought an evening newspaper and sat on a seat in between the ticket barriers of platforms 4 and 6, which was a position about central in the concourse. Cooper slipped behind the newsagent's kiosk and Talbot positioned himself close to the ticket office. Both Sergeants had a clear view of Hadley, who held his paper up to cover part of his face as he scanned the travellers, searching for the suspects amongst the people who milled about. Hadley occasionally glanced up at the station clock and watched with eager anticipation as six o'clock came ever closer. The scene was one of bustle and noise, punctuated by the slamming of train doors, the blowing of guards whistles followed by the pant of steam engines and the clunk of couplings taking the strain as the engine's pulled the trains away. Hadley waited patiently and scanned the travellers ever more closely but he saw no sign of any of the wanted men. The next time he glanced at the clock it said six fifteen and he began to question everything that he had assumed. Was Lansbury telling lies about the rendezvous at Waterloo to give Isaacs and the others a chance to evade arrest? Did Mrs Wainwright tell the three men who called on her that Miss Vervorde and her 'brother' had gone to Gravesend? If that was the case, then they would have caught the first available train from Waterloo. Hadley wrestled with his thoughts until half past six when he gave a subtle signal to Cooper to join him. The Sergeant walked over from the kiosk in a leisurely fashion then sat beside him.

"I think that either Lansbury has lied to us or the others have discovered that Boeker has gone to Gravesend with Miss Vervorde and they are all well on their way there now, Sergeant" said Hadley.

"Give it another half hour before we stand the constables down and go to Gravesend, sir" said Cooper.

"But time is of the essence, Sergeant" whispered Hadley.

"I realise that, sir, but Isaacs place is under surveillance and Inspector Huntley is briefed to arrest anyone who approaches the house, so an hour or so either way will not alter the outcome."

"I suppose you're right."

"Yes, I think I am, sir and I know that you want to be there when the arrests are made, but you can't be in two places at once."

"You're beginning to sound like my wife, Sergeant" Hadley said with a grin.

It was exactly seven o'clock when they left the seat and Cooper told the constables that the surveillance was over. Hadley wandered over to Talbot and informed him that he was closing down the operation.

"So we're off to Gravesend now, sir" said Talbot.

"By the next available train, Sergeant" replied Hadley.

"Well if they're all down there now it will make for a very interesting evening, sir" said Talbot.

"You're absolutely right, Sergeant."

Cooper sent the constables back to the Yard before he joined

Hadley and Talbot at the ticket barrier. They caught the packed seven thirty train to Gravesend, it was full of travellers returning from a day's sightseeing excursion in London. When the train arrived, Hadley was glad to get out of the overcrowded carriage and breathe the cool air that wafted off the Thames. After taking a trap to the police station they were immediately shown up to Inspector Huntley's office.

"I'm glad you're here…" Huntley began.

"Have there been some developments?" interrupted Hadley as he sat down.

"Yes, a short while ago, a woman went to the house in London Road and my men arrested her at the door" replied Huntley.

"Was she Hannah Vervorde?" asked Hadley.

"Yes she was" replied Huntley.

"Was Hans Boeker with her?" asked Hadley.

"No she was on her own when she arrived at the house" said Huntley.

"That really concerns me, now either Boeker has sent her to the house alone because he suspects we're watching the place, or the others have managed to get hold of him somewhere between Waterloo and Isaacs house, which means they've now got the diamonds!" said Hadley.

"I'll organise more of my men to search the town" said Huntley.

"Good and make sure they're armed."

"I will."

"Sergeant Cooper will give your people a description of the suspects and when he's done that I'd like to interview Miss Vervorde and Van de Haas" said Hadley.

"Very well" said Huntley with a nod before he and Cooper left his office to organise the immediate search of Gravesend for the suspects.

Twenty minutes later, Huntley and Cooper returned.

"The search is now under way" said Huntley.

"Thank you, that's good, now we'll hear what Miss Vervorde has to say for herself!"

CHAPTER 18

Hannah Vervorde looked frightened as she stared up at Hadley and the others as they entered the interview room. Hadley introduced himself and his Sergeants to the attractive, pale faced young woman after he sat at the table opposite her.

"Miss Vervorde, I will ask you questions that you must answer truthfully because men's lives depend upon what you tell me, do you understand?"

"I've done nothing wrong" she whimpered.

"I'm sure that is true, but you may have committed offences unwittingly" said Hadley.

"I'd never break the law, I'm a ward sister…"

"At the London Hospital, I know" interrupted Hadley to her surprise.

"Tell me what I've supposed to have done?" she asked plaintively.

"You left your lodgings in Turner Street this morning with a man, where is he now?"

She hesitated before she replied in a whisper "I don't know."

"Miss Vervorde…"

"I don't know I tell you!"

"What's his name?"

"Hans Boeker" she replied and Hadley smiled then glanced at Cooper who gave a slight nod.

"How do you come to know him?"

"He's a friend of my brother's, they work together in South Africa and they are in London on business" she replied.

"Did he tell you that he was carrying four precious diamonds in his small case?"

"Yes, he said that something had gone wrong with the business and he was afraid that they would be stolen from him by a gang of wicked men before he could deliver them to the rightful owner" she whispered.

"Do you know who that is?"

"No, Hans didn't tell me, all he said was that a man was coming over from Amsterdam to look at the diamonds and his friend Mr Isaacs had organised everything" she replied. Hadley waited for a few moments as he tried to piece the information together in his mind.

"Now tell me exactly what happened after you left your lodgings this morning and leave no detail out if you please" said Hadley. She glanced down at her hands which she clasped and then squeezed nervously.

"Hans said that he had to get to Mr Isaacs, who lived here in Gravesend as he would help him, so he asked me to come with him and I agreed. We went to Waterloo station and caught the train."

"Do you know if anybody followed you?" asked Hadley.

"I don't think so, but Hans was very anxious and kept looking back all the time" she replied.

"Continue if you please."

"When we arrived here we stopped for lunch at the Railway Hotel and waited for awhile before we walked to the house in London Road…"

"But you were alone when you arrived at the house" interrupted Hadley.

"Yes, that's because Hans thought that the men who wanted to rob him might be watching the house, so he asked me to go alone, knock at the door and ask for Mr Isaacs" she replied.

"Go on."

"I was to wave to him if it was all clear but before I knocked at the door, two men came up to me, said they were policemen and I was under arrest, but they wouldn't tell me why, then I was brought here and I have been locked up in a cell until now" she said with feeling.

"Do you know where Hans Boeker is?"

"No, I've no idea, I left him at the end of the London Road watching me walk to Mr Isaacs house and I'm sure he would have seen the two policemen taking me away and he must have thought they were the men he was afraid of" she replied.

"Oh bloody hell" whispered Huntley.

"Did Boeker say anything else that might give us a clue to his whereabouts?" asked Hadley.

"No, only if anything should go wrong then I was to wait at the Railway Hotel for him and if he didn't turn up, to catch the last train back to Waterloo tonight" she replied.

"Inspector Huntley, will you send armed surveillance officers to the hotel to arrest Boeker if he turns up there, they'll know him by the small case chained to his wrist" said Hadley.

"Right away" nodded Huntley.

"Why do they have to be armed?" asked Miss Vervorde in alarm.

"Because Hans Boeker is an armed and dangerous man who's already murdered one police officer, for which he will certainly hang, provided we don't shoot him first" replied Hadley.

"Oh dear God no!" she whispered before she burst into tears.

"Compose yourself, Miss Vervorde…"

"Hans is a gentle person who could never hurt anyone" she interrupted.

"He may appear all goodness and light to you, Miss, but underneath he's proved to be a ruthless killer" said Hadley.

"I don't believe you."

"We thought at first that he murdered your brother…"

"My brother? What has happened to him?" she asked with her eyes staring wildly at Hadley.

"He has been murdered, Miss" replied Hadley.

"He couldn't have been murdered, Hans told me that Dik was seeing some important people on business and would stay with them for a few days then he would come to see me before he returned home to Africa" she said with her eyes wide with fear.

"I'm sorry, Miss I assumed that you knew of your brother's death" said Hadley

"Oh God no" she whispered before she started to sob. Hadley looked at Cooper and said "Sergeant, will you arrange for someone to be with Miss Vervorde and give her the details of her brother's murder."

"Of course, sir."

"Miss Vervorde, I have no more questions for you at the moment and someone will be with you soon to help you" said Hadley. She raised her tear stained face to him and said with a sob "I think I just want to go home." Hadley nodded and replied "in a while we'll see you safely home, Miss Vervorde."

In Huntley's office they discussed the events so far.

"That poor deceived woman obviously knew nothing" said

Hadley.

"It's strange that she didn't know of her brother's murder, sir" said Cooper.

"It's quite understandable, the Press reported another murder of a foreign person and being a busy ward sister at the hospital, she could well have missed the report" replied Hadley.

"But even so, you'd have thought that someone would have contacted her, sir" said Cooper.

"Well who would do that? Detrekker was already dead and Boeker wanted to keep her brother's death from her whilst he stayed in hiding at her lodgings" said Hadley.

"I suppose so, sir."

"What do you plan to do now, sir?" asked Talbot.

"With Inspector Huntley's constables searching Gravesend for our suspects and surveillance men at the Hotel waiting for Boeker, I think all we can do at the moment is wait patiently, Sergeant" replied Hadley.

"In the meantime, perhaps you would like to book in at the Lion Hotel where I've reserved rooms for you" said Huntley.

"A very good idea" said Hadley.

"The Hotel is just along in West Street, which is at the end of this road, you can't miss it" said Huntley.

"We'll go there now, tell me, is the food good?" asked Hadley.

"It certainly is" replied Huntley with a smile.

"And what about the beer?"

"I'm sure you won't be disappointed" replied Huntley and they all smiled.

"We'll return after we have booked in and had something to eat" said Hadley.

"That's a good idea, because I've a feeling that we've a long night ahead of us" said Inspector Huntley.

"I'm sure that you're right, Inspector and when we get back we'll start with Van de Haas and see if he can shed any light on our darkness" said Hadley.

The Lion Hotel was a moderate establishment and Hadley was pleased to find that his room was spacious with a large comfortable bed, although he had some doubts about the amount of time he would be able to spend in it. When they met in the lounge bar before dinner, Cooper and Talbot reported that they also had suitable accommodation. After just one pint of local stout the detectives went into the dining room and enjoyed a meal of lamb cutlets followed by spotted dick with custard. Fully refreshed they made their way hurriedly back to the police station as Hadley was now anxious to interview Van de Haas.

The Dutchman was about forty years old, slightly built with a round face and hard blue eyes. He wore a pair of gold rimmed spectacles which he peered over at Hadley, sitting opposite him at the table in the interview room. Hadley introduced himself and his Sergeants but before he could finish, de Haas interrupted angrily.

"Why have I been arrested?" he demanded.

"Because you are connected with a known person who has committed a serious offence and…"

"You've no right to hold me and I demand to be set free!" interrupted de Haas.

"All in good time, sir" said Hadley calmly.

"And when will that be?"

"When I'm content, sir" said Hadley firmly.

"Dear God, you English are so pedantic!"

"And that's how we get results, sir. Now tell me, why are you here in Gravesend?"

De Haas studied his hands for a moment as he gathered his thoughts.

"I came here on business, Inspector."

"What kind of business?"

"You probably are not aware of this, but I am one of the leading experts in Europe on the cutting and presentation of fine gems, Inspector."

"I am aware of that fact, sir" replied Hadley and de Haas looked surprised but pleased.

"Ah, I see that my fame spreads even as far as the British police."

"We only know you because you're connected to the theft of diamonds, sir."

"I never break the law, Inspector!" he exclaimed angrily.

"Go on, sir."

"I was originally requested by a gentleman called Count von

Rausberg to examine and advise on how to cut and best present four large diamonds that he had purchased on behalf of the German Government."

"And did you?"

"No because, as you must know, they had been stolen by someone who was delivering them to London from South Africa" replied de Haas.

"Do you know who the thief is, sir?"

"No, Inspector."

"Tell me why the diamonds came to London instead of directly to you in Amsterdam?"

"It was arranged that my friend and colleague in the diamond business, Mr Solomon Isaacs would examine the stones first for his valuation of them before Count Rausberg brought them to me" he replied.

"So if the diamonds are now missing, why are you here?" asked Hadley.

"I received a message from Solomon telling me that Count Rausberg had now recovered the stones and as he was in a great hurry to get back to Berlin, after the delay caused by the theft, it would be helpful if I examined them here before he left" said de Haas.

"And you believed him, sir?"

"I had no reason to doubt what my friend said, Inspector."

Hadley said nothing for a few moments and then asked "do you know a man called Ralph Brandon-Hall?" The Dutchman looked surprised and appeared uncertain how to answer but he finally stammered "yes, yes, I think I've met him a couple of times in the past."

"Do you recall who he is?"

"Yes, I think he's something to do with diamond mining in South Africa, Inspector."

"Have you ever been to meetings with Sir Robert Salisbury at his country house at Chieveley?" asked Hadley and the Dutchman looked uneasy on hearing that.

"Yes, I have had the honour of meeting Sir Robert occasionally."

"Did the invitations come from Sir Robert or Mr Isaacs?"

"I don't recall to be honest, Inspector."

"This is important, so try and recall, Mr de Haas!" exclaimed Hadley and the Dutchman's face grew pale.

"I think the first invitation came from Solomon and then they were from Sir Robert himself" replied de Haas.

"Tell me about these meetings at Chieveley."

"They were social occasions really, Inspector."

"Did you take your wife then?" asked Hadley.

"Er, no I didn't actually."

"Why was that I wonder? In my experience, lady wives can't wait to get all dressed up in posh party frocks to attend society occasions" said Hadley.

"My wife does not travel well, Inspector and a sea crossing to England would cause her delicate health to falter" de Haas replied.

"How unfortunate that your wife should miss such regular parties because of her poor health" said Hadley as he noticed the Dutchman's face pale again before he glanced down at his hands, clasped before him on the table.

"Yes, Inspector" he whispered and they both knew that he was telling lies. Hadley waited for a few moments before he asked "did Count Rausberg tell you the size of the stones?"

"He said that their size was considerable and all necessary precautions must be taken to ensure that they were not stolen" replied de Haas.

"But apparently any precautions taken did not prevent the theft" said Hadley.

"No, Inspector." Hadley waited for a while before he said "Mr de Haas, I suspect that you along with Isaacs and Count Rausberg are all conspirators in the theft of the diamonds…"

"Absolutely not!" interrupted de Haas.

"Oh yes, sir, and Sir Robert Salisbury was either the instigator of this wicked plan or the reluctant, lack lustre participant by default!"

"No!"

"Time will tell and the truth will be revealed" said Hadley.

"You're a fool!"

"So I've often been told, but I am a successful fool, as those that I have investigated know to their cost when they faced either the hangman or the interior of Dartmoor prison!" said Hadley, his hard blue eyes glinting at the Dutchman.

"You can't frighten me!"

"I didn't intend to, but I'm going to charge you with conspiracy to steal diamonds and perverting the course of justice, good evening Mr de Haas" said Hadley as he stood up and left the room followed by his Sergeants.

The detectives returned to Huntley's office where they discussed the investigation and waited for something to happen. Hadley wondered if Boeker had told the truth to Miss Vervorde about meeting him at the hotel if events took an unexpected turn. Possibly he just wanted to be rid of her in which case the surveillance officers waiting for him were wasting their time.

"Boeker has got to show his face at sometime, sir" said Cooper.

"He's like will o' the wisp, he just seems to disappear in the mist, Sergeant" said Hadley.

"He can't hide forever, sir" said Talbot.

"With my men searching the town, he's bound to be caught soon" said Huntley.

"Well I just hope that you are all right, gentlemen" said Hadley with a hopeful smile.

"I think we all could do with some tea" said Huntley.

"A very good idea" said Hadley as a constable knocked and entered the office holding a brown envelope.

"This telegraph message for Inspector Hadley has just arrived, sir."

"Thank you" said Hadley as he took the envelope and opened it. The note read 'Hadley, Sir Robert Salisbury and his daughter have left the Yard secretly and their whereabouts are unknown, be advised that they may come down to Gravesend. The Commissioner fears the worst for their safety and demands their arrest into protective custody. Bell.' Hadley handed the note to Huntley who read it out aloud to the astonished Sergeants before he said "Oh bloody hell, this means I've got more suspects to look for!" Hadley smiled and Cooper asked "why should Sir Robert leave the safety of the Yard, sir?" asked Cooper.

"Because he's up to his neck in this conspiracy and as I said at the very beginning of the investigation, we're dealing with desperate men who see before them diamonds of incalculable value and they will stop at nothing to have them" replied Hadley.

"What are your plans now, sir?" asked Talbot.

"After we've had a cup of tea, I think we'll brave the night air and go to Isaacs house then to the Railway Hotel to assist the surveillance officers in the hope that our suspects show up" replied Hadley.

CHAPTER 19

Inspector Huntley remained at the station when the three detectives went in a trap to the end of the London Road. They walked casually down towards number 58 in the warm evening as the mist from the Thames rose and swept along before them in ghostly eddies. They approached the two surveillance officers standing in a narrow alleyway between two houses opposite Isaacs home. Hadley made himself known to them as they stepped into the alleyway.

"Nothing to report I'm afraid, sir" said the older officer.

"Somehow I am not surprised" said Hadley.

"Why's that, sir?" asked Cooper.

"Because I'm beginning to think that Boeker probably scuttled back to London when he saw Miss Vervorde being arrested and Isaacs never intended to come here in the first place" replied Hadley.

"But what about Sir Robert, sir?" asked Talbot.

"I think that the Chief is wrong about Sir Robert coming here, he's probably hurried down to Brandon-Hall's place in Teddington or he's returned to Chieveley, Sergeant."

"It looks like we're on a wild goose chase again, sir" said Cooper.

"I'm beginning to think that way, Sergeant."

"What now then, sir?" asked Cooper.

"We'll call in at the Railway Hotel to see if there's been any sign of Boeker then we'll see if we've missed the last train back to Waterloo" replied Hadley.

The surveillance officers confirmed that there had been no sighting of Boeker and when Cooper checked the time of the last train he was informed that it had left for Waterloo half an hour ago. They returned to the police station where Hadley told Huntley of his fears and suggested that he stand down all his officers from the surveillance as well as the search of the town. They walked in silence to the Lion Hotel where Hadley treated the Sergeants to a pint of stout in the bar before they retired in gloomy mood to bed. He spent a restless night worrying about the investigation and was quite glad when it was time to get up.

After a full breakfast, Hadley felt better and was in a positive frame of mind when he arrived at the police station where he thanked Huntley for all his help.

"Glad to have been of service to Scotland Yard" said Huntley with a smile.

"Thanks, I'll put it all in my report" said Hadley.

"Now, what about Miss Vervorde and de Haas?" asked Huntley.

"We'll take them back with us" replied Hadley.

"I'm glad about that" said Huntley.

"Yes I'm sure you've enough to deal with here no doubt" said Hadley.

"Indeed I have and it's the paperwork that really gets me down."

"I know the feeling!" said Hadley with a smile.

The detectives caught the ten o'clock train to Waterloo with a composed Miss Vervorde and an angry Dutchman who complained about his treatment nearly all the way to London. When they arrived at the station, Talbot was instructed to take Miss Vervorde home in a Hansom whilst Hadley, Cooper and de Haas went to the Yard in a trap. As soon as the Dutchman was in custody he was formally charged whilst Hadley went up to report to Chief Inspector Bell.

When Hadley entered the Chief's office he looked surprised to see him.

"I didn't expect to see you back so soon, Hadley."

"No, sir" said Hadley as Bell waved him to a seat.

"Have you arrested Boeker and recovered the diamonds?"

"No sir."

"Why not?"

"Because I think he's come back to London, sir."

"Oh dear God, the Commissioner will be very disappointed to hear that."

"I'm sorry, sir."

"What about Sir Robert then?"

"I'm sure he's not in Gravesend either, sir."

"Where is he for heaven's sake?"

"I think he's either gone to Brandon-Hall's house or back to Chieveley, sir."

"I see" said Bell in a worried tone.

"And may I ask how he managed to slip away from here with a constable on duty outside his room?" asked Hadley in a firm tone.

"We're not sure at the moment, Hadley, but the Commissioner has ordered an inquiry into it."

"Well I hope somebody's head will roll!" said Hadley angrily.

"Quite so, now any sign of Isaacs or the Count?" asked Bell hastily changing the subject.

"Not yet, sir, but if any of them show themselves at either the shop in Hatton Garden, the house at Clapham or Brandon-Hall's house in Teddington the surveillance officers will arrest them" replied Hadley. The Chief Inspector then averted his gaze to his paperwork and folded his arms on his desk as if struggling with some inner torment before he cleared his throat and said "Hadley, I had to withdraw the officers from surveillance duties…"

"What?" interrupted Hadley angrily.

"Well I thought you had all the suspects at Gravesend and so as we are very short of manpower at the present I had to take the decision…"

"This puts us back right where we started, sir!" exclaimed Hadley.

"Nonsense, I'm sure it only a matter of time before you have arrested them and recovered the stones" said Bell with a half smile.

"You may think so, sir."

"I've every confidence in you Hadley, after all you've managed to arrest Isaacs henchmen as well as the two South Africans, so I think that you're making steady progress and as I said, it's only a matter of time" beamed Bell. Hadley remained silent for a few moments and glared at the Chief before he said in a firm tone "for your information, sir, I've arrested the Dutchman, Van de Haas, he's in custody at the moment being charged with conspiracy to rob."

"That's more good progress" said Bell.

"You must now give me permission to go anywhere that the investigation leads me, sir."

"Yes, you have my unreserved permission to do whatever you wish as long as you recover the diamonds before the German Ambassador demands another interview with the Commissioner" said Bell.

"And when is that likely to be, sir?"

"I've no idea, so you'd better get a move on and look lively" replied Bell.

"I now intend to act very decisively and my actions may offend certain people, sir" said Hadley.

"Well provided you are not too unreasonable in the course of your duties, then I'm glad to hear it."

Hadley nodded and left Bell's office without saying another word.

Hadley briefed his Sergeants on Bell's decision to stand down the surveillance officers from duty to their surprise and dismay.

"Well any of the suspects could have come and gone without so much as a by your leave" said Cooper.

"That's quite so, Sergeant."

"So whilst we were kicking our heels down at Gravesend, they were running amok in London" said Talbot with undisguised disgust.

"That's a possibility. So, we've got to take action to find Boeker and the rest of them, first of all we'll call at the shop in Hatton Garden" said Hadley.

"Right, sir" said Cooper and Talbot nodded as George appeared then asked if they were ready for a pot of tea.

"I'm afraid not George, we're desperate men short of time!"

"Very good, sir" replied George calmly then Hadley looked at his Sergeants and said with a smile "if you're armed and ready then I suggest we go, gentlemen!"

Hadley took a police four wheeler from the Yard and told the driver to 'whip up' and get them to Hatton Garden as fast as possible. The carriage pulled up outside Isaacs shop and the detectives hurried into the glittering emporium. The sales assistant recognised Hadley immediately and asked if he could help.

"Is Mr Isaacs here?"

"I'm afraid not, sir, can I be of any assistance?"

"Do you know where he is at present?" demanded Hadley in an angry tone.

"I'm not really sure, sir" the assistant replied anxiously.

"What exactly does that mean?"

"Well when he came in last evening…"

"What time was that?" interrupted Hadley.

"Just before we closed at six o'clock, sir."

"Go on."

"He said he would be away on important business for a day or so and I was to carry on as usual, sir."

"Did he give you any clue as to where he was going?" asked Hadley.

"Not really, sir, it was the other gentleman with him who said it would be good to be in the country" replied the assistant.

"What time did they leave here?"

"About half past six, Mr Isaacs came down from his office with his case and told me to call a Hansom."

"Go on please."

"I did as I was asked and heard Mr Isaacs tell the driver to take them to Paddington Station, sir."

"Thank you, you've been very helpful" said Hadley with a smile.

"You're welcome, sir, I'm sure."

The Sergeants climbed aboard the carriage as Hadley told the driver to make haste to Teddington. The two black mares set off at a fast trot through the busy traffic and as the carriage swung into the Clerkenwell Road it nearly collided with a London Omnibus full of passengers, which swerved violently to avoid a crash. The omnibus driver shouted at the police driver as the passengers on the open top deck nearly fell over the side of the 'bus. Several women screamed with alarm and one lost her hat, which drifted down into the road before it was trampled on by horses pulling a brewer's dray loaded with beer barrels.

"London get's busier by the day" said Hadley calmly as the police driver hurried his mares along the road, seemingly oblivious to the mayhem he had caused.

"It certainly does, sir, and I'm sure we'll appreciate the quiet countryside at Chieveley after we've been to Teddington" said

Cooper.

"You're absolutely right, Sergeant."

"Do you think that Sir Robert is at Chieveley, sir?"

"Without doubt, Sergeant, I'm sure he'll be there to welcome Isaacs and his guest, along with others" replied Hadley.

"It will be quite a party then, sir" said Cooper.

"I think so, Sergeant, the only question is, are the diamonds going to be there with Hans Boeker?"

"I'm sure we'll know by the end of the day, sir" said Cooper with a smile.

"That's for sure" said Hadley as the carriage raced on out of the City and towards Teddington.

When the detectives arrived outside number 12, Riverside Walk, Hadley briefed his Sergeants to be ready with their revolvers if there appeared the slightest risk of danger to themselves. With grim determination they hurried up to the front door and rang the bell. The butler appeared and asked if he could help.

"Is Mr Brandon-Hall at home?" asked Hadley.

"No, sir, I understand that the master has gone out for the day" replied the butler.

"Is Rupert Brandon-Hall in?"

"No, sir, he's gone with the master but Miss Angelina is at home."

"I'd like to speak to her please" said Hadley and the butler gave a nod and opened the door wider for them to enter.

"Please wait here if you would, sir" said the butler before he disappeared into the drawing room. He returned a few moments later and said "Miss Angelina will see you now, sir." They followed him into the room where Angelina stood up by the fireplace. After greetings, Hadley asked "do you know where your father and brother have gone, Miss?"

"They're on the river, Inspector" she replied with a smile.

"On the river?"

"Yes, they went this morning in Papa's steam cruiser for a trip" she replied brightly.

"Have you any idea where they have gone, Miss?"

"No, Papa didn't say, but I assume it's just one of his cruises up and down the river as the mood takes him" she replied.

"What is the name of your father's boat, Miss?"
"She's called the African Queen, Inspector."
"How very apt."
"Yes it is."
"Was there anybody else with your father?"
"No, just Rupert and the crew of course."
"Of course, now when do you expect him back?"
"Sometime later this evening, Inspector."
Hadley thought for a few moments before he said "thank you for your help, Miss."
"You're welcome, Inspector, shall I tell Papa that you called?"
"That won't be necessary thank you, Miss."
"Very well."
"Good day to you, Miss."
"Good day, Inspector."

Once they were outside and climbing up into the carriage, Hadley told the driver to go at the fastest possible speed back to the Yard. As the carriage swayed from side to side, Hadley told his Sergeants his fears and the action he proposed to take next. When they arrived back in the office, Hadley went to see Inspector Drury, who commanded the River Police section. He explained what had happened and requested that a Police launch with armed officers should be sent off immediately to search for the 'African Queen' and arrest everyone on board. Drury agreed and issued instructions to his Sergeant. Back in his office Hadley sent a telegraph to the Newbury police informing them that the detectives were on their way and requesting the assistance of a Sergeant and four constables.

"Now then gentlemen, if you're ready we'll set off to Newbury" said Hadley.

"And then we'll see what's what" said Cooper.

"Indeed we will, Sergeant."

"I'm really looking forward to this little trip" said Talbot with a smile.

"So am I, Sergeant!"

Catching the express from Paddington, Hadley and his Sergeants arrived at Newbury at two o'clock. They stopped for tea and sandwiches at the station kiosk before making their way to Newbury Police station. The Duty Sergeant showed them immediately into Inspector George Wilkes' office. After introductions Hadley briefed Wilkes on the investigation so far and he was taken aback by the seriousness of the case as well as the involvement of Sir Robert Salisbury.

"I can hardly believe what you're telling me" said Wilkes.

"I can hardly believe it myself, but there it is and of course the driving force behind all the violence and conspiracy is the sheer incalculable value of these four diamonds" said Hadley.

"Well, my men are ready to assist you in whatever way they can, Inspector Hadley" said Wilkes.

"Thank you, Inspector."

"It's not often that we country boys get the chance to work alongside Scotland Yard" said Wilkes with a smile.

"No, I don't suppose you do" said Hadley.

"Around here there's the odd theft but mostly it's poachers we have to deal with" said Wilkes and the detectives smiled when they recalled their imprisonment in the wine cellar and the maid's comments.

"So I understand" said Hadley with a grin.

"Now I've arranged for my best man, Sergeant Grover, and four constables to assist you and if you would care to brief them now, Inspector, you can then get under way to Chieveley" said Wilkes.

Half an hour later they set off in convoy for Chieveley, with the detectives leading the way in a trap, followed by Sergeant Grover and his men in a police wagon. As they headed up the Oxford road towards Sir Robert's country house, Hadley felt the tension rising within him as his expectations of a violent confrontation with the conspirators could soon be realised. He remained silent until the trap turned into the driveway of Chieveley Manor and, glancing at his Sergeants', said "this is it, gentlemen." They both nodded as Hadley felt the comfort of the revolver in his coat pocket.

CHAPTER 20

When the trap and wagon pulled up outside the entrance to the house at Chieveley, Sergeant Grover deployed two men to go to the rear of the building whilst the detectives made their way up the steps to the imposing front door. Cooper rang the bell and they waited until Wilson opened the door and he stepped backwards in amazement at the sight of the officers.

"Sir..."

"Good afternoon, Wilson, please announce us to Sir Robert" said Hadley as he pushed the door open and strode into the hall way followed by Cooper, Talbot, Grover and two constables.

"But sir..." began Wilson.

"Now if you please, otherwise you'll face more charges other than those of imprisoning police officers" said Hadley firmly. Wilson stood open mouthed for a moment before he blurted out "the master is in the study, sir." Hadley nodded and approached the door to his right and said "in here?"

"Yes, sir" whispered the anxious butler. Hadley did not wait for Wilson but burst through the door followed by all his officers and confronted a startled Sir Robert seated at his desk and Solomon Isaacs, who leapt to his feet from his chair.

"You are both under arrest. I suggest that you come quietly gentlemen!"

"You're a tiresome, meddling fool out of your depth, Inspector!" exclaimed Isaacs as Sir Robert held his head in his hands.

"You will be taken to Newbury Police station immediately and then to Scotland Yard where I will formally charge you both" said Hadley.

"With what may I ask?" said Isaacs.

"All in good time, sir, all in good time, now do either of you know the whereabouts of Hans Boeker?"

"No and if we did, we wouldn't tell you, Inspector!" exclaimed Isaacs.

"I'm amazed that you persist in making your position worse than it already is" said Hadley.

"And I'm amazed that you're here" said Isaacs.

"I often amaze people, sir."

"It will be your downfall, Inspector" said Isaacs as he narrowed his hard eyes.

"We'll see, Sergeant Grover, take these men out to the wagon and lock them in" said Hadley.

"Yes, sir" replied Grover and as he strode towards Isaacs two men appeared from the hallway and grabbed the constables before hurling them to the floor. Grover turned as his men fell and one of them collided with Talbot knocking him backwards as Cooper reached for his revolver. Hadley stepped back and drew his revolver as Grover lashed out with his truncheon at the nearest assailant who was a large, heavily built man. The truncheon slammed hard into the man's shoulder and he shouted out with pain as he fell to the floor.

"Hold up or I'll shoot!" shouted Hadley as the constables struggled with the other man before Grover stunned him with a heavy blow to his head. Sir Robert stood up looking completely shattered by what he had just witnessed, whilst Isaacs grinned.

"Who are these men?" asked Hadley.

"They're mine, I had to replace Grenville and Lansbury, who you still have in custody" said Isaacs.

"Two more for the wagon, Sergeant Grover" said Hadley.

"Yes, sir" he replied calmly.

"Now f you have any other thugs concealed about the house I suggest that you advise them to desist from any heroics otherwise they are liable to be shot" said Hadley firmly as he pointed his revolver in the general direction of Isaacs and Sir Robert.

"I do believe that you really mean it, Inspector" said Isaacs with a curious smirk.

"With one of my officers already killed I'm more than ready to redress the balance in favour of the Metropolitan Police" replied Hadley.

"You're prepared to shoot men down in cold blood, Inspector?"

"Without a moment's hesitation and the temperature of my blood will not affect my decision" replied Hadley.

"That won't look very good on your record" said Isaacs.

"Let me worry about that, sir."

"Inspector, surely we can discuss this unfortunate situation calmly before any drastic action is taken" pleaded Sir Robert.

"I'm afraid it's too late for that now, sir" replied Hadley as the front door bell rang. They remained silent as Wilson opened the door and then they heard voices. Hadley waved at Talbot and Cooper to hide behind the open study doors as he turned to face Count von Rausberg and Herr Schoender as they entered the study. The Count and his assistant looked startled for a moment as Hadley wished them "good afternoon, gentlemen."

"What are you doing here?" asked the Count.

"I may ask you the same question, sir" said Hadley.

"It's none of your business why I am here!" exclaimed the Count angrily.

"Oh I think it most certainly is, sir" said Hadley with a smile as Grover and his constables dragged the two assailants from the room passed the shocked Count.

"What is going on here?" demanded the Count.

"These gentlemen are under arrest and now so are you Count Rausberg along with Herr Schoender" said Hadley.

"Gott in Himmel! You are mad!" exclaimed the Count.

"I think not, I'm just ambitious" said Hadley.

"My Government will have something to say about all this, Inspector" said the Count.

"And so will Her Majesty's, sir, I can assure you of that!" replied Hadley.

"How dare you speak to me in that manner!"

"You, along with other foreigners, have come to London and conspired to steal diamonds whilst not hesitating to use violence on our streets" said Hadley.

"I have done no such thing!"

"You will be free to put your case after you've been formally charged at Scotland Yard" said Hadley.

"I'll make sure that you are thrown out of the police for this!" exclaimed the Count.

"Sergeants, take them out to the wagon and then come back for these two" said Hadley as he waved his revolver towards Sir Robert and Isaacs.

"Right, sir" said Cooper as he and Talbot pointed their revolvers at the Count. There was a few moments silence before the Count glanced at Isaacs and asked "is he here?"

Isaacs shook his head and whispered "no".

"Who are you expecting?" asked Hadley, sensing that it might be Boeker but no one replied, then the Count left the study followed by Schoender and the Sergeants.

"I would remind you both that it is now in your own best interests to assist me in my investigations" said Hadley.

"When we get back to London and have spoken to the right people the only thing you'll be investigating is the amount of un-cleared horse droppings in Parliament Square!" said Isaacs with a grin.

"Time will tell, but in the meantime it is my duty to recover the diamonds and I…" Hadley was suddenly interrupted by the sound of two gun shots. He did not hesitate and ran from the study out into the hallway then through the open front door. He stopped and surveyed the scene before him. Cooper was crouched down by the front wheel of the police wagon pointing his revolver towards a trap whilst Talbot lay face down and bleeding on the gravel some yards away. The Count and Schoender were behind Cooper and they began to move away back towards the house. Hadley drew his revolver and hurried down the steps as another shot rang out from behind the trap. The driver leapt down from his seat and ran away back down the driveway. Grover and his men were pinned down inside the wagon with the prisoners and could offer no assistance. As Hadley reached Cooper he saw the man with a gun hiding behind the back of the trap.

"I think it's Boeker, sir" said Cooper.

"You may be right, Sergeant" replied Hadley as Talbot groaned and tried to lift himself up. He glanced at Hadley before he whispered "help me, sir." The Inspector ran the few yards to the wounded man and grabbing him by both arms, dragged him out of the line of fire. Talbot had been hit in his left side and was bleeding profusely. Hadley stuffed his handkerchief against the wound and told the Sergeant to hold it tightly in place. Whilst Hadley and Cooper's attention was diverted by Talbot, the man hiding behind the trap saw his opportunity to escape, jumped up onto the driver's seat and slapped the reins. The horse whinnied loudly as the trap spun round and set off at speed down the driveway towards the entrance to the Manor. Hadley and Cooper both stood and fired at the disappearing trap with its driver bent low for cover. Hadley saw one of his rounds hit and splinter the back of the driver's seat but it was to the left of the crouched man. Within moments the trap was out of range as Grover and his constables emerged from the police wagon..

"Stay here and take care of Talbot, Sergeant" said Hadley.

"Right, sir" replied Grover.

"Come with me, Sergeant" said Hadley to Cooper and he nodded as the Inspector leapt up on to the police trap. He picked up the reins and with a shout the two detectives were in hot pursuit of the mystery gunman. As the trap bounced with speed down the driveway, Cooper managed with great difficulty to re-load his revolver.

"What happened back there, Sergeant?"

"We were just about to get the Count and Schoender into the wagon when the trap arrived, I glanced up and without any warning the man produced a gun and fired at Talbot, sir."

"He'll pay for that!"

"I fired back and he jumped down behind the trap then discharged another shot" said Cooper.

"I'm almost sure now that the man must be Hans Boeker, Sergeant" said Hadley as they reached the end of the drive and swung out into the road towards the village. Hadley could see the trap in the far distance and he slapped the reins for more speed from the panting horse in front of him. They travelled on with the detectives keeping a close watch on the trap ahead, which was slowly pulling away from them.

"That's a fine horse he's got there" said Hadley and Cooper just nodded as the gap between the two traps became greater.

"We'll catch him, sir" said Cooper as the wind whistled around the detectives and the Sergeant clung to his bowler hat. They raced on and as they approached Chieveley village Hadley said "I'll stop outside the pub, you go in and tell the landlord to find the Doctor and send him out to take care of Talbot!"

"Right, sir."

Hadley stopped the panting horse outside the Lamb pub and Cooper rushed into the bar, returning just a few moments later. Hadley slapped the reins once again and they were on their way in pursuit of Hans Boeker. When they rounded a bend in the lane just before it joined the Oxford road, Hadley glimpsed the trap in front as it began to slow.

"By God, I think we've nearly got him!"

"Yes it looks like it, sir, when we get within range shall I shoot him?" asked Cooper as he produced his revolver.

"Only if it looks as if he is going to fire at us, Sergeant."

"As you say, sir."

The gap between the traps narrowed as Hadley spurred on the tired horse to greater effort. After they had turned onto the Oxford road and were heading down to Newbury, the fugitive trap slowed right down to a walk and Hadley rapidly overhauled it. As they drew near he said to Cooper "be ready to fire if necessary when Boeker sees us, Sergeant."

"I'm ready, sir."

The last few yards between the vehicles were quickly covered and as they drew alongside the trap the driver turned to face them. To their complete surprise it was not the gunman but the driver who had run away from the shooting. He paled visibly when he saw Cooper's revolver pointing at him and he pulled up his horse. He raised both hands in the air and shouted "don't shoot me, for Gawd's sake!"

"Where's the other man, your passenger?" asked Hadley as he stopped the trap.

"I left him in the lane by the Manor" replied the wide eyed driver.

"What!"

"He caught me up after I run away and told me to get back to Newbury as fast as I could" said the driver.

"He must have switched places with this man as soon as he turned out of the drive, Sergeant" said Hadley.

"And then hidden somewhere in a ditch, sir."

"Yes and is now back at the house causing no end of mayhem!" said Hadley as he turned the trap around in the road and slapped the reins. The tired horse went as quickly as it could, panting and sweating in the warm afternoon sun.

"I just wonder what awaits us when we get back, Sergeant."

"I'm sure that Sergeant Grover and his men have the situation under control, sir."

"I'm not so sure, Sergeant, remember they're a country force only used to dealing with the occasional thief and poachers" said

Hadley.

"That's true, sir."

"Armed and desperate men may prove too much for them to handle, Sergeant."

They remained silent all the way back to the Manor and Hadley became very anxious when he turned into the drive way and noticed that the police wagon was no longer outside the entrance to the house.

"Where's that gone to I wonder?" he said in a half whisper.

"And the Count's carriage is also missing, sir."

Hadley stopped the very tired horse in the shade of a large tree at the end of the drive, some fifty yards from the steps to the house. The detectives hurried across the gravel drive and up to the closed front door. Cooper rang the bell whilst Hadley drew his revolver. Wilson opened the door and the detectives pushed passed him into the hall.

"Where is everybody, Wilson?"

"They've all left, sir."

"Where have they gone to?"

"The police officers took the men they arrested back to Newbury and Sir Robert and Mr Isaacs have left with the Count, sir" replied Wilson with a smug grin.

"Have they indeed."

"Yes, sir."

"And I don't suppose for one moment that Sir Robert told you where he was going?"

"You're quite right, sir, the master never said a word to me about his intentions" replied Wilson.

"How convenient!"

"It is, sir."

"Did he say anything else?"

"Only that he would not be back for dinner this evening, sir" replied Wilson and Hadley glared at him for a few moments before the butler asked "will that be all, sir?"

"No Wilson, I think you're lying!"

"Me tell lies, sir? I would never do such a thing, sir!"

"We have just driven back from the Oxford road and we did not pass the police wagon supposedly on its way to Newbury!"

"Well then it must have gone the other way on the Wantage road, sir."

Hadley looked surprised when he heard that but was unsure if Wilson was telling the truth or not.

"Where's Sergeant Talbot?" demanded Hadley.

"Who sir?"

"My injured officer!"

"Ah, Doctor Thompson has taken him off in his trap to the Cottage Hospital in Newbury, sir."

"By the Wantage road no doubt?"

"Most probably, sir, after all it's the shortest route to Newbury from here, it saves going through the village and that's why everybody uses it" said Wilson. Hadley looked hard at the butler who cast his eyes down and he knew that the man was lying to protect his master.

"Right, we'll travel on the Wantage road to Newbury and see if what you say is true, Wilson."

"Very good, sir."

"I presume, instead of turning left at the end of the driveway for the village, we turn right?"

"Yes indeed, sir, you travel about a mile or so then you'll meet the Wantage road and if you turn left there, you will be on your way to the town by the shortest route" replied the butler.

"Thank you, Wilson, we'll be back tomorrow" said Hadley with a nod. The detectives left the house and climbed back onto the trap.

"He's lying to us, Sergeant" said Hadley as he slapped the reins for the horse to walk on.

"I'm sure he is, sir."

"It would not surprise me if Grover and his men were not held captive here along with Talbot and Doctor Thompson" said Hadley with concern.

When the trap reached the end of the drive, Hadley turned left towards the village.

"Aren't we going to Newbury on the Wantage road, sir?"

"No, Sergeant, we're going to Chieveley" replied Hadley.

"Why, sir?"

"To make inquiries before we send someone on a fast horse to

Newbury with a message for Inspector Wilkes, whilst we wait for nightfall, Sergeant!"

"So do you plan to go back to the Manor after dark, sir?"

"I do indeed and I think that we may surprise our suspects!"

"But what if they have all left as Wilson said, sir?"

"Then I've made a big mistake, Sergeant."

"Oh bloody hell, sir."

"Only time will tell, Sergeant but Wilson thinks we're coming back tomorrow and that might lull whoever is there now into a sense of false security."

CHAPTER 21

Arriving at the Lamb pub Hadley tied the horse to a post by a water trough, where the animal drank heavily as he patted it on its neck. Following Cooper into the bar, which was by now quite busy with locals, they ordered pints of ale from the landlord who asked "has the Doctor seen to your man, sir?"

"Yes, thank you and he's taken him to the Cottage Hospital" replied Cooper.

"Oh, I didn't see him come by here" said the proprietor in a thick Berkshire accent.

"Apparently he went on the Wantage road" said Cooper.

"Now why would he want to do that, I wonder?"

"We've been told it's the shortest route to Newbury" said Hadley.

"I don't think so, sir."

"Is it much further?" asked Cooper.

"I would say so by several miles, sir" replied the landlord. On hearing that Hadley looked at Cooper, raised his eyebrows and said "I think that proves my point, Sergeant."

"Indeed it does, sir."

Hadley sipped his ale then asked "I need to send an urgent message to the police station in Newbury, is there anyone who would deliver it for me?"

"Yes, young Richard Towns, the blacksmith's son, he's a good reliable lad" replied the landlord.

"Can someone get him for me?" asked Hadley.

"Yes, sir, I'll send Gladys right away for you."

Whilst the pretty barmaid hurried off to the blacksmiths to find Mr Towns, Hadley wrote a note to Inspector Wilkes on a page taken from Cooper's notebook. When Gladys returned with the young man, Hadley gave him the note and a guinea for his troubles then asked him to deliver the message as quickly as he could.

"Shall I wait for a reply, sir?" asked Towns.

"That will not be necessary" replied Hadley.

The young man nodded, left the pub and climbed up onto a fine chestnut mare then galloped off towards Newbury in the evening dusk.

"What now, sir?"

"I think we'll have something to eat and then make our way back to the Manor, Sergeant."

It was dark when they left the pub and climbed into the trap but the night was clear with the moon spreading silver light on their way ahead. As the trap turned into the drive way of the Manor, Hadley pulled the horse up and then led it off the gravel onto the grass beyond the elm trees that bordered the drive on either side.

"Now we'll see who is there, Sergeant" said Hadley as they began to make their way on foot along the line of trees towards the house. As they drew near they could see a figure standing outside on the steps. They stopped and remained still behind the last tree before peering cautiously out.

"I think that he's one of Isaacs' men, sir" whispered Cooper.

"If he is, that means that Grover and his constables did not get back to Newbury and are prisoners here, Sergeant."

"Yes, sir and they're probably all locked up in that damned room in the wine cellar" whispered Cooper.

"I'm sure you're right, now let's go round to the back of the house" said Hadley.

"We should wait until our friend goes inside before we make a move, sir."

"Yes, quite right, Sergeant" said Hadley as he knew that the open ground between the end of the drive and the Manor would be impossible to cross without being seen by the man on the steps. They waited behind the tree and occasionally looked towards the man, who wandered up and down oblivious to their presence. After about twenty minutes the front door was opened by the other Isaacs man and his colleague was called to come in to the house.

"Let's go, Sergeant" said Hadley and Cooper nodded before he followed on. The detectives crossed the moonlit open space quickly and made their way to the back of the house. As they passed the stable yard, Hadley saw the police wagon parked against the far wall and just pointed to it.

"You were right, sir" whispered Cooper and Hadley nodded.

When they approached the house more closely they could see the servants in the busy kitchen. Suddenly Wilson appeared and began waving his arms about. All the servants then appeared to hurry more at his command.

"Something is up, sir" whispered Cooper as they crouched down by the wall in the kitchen garden.

"It seems so, now what we have to do is get into the house, Sergeant."

"We'll probably have to wait until they've all gone to bed, sir."

"Only the servants then we can slip in through the kitchen."

"They'll lock the door before they turn in, sir."

"I'm sure they will but I trust you have your little tool set for such occasions as these" whispered Hadley and Cooper nodded.

An hour later the servants in the kitchen began to drift off, one by one, until only a large red faced woman was left. Hadley assumed she was the cook and he smiled when he saw her glance around the kitchen once more before she took the oil lamp from the table and left the room. The detectives hurried to the back door and Hadley grabbed the handle. As he tried it, to his surprise, the door opened and within a moment they were inside the warm, dark kitchen.

"How very careless of them to leave the door unlocked, you never who's about these days" whispered Hadley and Cooper grinned. When they opened the door to the servant's corridor they could hear the sound of muffled voices punctuated with laughter coming from upstairs.

"That's Sir Robert and his guests enjoying their after dinner stories" whispered Hadley.

"Not for very much longer, sir."

"On the contrary, Sergeant, we'll find Grover and his men, leave the house until first light then we'll pounce on the bastards, they'll be drunk and half asleep, I promise you that they won't know what's hit them!"

"I hope you're right, sir."

"I hope so too, Sergeant, now let's find our way down to the wine cellar."

Proceeding along a corridor they found the door to the wine cellar. Hadley opened it and he could smell the aroma of the wines and spirits drifting up from below. They cautiously descended the steps after closing the door behind them and Cooper struck a match to light their way. Finding a large candle on a shelf at the bottom of the stairs, Cooper lit it. The flickering light gave a ghostly shimmer on the white washed walls and they heard whispers from the room at the end. Suddenly a voice said "it's Inspector Hadley and his Sergeant!"

"Yes, we're here" whispered Hadley as he approached the room and flung back the two large bolts that held the door to the small prison. Grover and his four men poured out with gratitude and relief on their faces.

"How did you find us, sir?" asked Grover.

"We guessed you were here because we've been held in there as well, Sergeant" replied Hadley and they all smiled.

"Over night, I might add" said Cooper.

"Yes, so you country boys don't know how lucky you are" said Hadley.

"It seems so, sir" said Grover.

"Now we'll leave the house quietly, wait for the dawn, then we'll come back before they are awake and arrest the lot of them in their beds!" said Hadley.

They filed up slowly and purposefully into the corridor and Hadley listened for any movement upstairs but all he heard was the muffled sounds of the conversations. Hadley led the officers out through the kitchen and into the garden then into the stable yard.

"I suggest that we organise a duty roster to watch the house in case our friends decide to leave, then make ourselves comfortable with the horses in the stables, gentlemen" said Hadley. They all nodded and followed him in through the door at the end of the block. After the first constable had begun his watch in the yard, the rest settled down to get some sleep amongst the bales of straw.

Hadley asked Grover "tell me what happened after we left and chased the gunman?"

"It all happened very quickly, sir, whilst I was attending to Sergeant Talbot, the German pulled out a gun and threatened to shoot us."

"I presume that it was the Count's man, Schoender, who threatened you."

"Yes, sir."

"What about Talbot's revolver?"

"Schoender took it, sir."

"Then what happened?"

"The two men who were in the wagon were set free and we were brought down to the wine cellar and locked up, sir."

"Do you know what happened to Sergeant Talbot?"

"No, sir, I'm sorry to say that we had to leave him where he was" replied Grover.

"When we arrived in the village, Sergeant Cooper arranged for the Doctor to be summoned and I just hope that he came and attended to Talbot" said Hadley wearily.

"I don't know if he did, sir."

"Never mind, we'll soon find out because I sent a message to Inspector Wilkes asking him to inquire into Talbot's condition at the Cottage Hospital then come at dawn with as many armed men as he could muster" said Hadley.

"That's good to hear but I don't think that will be many, sir."

"Why is that?"

"Because we're nearly all here, sir" replied Grover.

"Well we'll have to wait and see then" said Hadley in a resigned tone.

"Yes, sir."

"Now let's all get some rest before the dawn breaks" said Hadley as he settled back against a bale of straw.

Hadley tried to get some sleep but the precariousness of the situation kept him awake. He hoped that Wilkes would find enough men to ensure that the arrests would go smoothly but he had doubts that troubled him. It seemed an age before the grey glimmer of dawn began to show and Hadley glanced at his fob watch. It was just after five o'clock and he decided to leave the men sleeping until five thirty then waken them. He glanced at Cooper, who was sleeping like a baby and then at Grover who lay motionless on the straw. The constables were dotted about in various positions, some snoring, but all fast asleep and Hadley thought it was a shame to wake them, but duty called. As soon as the time had come, Hadley shook Cooper and then Grover.

"Wake up, Sergeants, it's time to get up!" They both stirred and struggled to sit up amongst the straw.

"What time is it, sir?" asked Cooper.

"It's five thirty, Sergeant."

"Oh good God" whispered Cooper.

As soon as they were all awake and ready to go, Hadley called the constable on watch in and briefed them on his plans for successful operation.

"First of all, we'll quietly harness the horses to the wagon" he said and Grover nodded.

"Now in the house there are seven suspects who we will arrest, they are Sir Robert, Isaacs, the Count and his man, the two thugs and I believe Boeker, who is the man who shot Sergeant Talbot before he escaped then doubled back here."

"How many of them are armed, sir?" asked Grover.

"Assume that they all are, Sergeant" replied Hadley.

"Will you wait for Inspector Wilkes to arrive, sir?" asked Grover.

"No, we'll start straight away, Sergeant" replied Hadley.

"Is that wise, sir?" asked Cooper.

"I think it's the best course of action because we don't know when Inspector Wilkes will arrive and I don't want to wait" replied Hadley.

"Right, sir."

"Now as Sergeant Cooper and myself are the only armed officers I propose that we carry out the arrest of each suspect, then you, Sergeant, handcuff them, then two constables will bring each person to the wagon and lock them in" said Hadley.

"Very good, sir" said Grover.

"Be ready for the un-expected, gentlemen, and take cover if there's armed resistance."

"We will don't you worry, sir" Grover nodded.

"Let's go then."

Hadley led them single file out of the stables and across the yard to the kitchen garden wall. He stopped for a moment and surveyed the house for any lights or movement. He saw nothing and moved forward across the garden to the kitchen door. He found that it had been locked during the night and cursed himself for not awaking them earlier.

"Sergeant, pick this damned lock and hurry please!"

"Yes, sir" replied Cooper as he produced his leather wallet containing his fine steel tools. He worked quickly and moments later there was a resounding click as he sprung the lock open. Hadley led the way into the warm kitchen and into the corridor. He stopped and listened for any movement before sending a constable to the front door to un lock it, ready for Wilkes arrival. He then went up the servant's stairs to the first floor, opening the door to the plush corridor and listening before he proceeded along to the first bedroom. He listened at the door before he drew his revolver and gently opened the door. Isaacs lay on his back in the middle of a four poster bed and Hadley strode in and pointed his revolver at Isaacs head whilst Cooper went the other side of the bed and did the same. Hadley shook the sleeping man until he was awake, his eyes suddenly wide with terror.

"Solomon Isaacs, you are under arrest!"

"Good God! How did you…"

"Come quietly now otherwise it'll be the worse for you" interrupted Hadley as he half dragged the bewildered man from the bed. Grover immediately handcuffed him and he was led away by two constables.

"Now for the next one" said Hadley.

In the adjoining bedroom they found Schoender who was roused by the same method, but he lashed out at Hadley who did not hesitate to bring the barrel of his revolver down hard across the head of the struggling German. Schoender was stupefied by the savage blow and was securely handcuffed by Grover before being half carried away with a bleeding head wound.

"Find his gun and Talbot's, Sergeant" said Hadley to Cooper. The weapons were discovered in Schoender's jacket and Cooper put them in his pocket before they moved to the next bedroom. The Count looked almost regal as he lay on his back in the middle of the four poster bed. Hadley and Cooper deployed in the same manner and the startled man tried to offer some resistance but when he saw the cold menace in Hadley's eyes he stopped and said "mein Gott! You'll be very sorry indeed for this!"

"Not as sorry as you, sir" replied Hadley as Grover handcuffed the Count. They left Grover waiting for the first two constables to arrive back from the stable yard to collect the Count, and proceeded to the next room. Sir Robert lay fast asleep on his side with his arm around a young woman. Hadley shook him until he opened his eyes and at the same time the woman awoke and opened her mouth to scream. Cooper immediately put his hand over her mouth as Hadley half dragged Sir Robert from his warm bed and said "you are under arrest, sir!"

"You have just made the biggest mistake of your life, Inspector!" said Sir Robert.

"So you all keep saying but time will tell" replied Hadley as Grover entered the room and handcuffed Sir Robert.

"And I advise you, Miss, to stay here quietly otherwise I shall arrest you, do you understand?" asked Hadley and the terrified woman nodded her head.

"Let her go then, Sergeant" and Cooper took his hand from her mouth.

They went to the next room and found it empty.

"We've got to find Boeker and the two thugs yet, Sergeant."

"Yes, sir and possible the Isaacs men are in the servants quarters."

"That's a good point."

Crossing the landing and opening the first door they found this bedroom was also empty but in the next one they discovered a young man, who Cooper recognised as the gunman in the drive.

"That's him, sir" whispered Cooper as they approached the bed.

"At last" whispered Hadley as he moved close and pointed his revolver at his head.

"Wake up Hans Boeker, you're under arrest!" exclaimed Hadley as he shook the man vigorously. Boeker opened his eyes and stared in terror at the detectives before he asked "who the devil are you?"

"Inspector Hadley of Scotland Yard, and as I said, you're under arrest!"

"What for?"

"Murder for a start" replied Hadley as he pulled him from his bed.

"You're mad!"

"You're absolutely right, I'm mad enough to shoot you down without a moment's hesitation if you try to resist in any way!" said Hadley, his blue eyes glinting with anger.

"I'm not called Boeker, you've made a mistake!"

"Well if I have, then I'll apologise after your trial for the murder of Constable Meredith in Hatton Garden and the attempted murders of Sergeant Talbot and Sergeant Cooper, does that suit you, sir?" asked Hadley as Grover came in with handcuffs followed by two constables. As Grover handcuffed Boeker, Hadley asked him "now where are the diamonds?"

"I don't know what you're talking about" he replied.

"It would save me a lot of time and you considerable personal grief if you tell me where they are" said Hadley.

"What do you mean by 'considerable personal grief'?"

"The diamonds that you, along with Detrekker and Vervorde, brought from Africa have been the cause of murder and mayhem in London…"

"That's nothing to do with me" he interrupted.

"And it is now my duty to recover the stones that I believe are the property of the German Government."

"Then do your duty, Inspector."

"I will and I must inform you that the Commissioner at Scotland Yard has given me permission to use whatever means to recover the diamonds" said Hadley.

"So?"

"Simply put, Hans Boeker, you will tell me where they are otherwise I shall use very unpleasant force against you."

"Are you threatening me?"

"No, I'm making you aware of your situation so you know what awaits you" replied Hadley.

"You can't do that!"

"As South Africa is a long way away, you may not have heard of our methods and success at Scotland Yard in bringing investigations to satisfactory conclusions with all law breakers either hanged or imprisoned for the rest of their lives" said Hadley.

"You can't frighten me!"

"I don't intend to, I just want to know what you've done with the diamonds."

"I've nothing to say!" exclaimed Boeker.

"Very well" said Hadley and he nodded to Grover "handcuff him to a chair whilst we search the room."

"Right, sir."

"If we don't find the stones here, you can leave us to question him whilst you look for Isaacs' men, Sergeant" said Hadley.

"Yes, sir" replied Grover.

"Cooper, give Talbot's revolver to Sergeant Grover before he goes."

"Yes, sir."

"Now let's tear this room apart!"

CHAPTER 22

Hadley and the other officers searched the room methodically for the case containing the precious diamonds but after ten minutes they had found nothing except Boeker's pistol which Cooper put in his pocket.

"Right that will do, gentlemen, I think we're wasting our time now" said Hadley and they stopped the search.

"I'll go and look for Isaacs men in the servants' quarters, sir" said Grover.

"Very good, Sergeant, and if they offer any resistance don't hesitate to shoot them" said Hadley in a matter of fact tone.

"No, sir."

"Please give me your truncheon" said Hadley and when Boeker saw Grover hand over his substantial weapon, he paled beneath his tan.

"Thank you. Come back and let me know when you've arrested those other two" said Hadley.

"Yes, sir" replied Grover before he left the room followed by his constables. Hadley then walked up and down in front of Boeker slapping the truncheon into the palm of his free hand. Cooper looked at Hadley then with a slight grin, asked "do you want me to gag him as we usually do, sir?"

"Not for the moment, Sergeant, we don't wish to deny him his last chance to tell us what we want to know before the pain starts" replied Hadley.

"Shall I get a sheet off the bed to catch the blood, sir?"

"Yes, that's a good idea Sergeant, we don't want to stain the carpet if we can help it."

"Right, sir."

"We don't usually have to bother with such niceties in the cells at the Yard you understand, Mr Boeker" said Hadley with a grin as Cooper began to pull the bed apart. Hadley stopped pacing and came close to Boeker, glared into his pale face and asked with menace "now for the very last time, where are the diamonds?" The man hesitated but before he could answer, Cooper asked "what side do you want the sheet, sir?"

"There, to my left, Sergeant" replied Hadley as he stood in front of Boeker casually swinging the truncheon with his right hand close to the top of his head. Cooper nodded before he spread the white sheet neatly on the carpet up to the chair legs. At this point, Boeker stammered out "I don't know where they are, I gave them to Isaacs last night and he's got them now!"

"Ah, the truth at last" said Hadley as Grover burst into the room and said "we've found Sergeant Talbot and the Doctor, sir!"

"Thank God for that, where are they?"

"They were locked in the first room we came to in the servant's quarters, sir."

"How is Talbot?"

"He seemed alright and perked up when he saw us, sir."

"I'm sure he did, now get this man down to the wagon whilst we go with your constables and search for Isaacs men" said Hadley.

"Right, sir" replied Grover as Hadley and Cooper hurried from the bedroom.

As they made their way along the corridor towards the servant's quarters, Cooper said "our play acting certainly loosened his tongue, sir."

"I wasn't acting, Sergeant" replied Hadley grimly as they reached the door at the end. They stepped through into the bare corridor beyond and Hadley nodded at the two constables standing by an open door.

"In here, sir" said one with a grin.

Sergeant Talbot looked up from his bed when Hadley and Cooper entered the small room. Doctor Thompson sighed with relief as Talbot said "I'm bloody glad to see you, sir."

"Likewise, Sergeant, how are you?"

"Without the Doctor here, I'd probably be dead, sir."

"Well thank God for him" said Hadley.

"We need to get him to the Cottage Hospital as soon as we can" said the Doctor.

"Of course, Doctor, we'll get him downstairs and off to Newbury in my trap" replied Hadley.

"Good, I'll prepare the patient for the journey and get him dressed" said Thompson.

"We've one last thing to do before we can get you away and that won't take long" said Hadley.

"Have you arrested them all, sir?" asked Talbot.

"Just Isaacs men remain at large, Sergeant."

"I'm pleased to hear it, sir."

Leaving the Doctor and his patient, they proceeded down the corridor to the next room. Hadley opened the door and strode in with his revolver in his hand. There were two young men fast asleep in single beds and they were not disturbed by Hadley's entrance. He shook his head and closed the door quietly behind him then went to the next room. He was just about to open the door when someone from inside the room opened it first and Hadley recognised the kitchen maid who had been in the wine cellar.

"Oh my Gawd! It's the poachers! It's the poachers!" she screamed out before Hadley could stop her.

"Quiet! Be quiet you foolish girl!" he hissed but it was too late and the next door along the corridor opened and one of Isaacs men stepped out.

"Seize him! Don't let him get away!" shouted Hadley as the man made a run for it down the corridor. The two constables rushed past Hadley whilst he and Cooper strode into the room that Isaacs man had left to come face to face with the other thug.

"You're under arrest!" said Hadley as he levelled his revolver at him. The man raised his hands and stood motionless before Cooper pulled his arms down to handcuff him. By now all the noise and commotion had disturbed the other servants and they came out of their rooms, filling the corridor.

"What's going on?" asked a voice that Hadley recognised and he turned to see Wilson standing behind him.

"We're arresting suspects, Mr Wilson and I think you'd better come along too" replied Hadley. The butler looked anxious and said "I'm not going anywhere without the master's permission!"

"Well you can ask him when you see him outside in the police wagon" said Hadley with a smile.

"What! Don't tell me that you've arrested the master?"

"Yes I have arrested him, along with all his foreign friends, Wilson."

"This is monstrous!"

"I'm not in the mood to argue with you this early in the morning, so come quietly, or else…!" said Hadley as Cooper led the handcuffed man out of the room. The butler gave a nod and with his nose in the air followed Cooper and the prisoner along the corridor. Hadley glanced around the empty room and then announced to the inquisitive servants in the corridor "I'm Inspector Hadley of Scotland Yard, I've arrested Sir Robert and his guests who were staying here…" he was interrupted by the loud expressions of surprise. He waited until the noise had died down before he continued "I advise you all to go about your normal duties and wait for further instructions." As he passed through the servants he stopped and looked at the maid who had shouted out and said in a whisper "as you now know, Miss, I'm not a poacher!" She blushed and looked down at the floor before she bobbed a little curtsy.

Hadley arrived in the stable yard as Isaacs man was being loaded into the police wagon.

"Has the other one been caught yet?" he asked Cooper.

"No, sir."

"Damn."

Suddenly the sound of horses approaching at the gallop along with the rattle of wheels made them look up. Into the yard came two police wagons and as soon as they clattered to a halt on the cobbles, Inspector Wilkes jumped out of the leading wagon followed by four constables each armed with a rifle.

"Good God! The cavalry has arrived!" exclaimed Hadley with a smile.

"Morning Hadley" shouted Wilkes with a grin as more armed officers poured out of the second wagon.

"Good morning Wilkes, I'm very pleased to see you and your men, how many have you brought with you?"

"Eight, including my Sergeant" Wilkes replied.

"I suppose there's no one left back at Newbury station?"

"Only one constable, a messenger and the cat, they can handle anything for the moment" replied Wilkes.

"Good, now I'm pleased to report that Sergeant Grover and his men have carried out their duties bravely in support of us and as a result we have all the suspects in custody, bar one" said Hadley.

"Excellent news!"

"Will you ask one of your men to retrieve the horse and trap that I left near the entrance last night and bring it here for the Doctor and Talbot?" asked Hadley.

"Of course, Sergeant Morris, detail one of the men to bring the trap up from the end of the driveway" said Wilkes.

The Sergeant nodded and Wilkes asked "is Talbot badly injured?"

"I don't know for certain, but the Doctor is anxious to get him to the hospital as soon as possible" replied Hadley.

"That's understandable. I knew that he must be here when there was no sign of him at the hospital last night. Now, what about this lot?" asked Wilkes as he pointed at the forlorn looking suspects sitting in the closed wagon.

"I just need to get Isaacs out and interview him in the house away from the others before you take them to Newbury because Boeker claims that he's got the diamonds" replied Hadley.

"Right" nodded Wilkes.

The sight of so many armed constables in the yard resigned all the handcuffed suspects to their fate and Hadley noticed their pale faces with satisfaction. Isaacs was summoned and then man handled out of the wagon by two constables who followed Hadley back into the house with the prisoner. Hadley and Cooper led the way to the study where Isaacs was told to sit. The constables were asked to wait outside and Hadley said nothing until Cooper had closed the door. Then Isaacs fixed Hadley with his hard eyes and with a curl of his lip said with contempt "when I get back to London, I'll have you stripped of everything, including your house and you'll be a penniless beggar on the streets of London whilst your family is condemned to the workhouse for the rest of their miserable lives!" Hadley glared back at Isaacs with a frightening intensity and waited for some moments before he asked calmly "Boeker claims that he gave you the diamonds last night, so where are they now?"

"The man's a bloody liar!"

"I'm not so sure."

"If I knew I wouldn't tell you!"

"That's exactly what Boeker said before he was otherwise persuaded" said Hadley.

"I'm not intimidated by a working class fool like you, so you're wasting your time!"

"Possibly…"

"Just get me back to London so I can contact my solicitor" interrupted Isaacs.

"Oh make no mistake, Isaacs, we're all going back to the Yard…"

"Good" he interrupted.

"Along with diamonds" added Hadley and Isaacs glared at him. Hadley waited for a few moments before he said "the stones must be here somewhere and I assure you that I will pull this place apart, brick by brick to find them, you've already witnessed the manpower that I can call upon to do it!"

"Go to hell!"

"And for your information I have arranged for more men to come and assist in the search as I correctly predicted that you and your fellow conspirators would deny everything from that perfect platform of total ignorance in Police powers!"

"You're a bastard and no mistake!"

"I'm only called that by guilty men who have been caught, Isaacs."

"I'm not guilty of anything as you will find to your cost when I get back to London!"

"Ah, there's the rub, we're not going without the diamonds and that means we'll stay here until they are found" said Hadley with a grin as Isaacs shook his head.

"I'm saying nothing."

"As you please, but the nights are getting cold and the police wagon will not be a very comfortable place to sleep" said Hadley.

"That's inhuman!"

"But that's the sort of thing working class bastards have to do to get results in this hard world, Isaacs!"

"You're an insolent bloody fool!"

"Now I suggest you calm down and reflect on your situation whilst I go and tell your hoity toity friends outside in the wagon that they are staying there until the diamonds are recovered" said Hadley.

"No matter what you do, you'll get nothing from me!"

"Consider this for a moment, if you tell me where they are hidden we'll all get back to the Yard in double quick time…"

"I've told you to go to hell!" Isaacs interrupted.

"And that means that your solicitor can make his representations on your behalf and who knows, you may be released on bail" continued Hadley.

"I'm saying nothing."

"Sergeant Cooper, please stay here with the prisoner."

"Yes, sir."

Hadley left the study and told the constables to remain vigilant whilst he went outside.

Inspector Wilkes was directing some of his men to carry out a general search of the stables and outhouses when Hadley arrived in the stable yard.

"I'm planning on keeping all of the suspects here until I recover the diamonds, Inspector."

"Locked up in the wagon, Hadley?" asked Wilkes in surprise.

"Yes, I've got to loosen somebody's tongue and this might just do it."

"Right, shall I tell them?"

"No thank you, it'll be my pleasure" replied Hadley.

He approached the wagon which was guarded by three armed constables and spoke to the resigned suspects inside.

"Gentlemen, Mr Isaacs refuses to divulge the hiding place of the diamonds, I know they are somewhere here because Mr Boeker admits that he gave them to Isaacs last night…"

"You fool" said Sir Robert to Boeker.

"It is probable that one of you know where they are and until I recover them, none of you will be leaving here."

"You can't do that!" exclaimed Sir Robert.

"Furthermore, I have sent for more men to search the house from top to bottom and I will tear the place apart until I find them!" exclaimed Hadley.

"If you cause damage to my home you will pay for it with a prison sentence!" said Sir Robert. Hadley ignored the threat and said "the search can be avoided if you tell me where the diamonds are." The suspects all exchanged glances and remained silent.

"As you wish, gentlemen" said Hadley as the two constables who were chasing Isaacs' man hurried into the yard.

"I'm sorry, sir, but I'm afraid we've lost him after he got away from the house and ran into the wood" said the older constable.

"Damn!"

"What's up?" asked Wilkes as he approached across the yard.

"Isaacs' man has given us the slip, sir" replied the constable.

"Right, Sergeant Morris, organise a search party of four men and go with them to the wood and find that man" said Wilkes.

"Yes, sir" replied Morris.

"And you go with the party to guide them" said Wilkes to the older constable who nodded. As they set off, the trap arrived that Hadley had left at the entrance to the Manor.

"Good, now we can get Talbot and the Doctor to hospital, Inspector" said Hadley.

"Leave that to us, you go and try and find those diamonds so we can all get back to Newbury" said Wilkes and Hadley nodded.

When he arrived back in the study Hadley asked Cooper to come out into the hallway and close the door behind him.

"Any luck, sir?"

"No, Sergeant, when I told them they were going to stay here until we recovered the diamonds they just remained silent except for Sir Robert who threatened me with prison if we damaged his house" replied Hadley.

"What's next, sir?"

"I think we'll leave Isaacs in there alone to contemplate for a while and see if that helps" replied Hadley.

"And if it doesn't, sir?"

"Then we have no alternative other than to pull the place apart, Sergeant."

"That could be a lengthy business, sir."

"Indeed it could" said Hadley as he heard the sound of approaching horses and carriage wheels in the drive way.

The detectives went to the front door and opened it as the carriage came to a dignified halt in front of the house. The driver leapt down, opened the door and lowered the folding step for the occupants to alight. A well built man stepped out first of all followed by two more, they then all stood back as Herr Stumpfel descended followed by Herr Konigsberg.

"Oh hell, it's the bloody Germans!" said Hadley.

"What bad timing, sir" said Cooper as Konigsberg ascended the steps to the house and smiled when he noticed Hadley standing at the open door.

"Good morning, Inspector" said the German.

"Good morning, sir."

"I expect that you have come here to recover the diamonds, is that so?" asked Konigsberg.

"It is, sir."

"And have you?"

"Not yet."

"Now that's a pity" said Konigsberg.

"Shall we go inside and discuss this, sir?"

"Yes of course, Inspector."

On entering the drawing room Konigsberg said "as well as Herr Stumpfel I have brought these three gentlemen from our Embassy to assist in the recovery of our diamonds, Inspector."

"Have you now, sir."

"Yes and I wish to speak to Sir Robert in private first of all, where is he?"

"He's under arrest and locked in a police wagon outside, sir" replied Hadley.

"Under arrest, Inspector?" asked the German in surprise.

"Yes, sir, along with the others" replied Hadley.

"What others?"

"The other suspects involved in this murderous conspiracy to steal the diamonds, sir."

"Gott im Himmel, surely you don't suspect Sir Robert of any wrong doing?"

"I do, sir and with respect, you have some questions to answer" said Hadley as the sound of two gun shots rang out.

CHAPTER 23

Hadley raced from the drawing room followed by Cooper. They ran out of the front of the house around to the stable yard where Wilkes and two of his men were hurrying towards them.

"What's happened?" asked Hadley.

"I don't know, but the shots came from that direction" replied Wilkes as he pointed towards the wood that bordered the estate.

"Get your men over there and let me know the outcome" said Hadley relieved that the prisoners in the wagon were not involved in the shooting and that it was probably Isaacs' man who was the target.

"Yes of course" replied Wilkes.

"I'll be in the house trying to placate our recently arrived German visitors" said Hadley.

"My God, a German contingent, that's all we need" sighed Wilkes.

"Yes, a policeman's lot is not a happy one" said Hadley with a smile and Wilkes nodded before he called for two constables.

When Hadley and Cooper arrived back outside the drawing room they heard Konigsberg talking loudly to his men in German. He stopped as soon as the detectives entered and he gave them a weak smile before he asked "nothing too serious outside I trust, Inspector?"

"No, sir, everything is well in hand."

"I'm glad to hear it, now I would like to speak to Sir Robert privately, Inspector, so would you arrange that for me?"

"I will, sir, but I shall be with him when you talk to him…"

"But I insist that my conversation is private!" interrupted Konigsberg.

"As I have said, I will be there, but you may be assured that I will keep everything you discuss highly confidential, sir" said Hadley and the German glared at him for a moment.

"Very well, Inspector."

"Sergeant, will you kindly summon Sir Robert to the house and ensure that he's accompanied by a constable as well as yourself?"

"Yes, sir."

"I suggest, Herr Konigsberg that when Sir Robert arrives, all your colleagues wait outside in the hall way" said Hadley and he nodded.

As soon as Cooper left the drawing room, Hadley made his excuses to Konigsberg and went across to the study where Isaacs was sitting calmly gazing out of the window towards the wood.

"I think that your man, who escaped from the house, has been shot resisting arrest, sir" said Hadley in an unemotional tone.

"Yes, he probably has" said Isaacs with disinterest.

"That's a shame don't you agree?"

Isaacs stared at Hadley and replied "there's plenty more like him in London so one less will not be a great loss to the underclass."

"Your compassion is touching" said Hadley and Isaacs grinned.

"Did I hear raised German voices just now?" asked Isaacs.

"You did."

"Who is it?"

"Herr Konigsberg from the German Embassy" replied Hadley.

"Here for the diamonds I suppose?"

"You suppose correctly."

"Well he won't find them."

"Don't be too sure about that, because he's going to speak to Sir Robert in a moment and who knows…"

"Don't listen to what that old fool says!" interrupted Isaacs and Hadley knew that Sir Robert was the weak link in the chain that all the conspirators feared.

"I shall listen with great interest to see if that misguided man will reveal the whereabouts of the stones" said Hadley.

"Oh God, he's a weak, stupid man" whispered Isaacs.

"Indeed he is, now I'll leave you now to contemplate your situation whilst I go and see what he has to say for himself" said Hadley as he left the study.

Sir Robert arrived in the drawing room handcuffed and somewhat dishevelled.

"Mein Gott! They are treating you like a dreadful convict!" exclaimed Konigsberg with shock at the man's appearance as Sir Robert nodded before he sat down on a chair.

"This situation could have all been avoided" said Hadley as he sat opposite Konigsberg and waved everybody to leave the room except Cooper.

"I understand that Herr Konigsberg wishes to talk to me privately, Inspector" said Sir Robert.

"He does, but I'm afraid I can't allow that and I must be present" replied Hadley.

"Well before we start, will you ring for one of the servants to bring us some tea?" asked Sir Robert.

"Of course... ring the bell please, Sergeant"

"Yes, sir" replied Cooper.

Whilst they were waiting for the maid to arrive they said very little other than to comment on the good weather before Sir Robert complained to Konigsberg about being roughly awakened from his sleep in the middle of the night. Hadley informed them both in a firm tone that it was a necessary action that undoubtedly had saved lives. Konigsberg 'tut tutted' in sympathy at appropriate times and raised a disapproving eyebrow when he glanced at Hadley. As soon as the maid appeared, Sir Robert ordered tea and toast for them but excluded the police officers. Hadley smiled as Sir Robert said "I'm afraid that in the circumstances you'll have to make your own arrangements for food and drink, Inspector, as I can see no reason why you shouldn't have to suffer some inconvenience like the rest of us."

"As you wish, sir" replied Hadley.

"Now let's not waste valuable time, Sir Robert" said Konigsberg.

"Indeed not, I am as anxious as you to return to London where this un-Godly mess can be sorted out once and for all" replied Sir Robert.

"This is good to hear, what knowledge do you have of the diamonds?"

"Hans Boeker arrived yesterday with a small case which he later claimed contained the stones" replied Sir Robert.

"Did he show them to you?"

"No, because before he could, he disappeared hurriedly in a trap back to Newbury after an altercation with our police friends and did not return until much later at night without the case" replied Sir Robert. Hadley knew that Boeker could not have possibly spoken to Sir Robert after he shot Talbot but he remained silent to see if anything else materialised.

"What did he say when he came back here?" asked Konigsberg.

"He complained about the actions of the police in chasing him back to Newbury and so fearing for his life, he left the diamonds in a safe place to be recovered later" replied Sir Robert.

"But he must have told you where he had hidden the stones" said Konigsberg in an irritable tone.

"No he didn't, he just said that they were in a secure place and he would get them as soon it was safe to do so" replied Sir Robert. The German looked at Hadley and said "I want to talk to Herr Boeker immediately, Inspector."

"Very well, sir, I'll have him brought here" replied Hadley as the maid arrived with the tea and toast for her master. Whilst the maid was attending to the two men, Hadley asked Cooper to bring Boeker from the wagon.

When Hans Boeker arrived he was looking very anxious and after being introduced to Konigsberg he appeared even more fearful. Hadley was now enjoying the drama as it began to unfold before him and he sat quietly waiting for the information that he was sure would lead him to the diamonds.

"I am Herr Victor Konigsberg from the Imperial German Embassy in London where I hold a very high position, Herr Boeker" said the German. Boeker nodded at Konigsberg and mumbled "yes, sir."

"As you must be aware, the Imperial German Government in Berlin purchased four uncut diamonds from The Transvaal Mining Company owned by the late Herr Detrekker…"

"Yes, sir, I did know" interrupted Boeker nervously.

"And they were brought to London by Herr Detrekker, Herr Vervorde and yourself for valuation before being presented to our Ambassador, Count von Hollenhoff."

"That is correct, sir."

"Unfortunately the other two are now deceased and as you are the only remaining person likely to have the stones, I now want you to tell me where they are" said Konigsberg firmly.

"They are in a very safe place, sir" replied Boeker.

"Where?" demanded Konigsberg, his face contorted with anger.

"I am not at liberty to say, sir" replied Boeker.

"Gott im Himmel! You'll suffer for this!"

"All I can tell you, sir, is that a higher authority than yourself in Berlin has ordered that the diamonds be delivered to him through a named person in Amsterdam" said Boeker anxiously.

"What are you saying?" asked Konigsberg angrily.

"I have told you the truth, sir so I advise you to contact your superiors in Berlin" replied Boeker and on hearing that the German raised his eyebrows in surprise. Hadley was quite unsure whether the young South African was telling the truth or not.

"Who is this person in Amsterdam?" demanded Konigsberg.

"His name is Van de Haas" replied Boeker.

"And where is he now?" asked Konigsberg.

"In custody at Scotland Yard" said Hadley firmly as Boeker and Konigsberg looked at him open mouthed.

"What!" exclaimed Sir Robert.

"Where you two gentlemen will be keeping him company as soon as I have recovered the diamonds" said Hadley.

"If the stones are here, Inspector, I will be taking them back to the German Embassy in London" said Konigsberg.

"I'm afraid that I can't allow that, sir" said Hadley.

"In that case your career with the Police will finish as soon as I have spoken to Count Hollenhoff and he has informed your Commissioner of your stupid and insolent behaviour" said the German.

"Time will tell, sir of that I have no doubt" said Hadley wearily as Konigsberg turned his fierce gaze back to Boeker.

"You have one last chance to tell me where the diamonds are" said the German.

"Or what?" asked Boeker.

"You will find out my friend sooner than you can possibly imagine!" exclaimed Konigsberg angrily as the maid entered the room. They all looked at her as she announced in a nervous tone "Mr Brandon-Hall and his son are here to see you, sir."

Hadley stood as the South African and his son stepped into the drawing room.

"Ralph Brandon-Hall, you are under arrest!" said Hadley. The father and son glared at Hadley before Brandon-Hall said "you're pathetic, Inspector, do you realise that?"

Hadley drew his revolver and said "Sergeant Cooper, take Mr Brandon-Hall and his son to the wagon."

"Right, sir."

"You can't do this!" exclaimed Brandon-Hall.

"I've just done it, sir and I've saved my colleagues in the River Police the job of finding your boat and arresting you!"

"What?"

"Your daughter told me that you were cruising on the river but I'm delighted that you've moored up somewhere and are here now" said Hadley.

"Oh did she" said Brandon-Hall.

"Yes."

"Just tell me why my son and I are being arrested, Inspector."

"You know full well, sir" replied Hadley angrily.

"Enlighten me if you would."

"Because you were a party to the forceful and unlawful imprisonment of myself and two of my officers!" exclaimed Hadley.

"You foolish man, I saved your miserable lives because Isaacs wanted to kill you!"

"What!"

"I thought that would surprise you, Inspector" said Brandon-Hall with a smug grin.

Hadley took a moment to compose himself before he said "take them away, Sergeant."

"You'll regret this, Inspector" said Brandon-Hall. After they were led away Konigsberg looked hard at Boeker and asked "are you quite determined to remain silent about the diamonds?"

"I have nothing more to say to you" replied Boeker.

"Very well then, that is the end of the matter" said Konigsberg which surprised Hadley and made him suspicious.

"If you have finished Herr Konigsberg then I'll arrange for Boeker to be taken back to the wagon" said Hadley.

"Please feel free to carry on, Inspector" said the German. Hadley nodded and went to the hallway to summon a constable to escort Boeker. As he was about to speak to the officer he heard

Konigsberg call out for Stumpfel, who immediately entered the room. By the time Hadley arrived back, Konigsberg was whispering to his assistant who was nodding at his master's words. As Boeker was led away by the constable, Stumpfel followed them out into the hall closing the doors behind him.

"Well, what now, Inspector?" asked Sir Robert.

"You will wait in the wagon with the others until I have recovered the diamonds" replied Hadley.

"You won't find them here, Inspector, you heard what Boeker said, he's hidden them somewhere safe in Newbury" said Sir Robert.

"I do not believe that for one single moment" replied Hadley.

"What do you believe, Inspector?" asked Konigsberg.

"I'm sure that the diamonds are somewhere in this house and Isaacs knows where they are and possibly Sir Robert knows as well" replied Hadley.

"I've no idea where they are, Inspector" said Sir Robert hastily.

"So you say, sir, and now I'm going to speak to Isaacs to see if he is ready to tell me what I want to know, and if he does then we can all return to London" said Hadley.

"I'm pleased to hear it" said Sir Robert.

Isaacs was staring out of the window at the group of constables who were escorting his man back from the wood when Hadley entered the study.

"It seems that your men didn't shoot him after all, Inspector" said Isaacs.

"Yes, that appears to be the case" replied Hadley as he glanced out of the window before he sat at the large desk.

"I suppose he'll face a long prison term" said Isaacs.

"That's for the judge to decide."

"The law is an ass, Inspector."

"Possibly, but the law is all we have to keep everybody in line and when carrying such a heavy load of responsibility it is better to have an ass than no ass at all" said Hadley and Isaacs grinned.

"How long to you propose to keep me here, Inspector?"

"You'll be off to London with your friends as soon as I have the stones" replied Hadley.

"Then we're in for a very long wait indeed."

"I understand from Brandon-Hall that you wanted to kill me and my officers" said Hadley as he fixed Isaacs with a hard look. The man looked uncomfortable and his face paled before he replied "you surely can't really believe that, Inspector?"

"Well, between you and me, sir" said Hadley in a quiet, confidential tone, "you're all such bloody liars I'm not sure whether to believe anything you say!"

"When did Brandon-Hall tell you this monstrous lie?"

"A short time ago."

"Is he here?"

"Yes, he's been arrested now and is in the wagon waiting to return to London" replied Hadley.

"What else did he say?"

"Never mind about him for the moment, I'm more interested in what Boeker said…"

"Another liar!" interrupted Isaacs.

"He said that he gave the stones to you last night."

"As I said, another liar" replied Isaacs as the sound of a gunshot rang out.

CHAPTER 24

By the time Hadley reached the front door, Cooper and all of Konigsberg's Germans were already outside and hurrying down the steps. He raced after them followed by the constables on duty in the hall and caught up with the Germans as they entered the stable yard where Cooper was already bending over the body of Boeker. Stumpfel was standing a few yards away from them holding a smoking revolver. The dazed constable who was escorting Boeker stood with his hands on his hips looking down at the body as Inspector Wilkes strode up shouting "arrest that man immediately!" pointing at Stumpfel who calmly tucked his revolver into his belt.

Hadley pushed through the Germans as they gazed down at Boeker with a pool of blood spreading from the gaping wound in his head and asked "is he dead, Sergeant?"

"I'm afraid so, sir" replied Cooper. By now Stumpfel had been held by two constables and a third disarmed him.

"Get him handcuffed and in the wagon!" said Wilkes.

"You can't arrest me!" exclaimed Stumpfel.

"And why not may I ask?" demanded Wilkes.

"Because I am a member of the German Embassy and claim diplomatic immunity" replied Stumpfel with a grin.

"What did you say?" asked Wilkes as Hadley turned to face the German. There was total silence for a moment before Hadley said 'you murdering bloody bastard!"

"He was trying to escape so in the interest of the Imperial German Government I was forced to shoot him" said Stumpfel.

"Do you really think that we believe that!" exclaimed Hadley angrily as Konigsberg arrived accompanied by Sir Robert.

"What's happened?" asked Sir Robert.

"Stumpfel has shot Boeker" said Hadley.

"Good God!"

"Take him away now!" said Wilkes.

"You cannot arrest him!" exclaimed Konigsberg.

"Watch me" replied Wilkes.

"I claim diplomatic immunity for him" said Konigsberg.

"Claim what you like, sir, but he shot that man in cold blood before police witnesses and he will hang for it!" said Wilkes angrily.

"No he won't, so release him immediately!" Konigsberg persisted.

"Under no circumstances whatever" replied Wilkes firmly.

"I'm afraid that you have no option, Inspector" said Hadley wearily as fully realised the situation.

"We can't let him get away with this, Hadley" said Wilkes.

"We have no choice in the matter, you'll have to release him" replied Hadley.

"Good God Almighty, what is the world coming to?" asked Wilkes.

"That's what I often ask myself" said Hadley.

Wilkes glanced at Stumpfel and giving a quick nod said "alright men, let him go." The constables released the German who then held out his hand for his revolver which was reluctantly returned to him.

"I think, Herr Konigsberg that it would be sensible if you and your entourage returned to London" said Hadley.

"I am not leaving without the diamonds, Inspector" replied Konigsberg.

"Your presence here is now both unwelcome and hampering my investigation, sir" said Hadley.

"Inspector, I intend to remain here until I have recovered the lawful property of my Government, so you may object all you wish but it will be to no avail" said Konigsberg before he turned away and headed back towards the house with his entourage Hadley gave a slight shrug of his shoulders and glanced down at the body of the murdered South African.

"With his death goes any chance of our finding out what he did with the stones and now we'll have to search the house" said Hadley.

"I can't believe what has just happened here" said Wilkes in a shocked tone.

"I agree it's hard to come to terms, but you have to remember that these diamonds are of such value that these people will kill without hesitation to get them" said Hadley.

"I'm sure you're right but how will the murder of this man help in the recovery of the stones?" asked Wilkes with a mystified look

"I really don't know for the moment" replied Hadley.

"Oh God, what a mess" whispered Wilkes as he shook his head.

"Ask your men to take the body into the house, please" said Hadley.

"Yes of course."

"I'd like to have a few words with the constable who was escorting Boeker" said Hadley and Wilkes nodded before he called the young man over.

"Yes, sir?"

"Constable, when you left the house with the prisoner and the man who shot him, did they speak at all?" asked Hadley.

"Yes, sir."

"What did they say, constable?"

"I couldn't understand it, sir, I think they were speaking German or Dutch, I really don't know for sure" he replied.

"Thank you, constable" said Hadley and the officer gave a nod then joined his colleagues who were about to lift the body of the South African.

Hadley gazed after the Germans and noticed that Stumpfel was walking close to Konigsberg and speaking to him in an excited fashion.

"Sergeant, I think that Stumpfel somehow tricked Boeker into revealing where the diamonds are hidden" said Hadley.

"Really, sir?"

"Yes and Stumpfel is busy telling Konigsberg now!"

"Then we've got them, sir!"

"Yes, we'll go through the kitchen and confront them in the hallway, Sergeant!"

"Right, sir."

"Follow us if you please, Inspector" Hadley called out to Wilkes who nodded.

The detectives hurried out of the stable yard and through the kitchen garden into the house. They arrived in the hallway before the Germans and Hadley heard sounds coming from the study. He did not hesitate but burst through the doors to see Isaacs on his knees behind the desk.

"What are you doing?" asked Hadley as Isaacs glanced up at him. Isaacs did not reply but made a hurried attempt to hide whatever he had recovered but before he could do so, Hadley was behind the desk with him. Hadley saw the chain first and then its attachment to the handle of the small black case. Before he could speak again, Konigsberg voice boomed out from the study doors.

"I'll take that, thank you, Inspector!"

Hadley whirled round to face the smiling German and Stumpfel who was holding his revolver and pointing it at him. Two other members of the entourage had also drawn hand guns and they were levelled at Cooper and Wilkes.

"Herr Konigsberg, you really disappoint me" said Hadley with a smile.

"I'm sorry about that, Inspector, but if you will now kindly hand me the case, I will not trouble you further and will return to London as you requested earlier" replied Konigsberg as Sir Robert arrived and asked "have you got the stones?"

"I will have them any moment now, Sir Robert" replied Konigsberg.

"Good, then we can leave" said Sir Robert.

"And where do you think you'll be safe from me, Sir Robert?" asked Hadley.

"In Germany, Inspector, as my life in England is now over" replied Sir Robert.

"What about your daughter?"

"She can stay here if she wishes, and I can assure you that she has had no part in this, now remove these handcuffs" replied the Knight.

"But you have played the major role in this affair" said Hadley as he nodded to Cooper to unlock the handcuffs..

"Yes and it would have been a lot easier without your interference, Inspector."

"Is that what you call it?"

"Yes I do, this could all have been accomplished without so much violence and you are responsible for several un-necessary deaths" replied Sir Robert.

"Like Hans Boeker's for instance?"

"Well that was necessary because…"

"That's utter nonsense and well you know it!" interrupted Hadley angrily.

"You gentlemen seem to forget that we've armed officers

outside who will prevent you from leaving" said Wilkes.

"And they have strict orders to use lethal force!" exclaimed Hadley.

"We shall see, Inspector, but I have a feeling that you will order them to let us pass unhindered" smiled Konigsberg.

"I must advise you that you are very wrong, sir" said Hadley.

"Get the diamonds, Stumpfel" said Konigsberg the German strode towards Isaacs who stood behind the desk clasping the case. The German wrenched it from Isaacs grip and gave it to Konigsberg.

"Now gentlemen, we are about to leave, but before I do, I wish to give you two alternatives" said Konigsberg.

"And they are?" asked Hadley.

"You can either remain quietly here until we have left or I'll give the order to shoot all four of you…"

"And claim diplomatic immunity" interrupted Hadley.

"Precisely" smiled Konigsberg.

"In that case we'll remain quiet and catch you later" said Hadley.

"How very wise, so please indicate to your officers outside in the drive that we are leaving" said Konigsberg before he turned and left the study with Sir Robert followed by the entourage. Wilkes went to the front door and waved at his constables that all was well, then Hadley along with the others watched Konigsberg through the study window as he and his party climbed aboard their carriage before it made off at speed down the long driveway.

"Let's get after them now!" said Wilkes as he ran back into the study.

"No need, Inspector" said Isaacs calmly.

"Why is that?" asked Hadley.

"Because I have the diamonds hidden here" replied Isaacs with a grin.

"Where are they?"

"Over here" replied Isaacs as he made his way to the imposing book shelves that lined one wall of the study. He removed two large books from the third shelf and produced a blue velvet bag containing the four large, dull, uncut stones. Hadley smiled and asked "when did you take them from the case?"

"Last night when everybody had gone to bed" replied Isaacs as he opened the bag and allowed the stones to roll out onto the desk top for them all to see.

"So you feared that something like this would happen?" asked Wilkes as they crowded round to gaze at the diamonds.

"I was sure of it, I mean, who could resist such wealth and beauty?"

"Boeker gave the diamonds to you when he double backed last night" said Hadley.

"He did."

"But Sir Robert knew that" said Wilkes.

"Yes, he did and he showed us the secret panel behind the bottom drawer of his desk to hide the case after we had all examined these priceless stones, fashioned by nature for man's enjoyment" said Isaacs.

"Now, I suggest you hand them over to me for safe keeping whilst you explain who you are working for" said Hadley.

"I'm working for me, Inspector, and I suggest that we hide the diamonds as Sir Robert and his German friends will be back here as soon as they look in the case" said Isaacs.

"No, sir, we will set off immediately with the diamonds and an armed guard to London" replied Hadley as he picked up the stones and placed them back into the velvet bag.

"You're making a mistake that will cost you your life, Inspector!" exclaimed Isaacs.

"I'll be the judge of that, sir" replied Hadley.

"Konigsberg will kill you all" said Isaacs.

"Inspector Wilkes, summon your men and let's get under way!" said Hadley as placed the velvet bag in his coat pocket.

"Right you are" nodded Wilkes with a smile before he hurried out.

Hadley turned to Isaacs and said "now, sir, I think we'll go outside and once you are safely on board the wagon, we can leave for London." Isaacs looked angry and perplexed as he left the study with the detectives following him. They paused on the steps of the house to await the arrival of the wagon from the stable yard which seemed to have been delayed.

"Sergeant, go and find out what's keeping them" said Hadley as he glanced at his fob watch. Cooper nodded and hurried down the steps to the driveway before making his way round to the yard.

Within moments the Police wagon appeared and to his horror, Hadley saw that the constables were inside the carriage whilst all the prisoners led by Brandon-Hall and his son were walking alongside. Cooper and Wilkes were being held at gun point by Brandon-Hall and his son, who grinned at Hadley.

"Your country bumpkins failed to search us for weapons, Inspector" shouted Brandon-Hall as the wagon came to a halt at the bottom of the steps. Hadley knew that the Newbury policemen had been less than worldly wise when it came to dealing with such desperate men. Minor thefts and poachers were indeed their mark and Hadley cursed himself for not being more thorough in his warnings to the officers.

"Well, Mr Brandon-Hall, it seems that you have the advantage for the moment" said Hadley.

"Indeed I do, sir" replied Brandon-Hall as he waved Hadley and Isaacs to come down from the house. They descended the steps slowly and Hadley glanced at Cooper who looked sheepish, whilst Wilkes was crestfallen.

"Mr Brandon-Hall, I suggest that you do not make your position worse than it is and release all these officers" said Hadley and Brandon-Hall laughed out loud.

"Get in the wagon, Inspector with all your stupid men" said the South African in a menacing tone.

"Before I do, you may like to know that Konigsberg along with Sir Robert has made off with the diamonds and they are probably about to board the London train as we speak" said Hadley.

"What!" exclaimed Brandon-Hall.

"It's true, Ralph, the German has got the black case" said Isaacs as the South African paled with concern and then glanced at his son.

"Quick Rupert, get all these fools into the wagon!" said Brandon-Hall.

Hadley was disarmed before he climbed up into the wagon with Cooper and Wilkes. To his surprise, Isaacs did not take the velvet bag from him and he wondered why. The detectives sat on the long benches and glanced at the constables sitting alongside before Brandon-Hall slammed the rear door shut and locked it. He peered through the small barred opening in the door and said 'we'll leave you in peace now and you'll have plenty of time to consider what fools you are before someone eventually lets you out." They heard the laughter from von Rausberg, Schoender and Isaacs as the horses were led round and the wagon proceeded back into the stable yard where it was parked by the wall at the far end. Then the horses were slipped from their harnesses and led into the stables by Isaacs' men.

"How did they manage to overpower you?" asked Hadley.

"Brandon-Hall held a pistol to my head and told the constables to lay down their rifles otherwise he would shoot" said Wilkes.

"I suppose that after they had witnessed the murder of Boeke in cold blood they didn't hesitate" said Hadley in a resigned tone.

"Of course, and who can blame them?" asked Wilkes.

"No one, Inspector, now do you know where the rifles are?" asked Hadley.

"Isaacs men have got one each and the rest were taken into the stables" replied Wilkes. They heard the sound of Brandon-Hall's carriage as it sped off down the driveway towards the road and Hadley asked "I wonder why Isaacs didn't take the diamonds?"

"We'll find out in due course, sir" said Cooper.

"I'm sure, so tell me, have you got your lock picking implements to hand, Sergeant?"

"I have, sir."

"Then get cracking and get us out of here!"

Within minutes Cooper had sprung the lock and they all left the wagon. The horses were brought out from the stables and harnessed whilst the rifles were found in a tack room at the end of the block.

"Right, gentlemen, let's see if we can catch the miscreants before they get to Newbury!" exclaimed Hadley.

The police driver slapped the reins and the wagon pulled away into the drive as Hadley shouted "don't spare the horses!" By the time the wagon reached the end of the drive it was almost at full gallop, it slowed to turn left into the road to Chieveley, the driver cracked his whip once again and the wagon accelerated at top speed towards the village. As they drew near they suddenly heard gun fire and Hadley glanced at Wilkes then said "be ready for a pitched battle if what I suspect has just happened!"

"So you think Konigsberg has discovered that the case is empty and was on his way back when he saw Brandon-Hall with the others going towards Newbury" said Wilkes.

"Exactly so and now they're busy fighting it out for the diamonds" said Hadley with a grin.

"God help us all!" exclaimed Wilkes.

"He will, never fear, Inspector" replied Hadley as the wagon swayed with speed down the country lane towards the village. Suddenly the driver began pulling up the galloping horses, accompanied by shouts to stop as he applied the handbrake. The wooden brake blocks squealed loudly as they came into hard contact with the steel rimmed wheels and the wagon came to a halt as more shots were heard. Hadley opened the door and jumped down to the road, he peered cautiously out from around the back of the wagon to see what was happening. Cooper, Wilkes and the armed constables clambered out of the wagon to join him. Brandon-Hall's carriage lay lop sided on the grass verge of the village green with one of its rear wheels missing. One of Isaacs' men stood close by pointing a rifle towards Konigsberg's coach. The horses pulling the German coach were restless after the apparent collision and despite the driver's best efforts to calm them, looked as if they were about to bolt. A man lay motionless on his back in between the carriages and Hadley was sure it was the other Isaacs' man. Stumpfel was taking shelter with the Germans from behind Konigsberg's carriage, his revolver levelled at Isaacs, who was crouching by the front wheel of Brandon-Hall's carriage. Konigsberg was leaning out of his carriage shouting at Brandon-Hall who, still seated in his carriage, pointed his revolver at Konigsberg. Count von Rausberg stepped down from the far side of Brandon-Hall's carriage, followed by Schoender, they immediately caught sight of the police wagon some fifty yards away and Schoender raised his gun and fired towards Hadley. The sound of the gun shot concentrated the protagonists and they all looked in alarm towards the wagon as Hadley snatched a rifle from a constable and returned fire over the heads of the Count and Schoender. All hell let loose as Stumpfel, along with his fellow Germans, opened fire at the police wagon. Schoender and Brandon-Hall did the same and a hail of bullets smashed into the wagon, sending splinters of wood in all directions, as the driver leapt for his life. Hadley shouted to his men to take cover away from the wagon just as a bullet struck Wilkes in his leg. The Inspector fell to the ground in agony before Cooper and Sergeant Morris dragged him away into the safety of the roadside ditch. Hadley pulled back the rifle's bolt to clear the breech and fired another round, in anger, at Schoender but missed when the German darted for cover behind Brandon-Hall's carriage. The Count followed him before Hadley could fire another shot. Konigsberg began to shout loudly in German and all his men climbed back aboard his carriage before it suddenly lurched forward towards the police wagon. Hadley levelled his rifle at the carriage as a volley of gun fire erupted from the constables hiding in the ditch. Hadley saw the bullets splintering the wood work as the driver pulled hard on the reins and the German carriage swung round in the road in a futile attempt to escape. As it swung round, two of its wheels mounted the steep verge, causing it to roll over and crash onto its side. The horses were thrown to the ground as the driver leapt to safety and the wheels were still spinning in the air when Hadley called to his men to follow him. On reaching the carriage he shouted "Konigsberg, tell your men to lay down their arms otherwise they will be shot!" Stumpfel's head appeared out of the window and he gasped "don't shoot! Don't shoot! Herr Konigsberg is badly injured!" Hadley handed his rifle to a constable and climbed up the carriage to peer down through the window. Stumpfel fell back inside on top of the others who were groaning, except Konigsberg, who lay pale and motionless against the far door. Hadley summed up the situation and called for the struggling horses to be freed from their harnesses and the carriage to be righted. Whilst giving instructions to the constables he saw Brandon-Hall along with his son, Isaacs, Count Rausberg and Schoender running away across the village green. All of a sudden several men appeared from the thatched cottages bordering the green, some were carrying shotguns and they confronted Brandon-Hall and his entourage. Schoender drew his revolver but before he could fire it, the man who was closest to him, lashed out with the stock of his shotgun and knocked Schoender's revolver from his grasp. Brandon-Hall and his colleagues were rounded up by the villagers, their shotguns at the ready, and herded back towards the police wagon.

Meanwhile, after the frightened horses had been released, the constables all heaved at the German carriage and slowly it was lifted up until it suddenly fell back onto its four wheels with a resounding crash. The doors were opened and the occupants were carried out then laid on the grass close to the dead body of Isaacs' man. Hadley glanced round to see more villagers approaching the scene, they were led by Richard Towns, the blacksmith's son, carrying a large hammer, and the publican from the Lamb. Hadley was pleased to see them and when the group holding Brandon-Hall at gun point arrived with the others he smiled and said "thank you, gentlemen, we'll take over from you now."

Cooper and Sergeant Miller searched Brandon-Hall and his entourage for weapons before they were placed in the wagon. Inspector Wilkes had been helped from the ditch and was being attended to by Sergeant Grover, who had used his belt as a tourniquet around the Inspector's blood soaked leg. It appeared that only Konigsberg and one of his men were seriously hurt, the rest had minor cuts and bruises. Along with Stumpfel, they were all disarmed before being placed in the wagon with the others.

"We know that the good Doctor is at the Cottage Hospital with Talbot, so we'll have to do the best we can for the injured before we get them to Hospital, Sergeant" said Hadley as he glanced down at Konigsberg laying pale and motionless on the grass.

"Yes, sir" replied Cooper as the rest of the villagers arrived and began to look around the scene.

CHAPTER 25

The Chieveley villagers rallied round and gave what assistance they could to the police whilst Richard Towns returned to the smithy and brought back a wheel to replace the shattered one off Brandon-Hall's carriage. With the help of the villagers the new wheel was fitted and the carriage checked for any other damage. Meanwhile, Konigsberg slowly regained consciousness and Hadley, with Cooper's help, half carried the shaken, injured man to Brandon-Hall's carriage. Hadley spoke to Wilkes and examined his leg, which appeared to be a messy but superficial flesh wound, much to their relief.

Fresh horses were brought for the damaged German carriage and at Hadley's request it was slowly led away by the blacksmith's son to be securely stored in the smithy. The body of Isaacs' man was removed to the Doctor's surgery for collection later by the Hospital. Once everybody was aboard the police wagon, Brandon-Hall's carriage and a trap lent by the publican, the convoy set off at a fast trot towards Newbury.

The carriage containing the detectives, Inspector Wilkes, Konigsberg and his man went to the Cottage Hospital whilst the wagon and trap went straight to the police station where Sergeant Morris and Sergeant Grover placed all the miscreants in the cells.

The three injured men received immediate treatment at the Hospital from Doctor Thompson, assisted by the duty Doctor and a stern Matron, accompanied by nurses in crisp white uniforms, whilst the detectives went in search of Talbot.

"It's good to see you, sir" said Talbot with a broad smile as Hadley and Cooper approached his bed in the small ward.

"Likewise, Sergeant, how are you feeling now?" asked Hadley.

"Much better, thank you, sir" he replied.

"Can't keep an old soldier down" said Cooper with a grin.

"Too right" said Talbot.

"But the Doctor was a help" said Hadley.

"Oh yes, without him I'd have not seen another day, that's for sure" replied Talbot.

"I expect that you'll be out of here in no time" said Hadley.

"Yes sir. Now tell me, have you got all the blighters?" asked Talbot.

"Yes we have" replied Hadley.

"And the diamonds?"

"Yes."

"Bloody good!" exclaimed Talbot and Hadley went on to give him all the details of the arrests then showed him the four diamonds.

"They're big but they don't look much do they, sir?"

"That's because they are uncut, Sergeant."

"To think that these stones have caused so much trouble" said Talbot.

"It's not the stones but men's greed is the cause of the trouble, Sergeant" said Hadley.

The detectives left the Hospital after Doctor Thompson confirmed that Wilkes injury was a superficial flesh wound and Konigsberg was suffering with concussion and a broken arm whilst his colleague had a broken leg. Arrangements were made to recover the bodies of Boeker from the Manor and Isaacs' man from the Doctor's surgery.

Immediately they arrived at the police station, Hadley sent a telegraph to Bell informing him that the arrests had been made and the diamonds had been recovered.

"That should cheer him up, Sergeant" said Hadley as he slumped down behind Wilkes desk.

"Indeed it will, sir."

"Now I propose to have a pot of tea and think for a moment, Sergeant."

"That's a very good idea, sir."

Hadley decided that they should travel back to London the next morning with all their prisoners and arrangements were made at Newbury station for them to travel in the guards van, as he felt that the presence of armed constables on the train would cause unnecessary alarm to the passengers. Hadley telegraphed Bell with the time of their arrival at Paddington and requested a police wagon with armed officers to meet the train. Stumpfel claimed diplomatic immunity and demanded to be released from custody but Hadley told him in no uncertain terms that he would not be freed.

Hadley had a meeting with all the officers and thanked them for their support during the very dangerous operation. He was able to report that Inspector Wilkes injury was superficial and Sergeant Talbot was making a speedy recovery. He finished by telling them that they would all be mentioned by name in his final report that would be seen by the Commissioner himself, no less. They all smiled when Hadley remarked that he realised the adventure at Chieveley had been more than the usual routine for them but it was something that they could proudly tell their wives and grandchildren.

Hadley visited the cramped cells and looked hard through the bars at the sorry, disconsolate prisoners, he felt nothing but contempt for them all. They said nothing to him but remained with their eyes downcast. They all knew their future would be spent in prison or worse and that their lives were destroyed by their greed.

Hadley and Cooper spent the night sleeping in a locked cell guarded by a constable for fear of anything else untoward happening to the four diamonds. Sergeant Grover woke them at eight the next morning with cups of tea and toast. By nine thirty the prisoners were handcuffed and ready to catch the ten o'clock train to Paddington. Sergeant Grover and four armed constables accompanied them to the station where they all waited at the end of the platform for the train to arrive from Bristol. Once aboard the guards van the prisoners sat looking morose and glaring at the detectives most of the way to Paddington. To Hadley's surprise Chief Inspector Bell was at the London station to meet the party along with ten armed officers and two police wagons.
"The Commissioner is delighted at the recovery of the diamonds, Hadley" beamed the Chief as he greeted the detectives on the platform.
"Yes, it is a great relief, sir."
"I told the Commissioner that I thought it was only right for me to be leading the arresting officers when you arrived back with the

prisoners and the diamonds" said Bell and Hadley nodded.

"I'm glad to see you, sir."

"Yes, it's such a high profile investigation with diplomatic overtones, I told the Commissioner that I needed to be here and he agreed" said Bell with a smile of smug satisfaction.

"Quite right, sir" said Hadley wearily.

"Good, now let's get these people back to the Yard where we can charge them" said Bell.

"Yes, sir."

The prisoners were escorted to the wagons whilst Hadley and Cooper said 'goodbye' to Sergeant Grover and his men, shaking hands warmly with each officer.

On arrival at the Yard the prisoners were taken to custody and placed two to a cell, which did not suit Sir Robert or Herr Stumpfel, who complained bitterly about the conditions whilst claiming diplomatic immunity. Chief Inspector Bell summoned Hadley and Cooper to his office after they had written a short report on the outcome of their investigations at Chieveley. Bell waved them to a seat and said "now show me these diamonds, Hadley." The velvet bag was produced and the four precious stones were laid out on the Chief's desk. He stared at them with his mouth open.

"Good heavens, they are enormous!" he exclaimed.

"Indeed they are, sir."

"That one is as big as a hen's egg!" exclaimed Bell as he touched the largest stone.

"Indeed it is, sir."

"They must be worth millions" whispered Bell.

"I have no doubt of that, sir."

"No wonder these foreign Johnnies were ready to kill for them" said Bell.

"Very true, sir and I'm pleased we've got them all under lock and key" said Hadley.

"Yes, but I'm afraid it will be a devil of a lot of blasted paperwork to get them in front of a judge before we can hang most of them and imprison the rest" said Bell.

"You're right as usual, sir."

"Now let's get the diamonds up to the Commissioner so he can see what we have accomplished before he contacts the German Ambassador with the good news" said Bell.

"Before we do that, sir, may we get Jack Curtis to photograph the stones?" asked Hadley.

"Whatever for, Inspector?"

"As evidence for the court, sir as well as for the record" replied Hadley. Bell thought for a few moments and then smiled.

"Yes of course, Hadley, and I could be photographed holding them, strike s pose as you might say, oh, yes, that would be one for the archives!" exclaimed Bell.

"It certainly would be, sir."

"The Commissioner would be suitably impressed."

"He certainly would, sir."

"Sergeant, go and find Curtis and tell him that he is wanted urgently" said Bell and Cooper nodded and left the office.

Hadley looked hard at Bell and said "I have to inform you that Konigsberg and his entourage are claiming diplomatic immunity from all their unlawful acts."

"Are they by God?"

"Yes and I fear that Sir Robert will escape justice with all his political contacts, as well as Solomon Isaacs."

"Possibly, Hadley, but don't worry too much about them for the moment, the most important thing is the safe recovery of these diamonds" said Bell.

"But justice is not properly served if the guilty men are not convicted, sir."

"Look, Hadley, we've got enough low life blackguards in this investigation to hang or imprison to satisfy the public and the Press."

"But the ringleaders are likely to escape their rightful punishment, sir" persisted Hadley.

"It was ever thus, Inspector."

"You appear to be content about it, sir."

"I am, Hadley, the avoidance of a serious diplomatic situation between our country and Germany is the most important aspect of this incident and as long as some of the suspects are hanged or imprisoned, justice will be satisfied along with her Majesty's Government."

"Yes, sir" said Hadley wearily.

Cooper arrived back with Jack Curtis, who was amazed when he saw the size of the diamonds on the Chief's desk. Hadley suggested that a ruler be placed by each stone so that the size could be easily determined by any observer at the court hearings. Then Hadley asked Curtis, as a personal favour, to photograph the stones in a group around his gold fob watch and finally several shots were taken of Bell holding the diamonds on a cushion, much to the detective's amusement.

"I think that was very well done, Jack" said Bell as the photographer began to pack away his camera and tripod.

"Thank you, sir, I was glad to be of assistance" said Jack with a cheerful smile.

"The Commissioner will be impressed" said Bell.

"That's good to hear, sir" replied Jack.

"When will the photographs be ready?" asked Bell.

"All being well, I'll have them for you by late this afternoon, sir."

"Excellent, I'm sure the Commissioner will want to release the photographs to the Press" said Bell.

"Is that wise, sir?" asked Hadley with concern.

"It's my suggestion but we'll let the Commissioner decide if it is wise or not, Hadley."

"Of course, sir."

"Now let's get up to his office and show him the diamonds!"

The Commissioner was both delighted and surprised by the four precious stones and he heaped praise on the detectives for the successful outcome of the investigation. Chief Inspector Bell occasionally interjected with comments regarding the decisions that he made that were critical to the final successful conclusion of the investigation. However, the Commissioner did not seem to be interested in Bell's comments but asked Hadley to go into great detail regarding the operations at Chieveley. Hadley gave the facts and did not embroider them in any way. When he had finished, the Commissioner said "very well done, gentlemen, I am pleased with your efforts and your dedication to duty."

"Thank you, sir" said Hadley.

"I have sent word to Count von Hollenhoff at the Embassy that we have recovered the diamonds and I understand that he is on his way here" said the Commissioner.

"That is good news, sir" said Bell.

"Yes and also Sir George West, the Home Secretary, has been advised and he will join us soon to formally hand over the diamonds to Count von Hollenhoff" said the Commissioner with a contented smile.

"So all is well, sir" beamed the Chief Inspector.

"Yes, except for all the paperwork that we have to produce for the Crown Prosecution Service" said the Commissioner as his clerk entered the office and announced the arrival of Sir George West. They all stood as the Home Secretary strode in followed by his personal assistant. After introductions, Sir George was shown the diamonds and he was also amazed at their size.

"By God, Commissioner, they'd make a pretty necklace for some deserving woman!" Sir George said with a smile.

"Indeed they would, sir" said the Commissioner with a nod.

"Now, Inspector Hadley and Sergeant Cooper, I understand that we have to thank you for the recovery of the diamonds" said the Home Secretary.

"And a number of other dedicated officers who assisted us, sir" replied Hadley.

"So I understand, please let the Commissioner have all their names and the details of their help in this matter" said Sir George.

"Yes of course, sir" replied Hadley as the clerk entered the office and announced the arrival of Count von Hollenhoff. The Ambassador smiled as he greeted the officers and shook hands with Hadley and Cooper. His two assistants from the Embassy were introduced before Sir George made a short speech about the co-operation and understanding between the British and German peoples. When he had finished the diamonds were placed on a white napkin carried on a small silver plate, both hastily procured by the Commissioner's clerk, and presented to the Count.

"On behalf of the Imperial German Government I thank you Sir George, you Commissioner and the dedicated police officers who have recovered these precious diamonds, which are the rightful property of the German Government" said the Count as he picked up each stone, looked at it carefully then placed it in a small black case, lined with blue velvet, held open by an assistant.

"Thank you, your Excellency, it was our pleasure and our duty to be of assistance to you and the German Government" said Sir George with a smile.

"Thank you. Now gentlemen, I am having a celebration Ball at the Embassy in two weeks time and to show my gratitude, I would be delighted if you and your wives would attend as my honoured guests" said the Count. Hadley, Cooper and Bell all looked at one another in amazement.

"I'm sure we'd all be very pleased to accept your kind invitation, sir" replied Sir George diplomatically.

"That is settled then" said the Ambassador with a smile.

"Yes, thank you, your Excellency" said Sir George with a polite nod.

"I will leave you now, gentlemen and once again I thank you all. Good afternoon" said the Count before he strode out of the office followed by his assistants with the case of diamonds.

There was a silence for a few moments as everybody gathered their thoughts.

"Commissioner, I'll leave you now as I have to report to the Prime Minister on the successful conclusion of this incident" said Sir George.

"Yes, of course, sir" said the Commissioner.

"I wish to see all the reports on the investigation and the suspects involved before they are passed to the Crown Prosecution Service."

"Yes, Sir George" replied the Commissioner.

"So, well done all of you. I know that the Prime Minister will be both pleased and very relieved at this successful outcome" said Sir George before he left the office.

The Commissioner thanked the detectives once again before he dismissed them so they could attend to their reports. On reaching their office Hadley asked George to make a pot of tea and Cooper said "an invitation to an Embassy Ball, blimey, Doris will want a very special posh frock for that, sir!" Hadley laughed out loud and replied "my wife will want a Ball gown and with only two weeks to find one it will be a bit of a rush, Sergeant!"

The next few days were taken up with taking statements and

charging all the suspects in custody, before those with the right connections were released on bail. During this busy period the detectives took several early lunches at the Kings Head to help clarify their thinking. Hadley was certain that Sir Robert would escape justice, along with Solomon Isaacs, because of their connections with prominent people in high places. This was confirmed when Hadley learned that Sir Digby Frobisher London's foremost Counsel had been retained to defend Sir Robert and Oswald Dingle-Smith, the most feared Barrister, was to defend Solomon Isaacs at the trial. Hadley expected Brandon-Hall and his son to receive lengthy prison sentences in spite of their defence being conducted by Sterling Beresford, another leading Barrister and that the black man Setsi Nkumo would hang. The news came through from Saint Bart's that Tousi Mombesi had died from his injuries after his dramatic jump from the roof which, as Chief Inspector Bell pointed out, would save the cost of his trial and the executioner's time. Mrs Johnson, the landlady that he had attacked, was making a good recovery at Saint Bart's, which pleased the detectives. Van de Haas was released without charge much to his relief and he returned to Amsterdam immediately. Grenville and Lansbury were charged with several offences including kidnapping before being released on police bail.

Count von Rausberg and Schoender faced serious charges of deception coupled with kidnapping and assault with a deadly weapon whilst Herr Konigsberg, Stumpfel and all the German escaped any prosecution by hiding behind the cloak of diplomatic immunity. Hadley believed that they were responsible for the deaths of Kruger and Isaacs' thug at Chieveley village.

Chief Inspector Bell claimed that it would be the trial of the century and already the Press interest was considerable. Hadley knew that he and Cooper faced many court appearances and harsh cross examinations in the coming months that would be pressing and difficult.

Sergeant Talbot arrived back from the Cottage Hospital in Newbury looking quite well and relaxed after his ordeal. He was able to report that Inspector Wilkes was making steady progress towards a full recovery and he sent his regards to the detectives. Hadley and Cooper were pleased to see Talbot and over a pot of tea, brought him up to date with what had happened.

A few days later the detectives were writing their final reports and were just about to formally close the investigation when Chief Inspector Bell sent for Hadley.

When he entered the Chief's office he was surprised to see a beautiful young woman seated in front of his desk. She was crying and dabbing her eyes as Bell looked at Hadley and said "I'm afraid we have another bad foreign business to deal with, Inspector."

"We've hardly finished with the last one, sir."

"I realise that but you'll have to leave everything for the moment and concentrate on this, Hadley."

"Very well, sir."

"This young lady is Miss Anastasia Kalamski. Her mistress, Countess Helena Petrovna, a member of the Russian Royal family, was shot dead this morning as they walked in Hyde Park" said Bell.

"Dear God" whispered Hadley.

"Take a statement from Miss Kalamski then start the investigation and let me have a report as soon as possible."

"Right, sir."

"The Commissioner is very anxious because he recently received some intelligence from the Russian Embassy regarding suspected assassins and the murder of the Countess confirms that we've now got murderous Russian revolutionaries running amok in London!"

"It never rains, sir."

"Quite so, Hadley, but it was ever thus!"

Follow Hadley and Cooper as they fight to bring the assassins to justice in

THE ROYAL RUSSIAN MURDERS

Printed in the United Kingdom by
Lightning Source UK Ltd., Milton Keynes
138570UK00001B/4/P